ANOTHER
WORD
FOR
MURDER

Crossword Mysteries by Nero Blanc

THE CROSSWORD MURDER
TWO DOWN
THE CROSSWORD CONNECTION
A CROSSWORD TO DIE FOR
A CROSSWORDER'S HOLIDAY
CORPUS DE CROSSWORD
A CROSSWORDER'S GIFT
ANATOMY OF A CROSSWORD
WRAPPED UP IN CROSSWORDS
ANOTHER WORD FOR MURDER

ANOTHER WORD FOR MURDER

NERO BLANC

BERKLEY PRIME CRIME, NEW YORK

THE BERKLEY PUBLISHING GROUP
Published by the Penguin Group
Penguin Group (USA) Inc.
375 Hudson Street, New York, New York 10014, USA
Penguin Group (Canada), 10 Alcorn Avenue, Toronto, Ontario M4V 3B2, Canada
(a division of Pearson Penguin Canada Inc.)
Penguin Books Ltd., 80 Strand, London WC2R 0RL, England
Penguin Group Ireland, 25 St. Stephen's Green, Dublin 2, Ireland (a division of Penguin Books Ltd.)
Penguin Group (Australia), 250 Camberwell Road, Camberwell, Victoria 3124, Australia
(a division of Pearson Australia Group Pty. Ltd.)
Penguin Books India Pvt. Ltd., 11 Community Centre, Panchsheel Park, New Delhi-110 017, India
Penguin Group (NZ), Cnr. Airborne and Rosedale Roads, Albany, Auckland 1310, New Zealand
(a division of Pearson New Zealand Ltd.)
Penguin Books (South Africa) (Pty.) Ltd., 24 Sturdee Avenue, Rosebank, Johannesburg 2196, South Africa
Penguin Books Ltd., Registered Offices: 80 Strand, London WC2R 0RL, England

This book is an original publication of The Berkley Publishing Group.

BERKLEY® PRIME CRIME
The name BERKLEY PRIME CRIME and the BERKLEY PRIME CRIME design are trademarks belonging to Penguin Group (USA) Inc.

PRINTING HISTORY
Berkley trade paperback edition / July 2005

Library of Congress Cataloging-in-Publication Data

Blanc, Nero.
    Another word for murder / Nero Blanc.
        p. cm.
    ISBN 0-425-20270-4
    1. Polycrates, Rosco (Fictitious character)—Fiction. 2. Graham, Belle (Fictitious character)—Fiction. 3. Physicians—Crimes against—Fiction. 4. Crossword puzzle makers—Fiction. 5. Crossword puzzles—Fiction. 6. Massachusetts—Fiction. I. Title.

PS3552.L365A86 2005
813'.54—dc22   2005044065

PRINTED IN THE UNITED STATES OF AMERICA

10   9   8   7   6   5   4   3   2   1

A Letter from Nero Blanc

Dear Friends,

Another Word for Murder is our tenth collaboration as Nero Blanc. It's absolutely fitting that our wonderful cover artist, Grace DeVito, should put a clock on the jacket. Time does fly when you're having fun.

We're often asked how a husband and wife can write together without harboring lethal thoughts about one another, and our response is always: good communication. As former actors, we value collaboration in the creative process; in fact, we began the series because we wanted to work as partners once again. Each of us has different gifts, and when one of us is in a slump, the other's in fine fettle. We become our own tag team, cheering each other on.

A big thank you to all our readers for making the journey so pleasurable. Thank you for your letters of encouragement, your thoughtful queries, and your genuine interest in Rosco, Belle, Al, Sara, Abe, and the gang. Remember our website www.CrosswordMysteries.com has puzzles to download.

Cheers—and, yes, we're hard at work on another Nero!

Please write to us soon,
Cordelia and Steve

For Jack and Ray
Good friends can be hard to find.

The authors wish to acknowledge the great talents of
F. William Parker
and his assistance in all things automotive
over many, many years.

CHAPTER

1

Lily was one of those children whose beauty and wholehearted delight in the world around them made total strangers stop in their tracks and smile. She was four, almost four and a half, with the kind of curly blonde hair normally associated with baby angels in Italian Renaissance paintings, and a face that glowed with a cherubic sense of fun.

She liked knock-knock jokes, storybooks, and picture books—except those with an over-abundance of green or purple. And she loved to talk. "Why" had once been her favorite word, and she'd been persistent in demanding answers. Now that it was five months past her birthday, the question had been replaced by her own set of improbable and marvelous theories. She was an authority on everything, including the fact that the family dog, a chocolate-brown Labrador retriever named Bear, was a real bear—because of "his big feets."

It was fortunate that Lily; her mother, Karen; Bear; and Lily's "very busy" father, "Doctor Dan" lived in the coastal Massachusetts city of Newcastle. Shaggy wild beasts of the *Ursus arctus* and *americanus* varieties had forsaken Newcastle's populous shoreline and its tree-dotted inland suburbs several centuries before. Not that this piece of information would have altered Lily's assessment. Her Bear was permitted to play in the large, cliff-side dog park with the city's other pets or swim at the several public beaches because he was a "gentle bear."

This reasoning led her to wonder about the species of another visitor to the dog park, a brown and black Shepherd mix named Kit who was often called "Kitty"—causing Lily to often suggest that the tallish dog with the four white paws might really be a cat. Belle Graham, who usually brought Kit to the park, was deemed "Cookie" because of the four-year-old's fondness for graham crackers, which she called cookies; however Gabby, the terrier and poodle combination who was Kit's companion was allowed to retain her name.

"'Cause she likes to bark," Lily stated, making it clear she'd heard the word "gabby" before, but not necessarily associated with a shortening of Gabriella. Cookie's husband "Rock"—Rosco to anyone over the age of six—was one of Lily's favorite people and one for whom she harbored just the smallest bit of a crush.

"Where's Rock?" she now demanded. Lily and her mother were standing on a broad, grassy rise overlooking the many-gabled building that had once been the Dew Drop Inn, a summer resort that changed hands every decade or so, but that never saw a lasting rebirth. A wide but dilapidated porch encircled the structure; on this sunny afternoon in late May, it exuded an aura of bittersweet nostalgia as if the rocking chairs that once lined its painted boards were still moving in gentle harmony.

"Rock needs to buy a new car," Belle said. "He's out looking at some right now."

"Finally biting the bullet, is he?" Karen asked with a chuckle. Like her daughter—and like Belle—Karen was also blonde, although her hair was now a tawny hue while Belle's and Lily's were the color of corn silk. Standing together, the threesome looked gilded and happy, just as the warm day spreading about them also seemed graced with prosperity and peace.

"Yup," Belle chortled. "He and Al Lever are starting their 'fact-finding mission.' I wasn't invited; I guess they thought I'd pick the first vehicle the salesman trotted out."

"Men and their precious machines." Karen shook her head while Belle laughed again.

"What's that weird relationship all about anyway?"

"True love?" Karen's blue eyes sparkled with mirth.

Belle smiled in return. "You may be right. Although Rosco knows absolutely zip about cars, when those goons destroyed his Jeep last November, he acted as if they'd attacked a member of the family.

"And it's taken six months for him to get up the courage to hunt for a permanent replacement. Now, I don't want to get overly clinical, but—"

"You're suggesting he should have passed his period of mourning?" Belle's laughter grew.

"The way my Dan runs through cars, he doesn't have time for grief. If it's hot off the assembly line, he's got to get it in our driveway. And I mean, *pronto*." Karen raised her hands in anticipation of her friend's next comment. "I know, I know. . . . Consumerism run rampant, the throw-away society, materialism at its worst, etcetera, etcetera. But Dan had such a hard-knock life as a kid that I just can't bring myself to criticize his spendthrift ways now. Besides, he insists he's actually *saving* money by leasing a couple of them. . . . Not that I believe him."

"You can only drive one at a time." But Belle stopped there; she liked Karen too much to point out the obvious: that she and her husband were fortunate to be able to indulge in such expensive habits. Instead, Belle offered a cheerful follow-up. "It's clear I'm going to have to construct a crossword for the legions of automotive buffs out there. How about 'Driven to Distraction' for a title?"

"I don't like cross words," piped in Lily. She was scowling fiercely, almost defiantly.

"But Cookie makes crossword puzzles for the newspaper, sweetheart," her mother soothed. "You know that because your daddy—"

"I don't like cross words!" Lily insisted while Karen gently tried to correct her daughter's mistake.

"Being cross and using cross words isn't the same as doing Cookie's puzzles, sweetheart."

But Lily's brain had already flown off in another direction. "Guess why Bear likes to swim?" she demanded of Belle.

"Why?" was the amused response.

"Because bears eat fish. Mommy and I saw them on TV. They catch them with their feets." Then she pelted away from the two adults, calling "Bear! Bear! Bear!" at the top of her lungs.

Karen laughed as she watched her daughter and the dogs flying over the emerald-green grass, a whirl of furry legs, pink, little-girl knees, and two very turquoise and glitter-strewn shoes. "Imagine being accosted with that decibel level *inside*. Sometimes Dan claps his hands over his ears, but it only makes Lily yell all the more. Personally, I think he does it to egg her on. Then he threatens to go outside to the driveway and sit in his latest ride with the windows rolled up and the sound system blaring. One time I came home from the supermarket and found them *both* ensconced in the Explorer. They were fast asleep: Lily sprawled across the rear seat, Dan behind the wheel. I didn't have the heart to wake them, but I did turn the music down lest the neighbors report us to cops."

"Maybe you should sell your house and move into a mobile home."

"If Lamborghini decided to make such a vehicle, I'm sure Dan would consider it."

CHAPTER

2

"It's been hit," Al Lever said as he straightened from the crouched position he'd assumed beside the right front fender of a three-year-old red Ford Mustang. He groaned slightly as he rose, then leaned against the car. "Man, my knees just aren't what they used to be." After that, he coughed twice and lit a cigarette.

Lever was Newcastle's chief homicide detective, a balding guy with a large paunch who relished playing the role of the gruff, hard-nosed police inspector—a demeanor that was all smoke and mirrors. He also had a solid knowledge of automobiles and how they worked, which was why on this particular Tuesday afternoon he'd taken some of his precious "liberty" time to accompany his former partner, Rosco Polycrates, on his mission to purchase a vehicle that would replace his ruined Jeep. Greek American male or not, Rosco lacked a major masculine trait: he knew very little about cars and what it was that kept them moving forward. This lack of expertise in automotive matters was a source of perplexed embarrassment to his brothers-in-law, and even to his sisters, although they consoled themselves that at least he could talk intelligently and ardently about the Boston Red Sox and

New England Patriots—in Greek, no less. You couldn't be a resident of Massachusetts and not be a Sox or Pats fan no matter what language you spoke, or how many.

Rosco broke other stereotypes, as well. His eight years as a detective with the Newcastle P.D. had taught him that he was too much of a free spirit for the bureaucracy of organized law enforcement. He didn't like filling out paperwork. He didn't like jouncing around in the city's unmarked cars. He hated carrying a gun, and he refused to wear socks except with running shoes. He'd left the NPD six years ago, opened his own private detective agency immediately thereafter, and never looked back—except for the bonds of friendship he continued to maintain with Lever and Abe Jones, who was the NPD's forensics honcho.

"What do you mean, it's been hit?" Rosco demanded. Unlike Al, he was trim and fit, and a devoted jogger, while Al's idea of exercise was walking up a flight of stairs—or maybe *half* a flight of stairs. "This is a great car. Look at it. I rented one just like it in Los Angeles when Belle and I went out there last winter."

"You rented a three-year-old Mustang?"

"Well . . . no . . . I guess not. It only had 700 miles on it; maybe it was new. . . . I mean, I don't know. . . . It looked just like this one. It was red."

"No one rents out three-year-old cars, Poly—Crates," Lever said as the cigarette smoke left his lungs, "especially in LA." His butchering of Rosco's last name had been a running gag between them for almost fifteen years and was predictably countered by Rosco's admonishing him over his sizable girth and ever-present smoker's cough.

Al pointed at the side of the car. "Look at that fender and door panel. See the ripples in the paint? She's been hit. And you have no idea how bad the damage might have been. Maybe the frame's been bent. And there's no way I'm crawling underneath to see if it's been straightened out properly, so let's move on."

Rosco laughed. "You wouldn't fit underneath, Al."

"Yeah, these Mustangs ride pretty low."

"Right."

Lever coughed again. "What? You think I've got the time to be trotting off to the gym three of four times a week like Abe does? Or playing handball with those kids on Congress Street? Or running around the park all day long like you, Mr. Slim-and-Trim? Wait'll you hit forty, my friend; watch how you fill out."

"Well, since I have less than two years to go, I guess I'd better start hitting those doughnuts and Camel Filters in earnest. That is, if I want to catch up to you."

"Ho ho . . . ," was Lever's sole response. Then he walked over to a Lexus SUV. "Here. This is what you need. This has some style."

"I'm not buying a white car, Al. Besides, I had a Jeep. I don't think I want another one. Actually, I don't think Belle could stand another Jeep. She'd chop my noggin off."

Lever shook his head slowly from side to side, thinking, *How could this guy be so dense?* "It's a Lexus, Poly—Crates, not a Jeep."

"It's a four-by-four; it has fat tires and it sits two feet off the ground. As far as I'm concerned, it's a Jeep."

Lever ignored the comment. Instead, he circled the Lexus twice, then stopped to study the large yellow sticker affixed to the driver's-side window. "The price is right. Only a year old, low mileage. Body's clean, no sign of any road-salt body-rot; the interior's sharp. Leather seats."

"I'm not buying a white Jeep, so forget it."

"I'm tellin' ya, Poly—Crates. This ain't no Jeep."

"Look, Al, I know it's not a genuine Jeep, but in my book, it's a wannabe; it's a clone. And it's white. I don't want a white car."

Lever sighed. "Okay, but you'd better be sticking with four-wheel drive if you want to make it through next winter without a serious fender-bender."

Rosco glanced up at the sparse and feathery clouds float-ing against the warm and bright blue sky. It was almost impossible to imagine icy roads and hazardous driving con-ditions. "Speaking of traffic accidents, what's the story on that hit-and-run on the west side nine months ago?"

"You mean when the Snyder boy was killed?"

Rosco nodded.

"No go." Lever released a frustrated and unhappy breath. "We're guessing the creep who did it was from out of town. None of the local body shops worked on anything matching that kind of probable front-end damage. At least, if they did, they're not talking about it."

Rosco nodded again. "The Snyders have hired a lawyer."

Lever dropped his cigarette to the ground and crushed it out with his shoe. "And let me guess; the lawyer has hired one Rosco Polycrates, owner and sole employee of the infa-mous Polycrates Detective Agency?"

"Elaine Vogel's the attorney. She called me this morning. I've worked with her before. This is pro bono on her part. The family just wants some answers so they can achieve a mea-sure of closure. You can't blame them. A kid dies, I'd want answers, too. I haven't said yea or nay at this point. I thought I'd talk to you first."

"No white Jeep, huh?"

Rosco shook his head, and Lever slid his hands into his pockets and ambled toward a green Subaru sedan. Rosco walked by his side. The lieutenant took a deep breath and said, "No one wants to nab the crumb-bum who killed the Snyder kid more than I do, Poly—Crates. So, sure, look into it. I'll give you all I've got. But to be honest, there's nothing there. Unless a mystery witness miraculously drops from the sky, the case is as cold as Lake Nippenicket in January."

Rosco didn't respond for a moment. "I hear what you're saying, Al . . . and I don't want to give the family false hope, but maybe they just need a little something more. . . . Anyway, who knows? It could be that this Porto Ristorante thing I've been working on for Northeast Mutual might supply some overlap info. There has to be an auto-body shop out there somewhere that doubles as a chop-shop. Maybe they fix fenders on the hush-hush. I find it, and who knows? You hit a kid with a car, well, there's got to be evidence that something happened to the vehicle. . . ." Rosco left the rest of the sentence unfinished.

"Porto Ristorante." Lever chuckled as he lit another cigarette. "I hate to say it, but the boys in robbery are still laughing over the dopes who got ripped off at Porto. The prevalent attitude down at that end of the station house seems to be a unanimous 'It serves them right.'"

"The insurance companies aren't doing a lot of laughing."

Porto Ristorante was one of Newcastle's newer and more expensive eating establishments. It featured high-end northern Italian cuisine, a formidable wine list, a chef of celebrity status, and a voluptuous Tuscan-red and Venetian-gold interior that commanded a sweeping view of the Newcastle harbor. The problem was that restaurant didn't have valet parking, although that hadn't prevented some clever thieves from offering that particular service one Friday evening in March; the Ides to be precise. Clearly the criminals had had a sense of humor.

As Porto's customers had arrived, bogus valet parking attendants outfitted in Porto-red jackets had supplied fake claim tickets to the drivers. Each ticket had a number on one side and a portrait of Julius Caesar along with the name *Marcus Brutus Valet Service* printed on the reverse. Any vehicle worth over fifty thousand dollars was never seen again. They'd vanished along with the keys and electronic garage door openers to twenty-two of Newcastle's pricier residences. A number of locksmiths had done very well with emergency house calls that evening.

Lever grunted with what sounded like another chuckle. "So what was the final tally on that job?"

"Seven Mercedes, twelve BMWs, two Porsches, and a Bentley."

"Yeah, well, you can forget about any chop-shops, bucko. The boys and girls in robbery say wheels like those go straight out of the country. The crooks probably drove them right onto a boat at pier six and were in Argentina before the owners finished their *limoncellos* and cappuccinos."

Rosco shrugged. "Maybe. But I've checked around; there seems to be a strong market for BMW and Mercedes parts, especially down in Connecticut."

The pair came to a stop in front of the green sedan. Rosco nodded in recognition. "My mom has a Subaru," he said.

Lever placed his foot on the bumper and lit another cigarette. "They're good cars. . . . All-wheel drive. Great in snow and ice. Good gas mileage. You can't go wrong with a Subaru."

"My mom has one."

"What? Just because your mother drives a Subaru, that means you can't?"

"What does your mother drive?"

"That's not the point. We're not talking about my mother, we're trying to get you a decent set of wheels."

"What's she drive?"

"A Cadillac, okay?"

"And what do you drive?"

"That's not the point. I just don't happen to like Cadillacs. It has nothing to to with the fact that my mother drives one. I'm not that immature, Poly—Crates."

"Uh-huh." Rosco walked to the rear of the Subaru, and Lever followed. "Nope. Looks too much like my mom's car."

"Okay, fine, no Subarus for Mrs. Poly—Crates's little boy."

They walked by two pickup trucks, and came to a dark blue Audi coupe. The bright sky reflected brilliantly in the freshly waxed hood, fenders, and roof. It appeared to be brand new.

"This is it," Lever said. "Look at this baby. Can't you see yourself cruising around Newcastle in this? I mean, is this class, or what? And with an Audi you get your all-wheel drive, too. You're set for winter." He looked at the sticker. "Look at this—less than three thousand miles. . . . This is your car, Poly—Crates. This is you."

Rosco shook his head. "My sister Zoe drives an Audi."

"Why do I even bother talking to you?"

CHAPTER

3

Dan Tacete pulled into his driveway that evening at six forty-five. The slow-sinking sun bathed his spacious home in a rosy glow, giving its many west-facing windows such a pink and vivid hue they looked like hammered sheets of gold and copper. Dan paid no heed to this spectacular sight.

Instead, he sat staring numbly through the windshield, his hands clenching the steering wheel, and his square, all-American jaw worried and tight. His neatly trimmed mustache stood out from his upper lip like a wire brush. By rights, what was worrying him should never have been happening. After all, he told himself, he was driving his least conspicuous car, the two-year-old white Ford Explorer that he kept precisely for the kind of work he did every Tuesday afternoon: the pro bono examinations, routine fillings, and other general dental care he provided for the Bay Clinic located a few blocks from the St. Augustine Mission for Men.

Despite every attempt at being low-key, despite the nondescript wardrobe, his customary Rolex and Guccis replaced with an inexpensive black plastic sports watch and running shoes, Dan had the sensation that someone had tried to follow him home. Several times, he'd noticed a gray Toyota four-door sedan in his rear-view mirror. It was an old car with numerous dents on the side doors, and it was not the type of vehicle ordinarily spotted in a tony place like Halcyon Estates. The fact that the driver's route coincided with his own was both odd and profoundly disquieting.

Before removing the key from the Explorer's ignition, Dan glanced into the rear-view mirror one last time. But his search revealed only the familiar: a semicircular drive opening into a tree-lined cul-de-sac. Every car in his sight-line was one he recognized as belonging to a neighbor or a neighbor's live-in household help; and all were parked and empty. Then he turned in the seat to survey the rest of the street, his broad, athlete's shoulders and frame fought against the shoulder harness until he impatiently stabbed at the clasp and released it.

There was no inkling of suspicious activity on any side. In fact, the road and sidewalks were remarkably devoid of people. No kids tossing frisbees, no skateboards, none of the other dads arriving home from work. But then it was six forty-five on a weekday. Everyone would have been inside enjoying their supper. By seven thirty or eight, the kids would be back outdoors—especially on a warm evening like this.

Dan opened the Explorer's door, stepped out, then beeped the car's automatic lock as he began walking toward the house. He turned once to look behind him, but the scene remained almost eerily empty.

"Karen? Lily-bet?" he called the moment he stepped in. "Where's my baby girl?" He shut and locked the door behind him and threw the dead bolt; something he only did the last thing at night.

Bear and Lily hurtled toward him, both canine and child making as much noise as possible. The foyer's marble tiles echoed and pinged while the cathedral ceiling heightened rather than lessened the sound. "Daddy! Daddy! Daddy! Daddy!" Lily screamed. Bear barked and jumped up on Dan, and the dog's weight and forward momentum nearly knocked him over.

"Down! Bad dog. Get down, Bear!" he said. His tone was far more forceful than was necessary; the stress of a long day coloring each of his words.

Watching the dog suddenly sink into an unhappy crouch, Lily began to cry.

"Tough day?" Karen appeared from the living room. She was wearing an apron; in her hand was a wooden stirring spoon coated with chocolate icing. She gazed lovingly at Lily. "And, did someone here forget to eat the chocolate frosting she was helping me put on the cake?" Mother bent down to daughter, who continued to weep. Lily made no further move toward her father.

"Daddy's cross . . . cross words."

"He's not cross with you, sweetheart. He's trying to teach Bear not to jump. Bear's too big a fellow to be jumping on people. If that had been you . . . well, your daddy and I don't want to see you get hurt, now, do we?"

But Lily would not be consoled. Instead, she eyed Dan with a child's pout while Karen cocked her head and gave her husband a complicitous glance.

"Someone's a little T-I-R-E-D," she spelled out. "I'll get her to bed and then you and I can have a leisurely, *grown-up* dinner. I'm experimenting with a new veal recipe."

"Sounds wonderful . . ." Dan paused, then squatted down to Lily's level.

"Daddy's sorry, baby. He's not mad a you—"

"Bear's a good bear," Lily insisted.

"He's a good bear when he doesn't jump. Mommy and I don't want him knocking you down . . . or your friends."

Lily sniffled once, but made no further reply.

"You get ready for bed, and then Daddy will come in and read you a story, okay?"

"Okay," Lily said, but the sound was still hesitant. Then she took her mother's hand and began trundling up the wide circular staircase that served as the foyer's focal point. As they reached the second step, Dan called to his wife.

"Karen . . . ?"

His wife turned; the difference in their physical stature made her eye level only slightly higher than Dan's. "Mm hm?"

"You haven't . . . you haven't noticed anything odd, have you? I mean, no one's tried to follow you home or anything? Tried to approach you?"

Karen smiled. "Mothers with four-year-olds don't usually impress the guys-trying-to-make-a-pass-at-pretty-ladies crowd."

"I don't mean men coming on to you . . ."

Karen looked at her husband. Her amused expression began to fade. "Why do you ask?"

"It felt like someone was following me when I left the clinic. . . . It could have been a coincidence, I know, but . . . well, there are some weird people out there . . . and we . . . we don't live in a house or community that's exactly low-profile."

Karen didn't respond. It wasn't just the house, she thought, but the number and caliber of the cars Dan owned that gave away their wealth; three in the garage and three more left to rest resplendently on the drive.

"I don't know what I'm saying, Karen. . . . I guess, just be careful, that's all."

"I always am, Dan."

"With Lily, too . . ."

"She's my daughter, Dan. Of course, I'm going to be careful with her."

"That's not what I meant." He drew in a long and heavy breath. "You're right. I *am* tired, and I'm probably overreacting. . . . Working at the clinic isn't easy. The equipment's less than adequate . . . and heck, the guys themselves are no walk in the park."

"You don't have to do it, Dan. Jack doesn't bother to donate any of his time—"

"Don't get me started. If Jack Wagner had his way, none of my indigent cases would ever walk through the doors of our practice, no matter how much they needed the services I

provide at the Bay Clinic. Unless, of course, Jacko could figure out a way to bilk the system . . . sign 'em up for implants and make the government pay. He can't wait for the
day Medicare gets a dental clause."

Karen kept silent.

"I'm sorry, hon, I didn't mean to go off on a tirade. Lily's
right. 'Cross words.' " He smiled at his wife and daughter.
"Look, I'll grab a quick shower. You get her nibs tucked in,
and then—"

But Karen interrupted, her pretty face serious and searching. "Look . . . Dan . . . if you think someone was really following you . . . maybe you should do something about it. Tell
the police."

"The cops? I can't call the cops. What would I tell them?
'It felt like I was being tailed?' I can only guess what they'd
say to that. Somehow I think the words 'too much money
and Gen-X paranoia' would be the first ones out of their
mouths."

"Okay . . . how about a private detective . . . ? Someone
you hire to—"

"We don't need a bodyguard, honey. Besides, private eyes
are all a bunch of sleazy characters—"

"Rosco isn't."

"Who on earth is that?"

But the question was overruled by Lily's shrill "Rock and
Cookie and the park."

"Are those names of dogs or people?" Dan asked with a
forced chuckle.

"You know 'Cookie' as Belle Graham—well, you don't really know her since you two haven't met yet. 'Rock' is her
husband, Rosco Polycrates. He's a private investigator, and
from what people in the dog park say, he sounds like a pretty
good one."

Dan shook his head. "I don't know, Karen. . . . I don't
want to get into a 'fortress' mentality. I probably just imagined that someone was following me. . . ." He bent down to

his daughter's height. "Okay, Lily-white, you let Mommy help you take a bath and get in your p.j.'s and then we'll read a story."

"The one about the elephants with the funny ears." Lily was finally smiling.

"Whatever you want."

As mother and daughter proceeded up the stairs, the phone rang.

"That's probably my altruistic partner right now, calling to see how many gold fillings I gave away today." Dan walked into the living room.

"Hello?" Karen heard him say, "Hello? *Hello? Who is* this?" She then heard the angry sound of the receiver being slammed down into its base.

CHAPTER

4

"Okay . . . ," Belle muttered to herself as she hunched over her desk, a sheet of graph paper spread before her, a pencil poised in her fingers, and a plethora of research books including her beloved *Oxford English Dictionary,* the O.E.D., lying within her reach. The other hand held a licorice whip, which she nibbled at distractedly—licorice being one of her major food groups and the other being deviled eggs laced with capers. At the moment though, Belle was far too deep in thought to take much notice of what she was eating. "A plant theme for spring . . ."

She blocked HOLLY into the crossword's Down line, then stared at it. "And the clue could be either *Actress Hunter* or ___ *Golightly.* . . . And then there's MAGNOLIAS, which can cross the 'L' in HOLLY, and the clue can be *Steel* ___, meaning that I can reference the clue with another that might be a shrub with BLUE flowers. . . . Maybe a hydrangea . . . ?"

Hoping for inspiration from her garden, Belle looked up and out the windows of her home office, a converted rear porch whose decor positively shouted crossword: the wood floor painted in bold black-and-white squares, curtains hand-blocked with giant puzzle grids and clues, ditto lamp shades, and a pair of captain's chairs with mix-and-match black-and-white canvas covers, as well as numerous ceramic plates and bowls displaying the tell-tale design. Any visitor not addicted to crosswords would have decided the person who'd chosen this singular theme was loony, indeed. Belle, however, loved it. "I guess I'm just a black-and-white person," she liked to joke. "Gray areas aren't high on my list—unless it's the stuff that makes brains tick."

She rose, walked to the open rear door, and gazed at the serene morning scene, at the birds hopping in and out of the trees, or taking quick flight skyward while the occasional seagull lofted raucously overhead. Hearing Belle move from her desk brought both dogs to her side in a trice. "It's not even ten o'clock yet, girls," she said with a smile. "You know you don't have another walk till noon." But Kit and Gabby heard the ambivalence of the tone and remained expectantly close with their faces staring through the screen door at the patch of greenery that spread behind the old house on Newcastle's historic Captain's Walk.

Belle laughed. "How am I going to finish this puzzle and then get back to editing the submissions for next year's crossword collection if we play hooky?"

Neither animal stirred.

"On the other hand, maybe doing some yard work will prove inspirational. . . . Perhaps my puzzle could involve a riff on plants and the emotional qualities connected with them: pure as a lily, sweet as a rose . . . and 'daisy,' which, as we all know, is an old slang term for something that's positively 'peachy.' What do you think, girls?"

The "girls" said nothing, of course, but Gabby, the younger, smaller, and more terrier determined, quivered while her wet, black nose sniffed the air with rabbitlike intensity.

"Okay, okay . . . ," Belle chuckled. "I can take a hint." She pushed open the screen door; and the three, according to their physical and emotional characteristics, either leapt or stepped into the abundant sunshine. There was a pleasing hum of bees, a perfumy scent of lilac, the tangy aroma of growing grass, and spring's fresh earth. The city garden, and the others adjoining it, were bursting with life and energy.

"This was definitely a good idea," Belle said. "While I get the rake, you two can start picking up fallen twigs."

Kit and Gabby were already concentrating on this task, although "picking up" seemed to involve more chewing and playing tug-of-war than actual gathering.

"Now, there's something to consider . . . ," Belle mused as she returned from the shed that held the manual lawn mower, a collection of flower pots in various stages of repair and a resident spider whose offspring took over the building on a yearly basis before blowing off toward other locales. " 'Rake,' as in this gardening implement in my hands; 'rake' when applied to an angle; and 'rake,' the abbreviation of 'rakehell,' or libertine. . . . Hmmm, maybe this is the beginning of a home-improvement crossword—for all the 'rakes' out there who favor low-slung tool belts—"

Her speech was interrupted by the front doorbell, which set in motion a series of outraged yips from Gabby and a couple of bossy woofs from Kit. "Girls! Stop! We go through this every day at the same time. You know it's only Artie bringing the mail."

Accompanied by her bodyguards, Belle walked inside, passing back through her office and into the living room with its eclectic thrift shop "finds." Through the beveled glass panes flanking the front door she could see the postman, his heavy, blue-gray bag hanging on its shoulder strap, his bulldog-thick frame bending to one side to accommodate the burden. Artie always rang the bell or knocked on the door, rather than simply leaving the mail and departing in silence. He was a man who liked to talk.

"Hiya, Belle. Hiya, poochies." He held up a flat, cardboard-padded envelope. "A submission for your new puzzle collection. . . . Says so right here."

Belle frowned slightly as she took it. "Constructors are supposed to send them to my office at the *Crier*."

"Yeah, that's how I thought you usually handled things. Can't be too careful these days."

"It's really for copyright reasons, Artie. The *Crier* mail room keeps a log of everything that comes into my box. Not that I'm planning on stealing another person's creation, but the editor-in-chief is a firm believer in legally protecting all parties."

"Speaking of protection, it's not such a swell notion that some of these crossword kooks have access to your home address. Like I said, can't be too careful."

Belle shrugged. "Where there's a will, there's a way, Artie." She studied the envelope. "A post office box in Newcastle . . . hmmm . . . but not a name I recognize—W. H. Everts? No Mr. or Ms. or Mrs., either."

"Maybe that's a good thing? Possibly another word game junkie has moved into town? But, hey, if you want to know where this Everts lives, you just let me know. All that stuff's on record downtown. Everts's gotta have filled out an address card in order to get a box." Artie shifted his large mail satchel from one shoulder to the other. "So, how's everything going with the hubby? Any hot new cases he's working on?"

Belle smiled. "You always ask me that, Artie, and you know I can't answer. . . . There are things Rosco won't even tell *me*."

"Yeah, right."

"It's true!" Belle laughed. "Well, thanks for this—"

But Artie wasn't yet finished gabbing. "Dynamite day, isn't it?"

"Gorgeous . . . but I'd better get back to work if I don't want my editor grousing at me."

"Sure thing. Me, too. Can't stand around all day yakking. . . . Make haste while the sun shines, or however that saying goes."

"I believe the word is 'hay' instead of 'haste,' Artie."

"Whatever . . . I never did learn those kiddie rhymes."

"And I don't think it was written for children."

"Not 'haste,' huh?"

"No. You could try 'Haste maketh waste,' though."

"Yeah, who doesn't know that one. Ben Franklin, right?"

"John Haywood."

"Huh. John Haywood. I knew there was some 'hay' in there somewhere." Artie shrugged. "Well, the sun's shining. I'm on my way. Forget the hay . . . and haste? That ain't my thing. People spend too much time running from here to there."

"Have a nice day, Artie."

Walking back to her office, Belle was still chuckling as she opened the envelope and removed the crossword. "Oh, this is clever," she said aloud. "It's a nursery rhyme theme . . . and gardens . . ." She looked at the dogs. "You don't think someone was peering over our fence just now, do you?"

Across

1. Contribution
7. Agile
11. Block letters?
14. Natural gas component
15. Garden worker
16. Chevy model
17. Fairy tale, part 1
19. Take the__
20. Rocky peak
21. "Pease-porridge__"
22. "__a cluck, there a cluck . . ."
23. Fairy tale, part 2
29. Salt form
31. The piper's son
32. "And__all in a row."
36. Engine additive; abbr.
39. Fairy tale villain
40. And so on
41. "See ya!"
42. Snake sound
43. Cockleshells' partner
47. "Big__"
48. See 11-Down
49. Fairy tale, part 3
55. Road sign
56. __of war
57. Middle grade
60. Nursery school subject
61. Fairy tale, part 4
66. River islet
67. Pilot's org.
68. Remove more fat
69. Navy noncom
70. Nitti foe
71. "__Fideles"

Down

1. Achievement
2. Air; prefix
3. Guessing-game players
4. Bronzed
5. Yoko__
6. Ring man
7. "Fire away"
8. __Rico
9. Little__Riding Hood
10. Centuries; abbr.
11. Seldom see eye-to-eye, with 48-Across
12. Chinny-chin-chin fuzz
13. Gets by
18. "__killed Cock Robin?"
22. Haw's partner
24. __lite
25. Grasshopper & ant eliminator; abbr.
26. Waterloo warrior
27. Flowers-by-phone folks; abbr.
28. MS-__
29. NYSE offerings
30. ACLU & NRA
33. Mr. Torme
34. Dune buggy; abbr.
35. Skating surface
36. Mauser mufflers
37. Like a beanstalk
38. Nosegay item
41. Parrot's nose
43. Arabian marketplace
44. Presidential nickname
45. Monopoly purchase; abbr.
46. The big__wolf
47. Pound sound
49. Stern or Hayes
50. Sunset__
51. Numbers game
52. Globe base?
53. Large bays
54. In the past
58. Amend
59. Salinger character

"BABY STEPS"

61. One-third of a Beach Boys hit
62. Function
63. __Angelico
64. Marry
65. Nice summer

CHAPTER

5

Smile!, the dental practice owned by Jack Wagner and Dan Tacete, sat squarely in the section of Newcastle that was viewed as the city's most up-and-coming neighborhood. Once-abandoned Victorian-era brownstones were being rehabbed into condominium apartments, art galleries, and boutiques, which meant that passersby peering through the buildings' first-floor windows were more likely to spot a wall-sized canvas or a minimalistic display of trendy Italian jackets than the suite of cherrywood furniture displayed during an earlier era—or the rubble and decay of ten years past.

In the case of Smile!, the view was of a well-appointed waiting area: black leather Eames chairs, attractive side tables, and standing lamps that looked as though they belonged in an exclusive country club rather than an office. The examination rooms were at the building's rear, so that entering Smile! it almost seemed as if the patient had made an error and wandered into an appointments-only gallery. Except for the smell, of course. No amount of potpourri and flowering plants could successfully eradicate the scent of mouthwash, paste tooth polish, and alcohol, or the nose-tickling aroma of local anesthetic. And nothing could disguise the persistent buzz of the high-speed drill.

On this day, the contrast between the comforting facade and the potentially painful truth was also reflected in a conversation between the practice's two partners. Facing each other over the inlaid wood of the reception desk, the two men all but glowered at one another. It was fortunate the desk lay between them; acting as an inanimate referee.

"Let's talk about this later, why don't we, Jack? Rob is my last appointment for the day, so I suggest we—"

"I'd like to discuss the matter with you *now*, if you don't mind." Wagner's lips attempted a polite and toothy smile, although his eyes did not. "The hours you spend here are getting harder and harder to predict. It's no way to run a business; and if I'm left to pick up the slack, as I was this morning, it's detrimental to the practice. When patients expect to see you, they're disappointed if I do the work and vice-versa. It has nothing to do with expertise or ability; it has to do with comfort levels. And if patients aren't encouraged to feel relaxed and safe, they will go elsewhere. I've seen it happen."

Dan glanced at Bonnie, the receptionist, as if seeking her support, but she lowered her eyes and pretended to study the list of that Wednesday's appointments. "As soon as Rob and I are done, I'm all yours, Jack. And I'm sorry if I was late getting in today—"

"And early leaving yesterday—"

"Yesterday was my scheduled afternoon at the Bay Clinic, which is something I cleared with you two years ago when we first established our—"

"Mrs. Harris called; she had an emergency. You're her doctor, not me. You need to be available, and you need to keep your cell phone turned on. Mrs. Harris was not happy."

Dan turned away and looked toward a patient who was sitting in one of the Eames chairs holding a copy of *Moderne* magazine. "All set to undergo some more torture, sport?" The tone was intended as a friendly one, but it had a definite bite.

"Hey, I can wait a couple of extra minutes, Doctor D," was the easy reply. Although he was more or less Tacete's height, Rob Rossi had a loose and rubbery manner, as if his bones had been jumbled together rather than stacked in an orderly fashion. Sitting in his chair with this casual and haphazard posture, he appeared shorter than he was—as well as a good deal younger and more boyishly earnest. "I don't have to show up for work till late. You guys take care of all the business you want to. I'll scan the mags or shoot the breeze with Miss Bonnie here."

"Good. Thank you." It was Wagner who responded. The words were cold. He put his hand on Dan's elbow and steered him through the doors that led to the examination rooms and offices. Despite the fact that Dan was the taller and probably the stronger of the two, he submitted to what appeared to be a command.

Once the partners had disappeared, Rob tossed *Moderne* onto a low glass-topped table and stood, stretched, then sauntered over to Bonnie. "What's up with Mr. Stuffed-Shirt, anyway?"

"You mean Doctor Wagner?"

"I sure as hell don't mean Doctor Dan."

Bonnie's eyes returned to the desk's surface. She didn't speak.

"I hope Wagner doesn't treat a kid like you the same way he treats his partner."

"I'm not a kid." Bonnie sat straighter, her jaw jutting high. Her curly red hair seemed to bristle, giving her a schoolgirl's defiant aura—which was belied by the soft and voluptuous figure of a young woman in her prime.

"Which is kinda obvious." Rossi grinned, draping himself over the desk as though he were leaning across a chummy bar—a position he knew something about since he was a mixologist at one of Newcastle's more notorious watering holes, The Black Sheep Tavern. "How come you never stop by the Sheep for a drink? Your brother does. Quite a bit, in fact."

Bonnie made no answer.

"Not your brother's keeper, huh?"

"No, I'm not."

"Uh oh, that's a frosty tone if I ever heard one. And, believe me, I know from ladies with ice cubes where their hearts should be." Rob leaned closer. "Hey, you don't want to hang out where Frank does, fine by me, but you and me could, you know—"

But Rossi's suggestion was interrupted by the increasing volume of the arguing partners. Despite the closed door leading to the rear cubicles and the obvious solidity of the building, the sound carried clearly into the waiting area.

"He has as much right to be here as anyone else, Jack—"

"Look, I'm not saying I want to stifle your generous impulses—"

"Oh no—?"

"But this kind of work could easily be done after regular office hours when our other patients aren't—"

"You mean, sneak them in at night like vampires—?"

"That's not what I'm—"

"Since they're clearly blood-sucking individuals who depend on society for help—"

"Come off it, Dan. I've never—"

"You come off it, Jack! Every time I need to bring one of my quote 'freebie' patients in here, you—"

"What I'm saying is, we've built up a solid practice in a comparatively short amount of time. We've got the elite of the city. They don't want to rub shoulders with—"

"With folks like Rob Rossi who opens beers and pours shots for a living? What, you don't think members of our 'elite' clientele don't hoist a few now and then?"

"That's not the point, and you know it. Maybe you could just suggest that these people try to adopt a certain dress code. How about slacks and shoes as opposed to torn jeans and sneakers?"

" 'These people'? What does that mean?"

There was a thud that sounded like a hand banging hard

upon an equally unforgiving surface. Bonnie rose from her desk and walked swiftly through the door leading to the back. Rossi couldn't hear her words, but whatever she was saying had the effect of silencing her two bosses.

When she returned she graced Rob with a bland and professional smile. "Doctor Tacete will be ready for you in just a moment, Mr. Rossi."

"You're some tough chick, Bonnie."

The receptionist resumed her seat, but made no reply.

"Remind me not to get into a fight with you," he added. "Hell, I should warn Frank to mind his P's and Q's. He grew up with you, though, so I guess he should know. Maybe he's the one should be warning me?"

"My brother does just fine without anyone's help."

Rob offered no response, and Bonnie's face suddenly crumpled into a troubled frown.

"Hey, he's a good guy, Bonnie. He'll straighten himself out. I know guys a lot worse off than Frankie, that's for darn sure."

A light on the receptionist's phone flashed. "Doctor Tacete will see you now, Mr. Rossi."

CHAPTER

6

When Bonnie O'Connell left the offices of Smile! at six fifteen that evening she actually gave Rob Rossi's invitation to stop by the Black Sheep some serious thought. Her workday had been filled with tension, and a frozen margarita was beginning to look like just the ticket. It had all started with Dr. Tacete's late arrival that morning and his insistence that he'd been trying to lose a car that was tailing him. Things like that didn't happen in Newcastle, and his tardiness had contributed greatly to the annoyance not only of Mrs. Harris but also of old Mrs. Whitehead—who, naturally, took out her considerable ire on the receptionist.

"Young lady, I always take Doctor Tacete's first appointment because I do not expect to be kept waiting. I'm punctual; I expect others to be punctual, as well." Bonnie could still hear the woman's ancient, Bourbon-and-cigarette scoured voice ringing in her ears.

The day had deteriorated from that point on, ending with the doctors going at each other's throats like a couple of wild dogs. It had seemed clear that after two years of building up a strong and lucrative practice, Dan Tacete and Jack Wagner had grown to despise one another, and the chill,

Bonnie knew, even extended itself to their wives. She guessed that it was only a matter of time before the men ended their relationship altogether; and the fear of losing her job, and the resulting lifestyle she'd been able to establish, only fueled her anxiety.

So she drove directly to The Black Sheep Tavern from work. Rob Rossi wasn't a bad-looking guy; and even though she was presently *involved* with someone, she was beginning to realize that the liaison had all the markings of a dead end. The time to move on could not be far away, so why wait for the ax to fall?

As she turned off Third Street and angled her car up Hamilton she could see the Black Sheep's weather-beaten sign swinging slightly in the breeze. Although the bar had no lot, street parking was readily available as this part of Newcastle hadn't yet caught the gentrification rage that was transforming other sections of the city. The neighborhood remained an area caught out of time, with the tavern being its single stable—and sustainable—business: an old bar whose patrons were solid, blue-collar locals or the few outside visitors who wanted to sample Newcastle's earlier and earthier ambience.

Bonnie opted to park as near to the entrance as she could, but as she drew closer she caught sight of her brother Frank's pickup truck resting on the opposite side of the street. She sighed and thought, *I'm not ready for Frank tonight,* and drove on without stopping. She then dropped by a Mexican restaurant three blocks from her apartment, picked up some takeout burritos and a Diet Coke, and arrived home a little after seven thirty.

Her apartment entrance was on the ground floor, a comfortable one-bedroom duplex in a newly completed complex on Newcastle's west side. The design was modern and bright, and she'd furnished it with care, opting to overspend on a sleek leather sectional couch and a wall unit that looked built-in. The bedroom boasted a massive Southwestern-styled four-poster bed that might have seemed out of place in coastal Massachusetts, but Bonnie had fallen in love with it the moment she spotted it on the showroom floor.

In fact, she loved the entire property: the outdoor swimming pool—which would be opening in a few weeks—the private gym, and the three tennis courts. The only downsides were high rent and poor security. Because of the townhouse-style layout, anybody could walk up to her front door and ring the bell.

True, the buildings had their own security staff; and the guards were friendly and efficient, but they couldn't be everywhere at once. Which meant that the occasional kid selling candy or raffle tickets, or college student looking for signatures on a petition was bound to appear on her doorstep. So when her door chime sounded at nine P.M., Bonnie wasn't startled, although it did seem a little late for solicitations. For caution's sake, she drew the safety chain across the door before she opened it.

"Heya, babe." Frank's crooked and hesitant grin meant that he'd clearly had one too many beers at the Black Sheep. His long, red hair had been sloppily pulled back into a makeshift ponytail; his rust-colored mustache was matted; he needed a shave; and his shirttail hung halfway out of faded black jeans that had gone too long without a washing. "No smile for your old bro?"

Bonnie let out a small sigh but not one loud enough for her brother to hear. "Hi, Frank." She slipped the chain from the door. "Come on in."

Frank stumbled past her, flopped onto the couch, and proceeded to light a cigarette—albeit with shaky hands. Then he placed his feet on the corner of the glass-topped coffee table. "I was down at the Sheep. Rob told me you might be stoppin' in when I saw him yesterday. Said he was finally gonna get up his nerve and ask you to come around when he was at Smile! this afternoon."

"It's a bar, Frank. People don't need an invitation to walk in." Bonnie's tone was stiff and unyielding, as was her body language.

He straightened up slightly. "Whoa, someone's testy tonight."

"It's been a long day. And I'm tired. What can I do for you?"

"Ain't you gonna offer me a beer, lil' sis?"

"Are you driving?"

"Is the pope Catholic?" He laughed, then hiccuped noisily.

Bonnie leaned against a large chair, facing her brother. "It looks to me like you've had enough booze already. Especially if you've got to drive home. I can make you some coffee if you'd like, but that's it."

"Nah . . ." He hiccuped again, then slumped back down into the leather cushion.

Bonnie sighed, loudly this time. She made no attempt to conceal her annoyance. "Better yet, why don't you just spend the night on the couch." She looked across the room at her TV. "I think the Sox are out in Oakland. There's probably a game on."

Frank chortled. "What? No boyfriend to cuddle up with tonight? High-rolling, sonny-boy didn't fink out on you again, did he?"

Bonnie furrowed her brow; her eyes were slits. "I don't need you coming into my house and talking like that, okay? I do my best to help you out, Frank, so have a little respect. My relationships are my business, not yours."

"Yeah, sure . . . . What the heck? My money says he ain't gonna be in the picture much longer, anyways."

"What's that supposed to mean?"

"That he's the type that moves on, that's all. Sets you up here, and then decides he'd like something closer to home or like that. . . . He's like a bass guitar player, know what I mean? You know how many bass players the bands I've been in have gone through in the last five years? A bunch. That's how many. They always think the grass is gonna be greener somewhere else so they take a powder on ya. That's all I'm sayin'. They all got some sorta racket goin' on. Your guy reminds me of all them damn bass players. They're all the same."

"Right. And just how many bands have you played for in the last five years? Not to mention rackets."

"That's different," Frank said indignantly. "I'm a drummer. Drummers gotta move on every now and then. Ya gotta stretch yourself artistically. 'Cause see, drummers stay in the same area of the world—just like me. Ain't that easy to pack up your drums and move from here to there. But bass players? They fly off; go to places like Los Angeles, New York, Europe, even . . ."

She crossed her arms over her chest and said, "Thank you for the advice. I'll keep it in mind."

"Any time." He inhaled deeply from his cigarette. "You know, Rob thinks you're hot stuff. . . . So, did he ask you to swing by the Sheep tonight or not?"

"Yes."

"Yeah, see, he said he was gonna. . . . Said he had an appointment with one of your docs this afternoon. But then it's weird, he didn't even show up for work tonight. Terry had to fill in for him."

Bonnie shrugged. "Maybe something came up."

"I was thinkin' that maybe you two was off doin' something together. Guess I was wrong."

She stifled another sigh, then stared at her brother until his glance shifted away, and his shoulders curved into a defensive V that made him look old and beaten. "What do you want, Frank? I'm tired and I'd like to go to bed."

"Well . . . I could use a little cash."

"Frank—"

"Without the lecture."

Bonnie turned and walked into her kitchen thinking, *That was a stupid question; of course, he's here for cash. That's all he ever wants.* She took a twenty-dollar bill from her purse, returned to the living room, and held it out to her brother.

Frank took the bill and said, "I'm gonna need more than this, sis. I gotta run a payment for my truck over to the car lot tomorrow or they're gonna repo it."

"How much is that?"

"Three hundred oughta' do it."

Bonnie let out a prolonged and unhappy breath. "I thought I saw an ad in one of the weeklies listing a gig for The Ravens at Oasis this weekend. That's who you're playing for now, isn't it? The Ravens? Can't you put off the car dealer until you get paid? I don't have three hundred dollars, Frank."

He stubbed his cigarette out in the ashtray. "Yeah, well, me and The Ravens had some artistic differences."

"They fired you." Bonnie said flatly. It was a statement, not a question. She knew the answer.

"If you listen to them, yeah, that's what they're gonna say, but the truth is I'd had it. . . . They ain't goin' nowheres. I mean, playin' a dump like Oasis, what's that?"

"A job."

"See, that's why I was hopin' your big, bad boyfriend would be here and not Rob. He'd front me the dough and not put me through the third degree."

Bonnie didn't respond. Instead, she returned to the kitchen, removed her checkbook from her purse, and wrote a check to Frank for three hundred dollars. Then she walked back into the living room and handed it to her brother. "I want you to leave, Frank. I have to get some sleep."

"Thanks, babe." He folded the check and slipped it into his shirt pocket. "Look, don't worry; I'm gonna get this back to you soon. I'm workin' on something else; it could be a really big deal. If it works out, I'll be able to wipe the slate clean."

"You have to go, Frank."

"Yeah, sure . . . sure . . . sure thing . . ." He stood and walked to the door. Bonnie watched the determined set of his back and shoulders, but also noticed how thin they'd become.

She could see the knobs of his spine poking through his shirt.

"Thanks for the jack, babe. What do you want me to tell Rob when I see him?"

"Why don't you just stay out of the Black Sheep?"

"Nah, that's where the action is; that's where you make your contacts in this town."

CHAPTER

7

Lily had been fussy all morning, and even the promise that Daddy was coming home early from work so that he could finally join in their afternoon jaunt to the dog park did little to lift the spirits of the fretful child. Karen was afraid her daughter was coming down with one of the constant colds her age group seemed prone to, and she kept placing her palm on Lily's forehead, waiting for and dreading the first sign of a fever.

"Go 'way," Lily ordered as her mother's fingers again passed across her brow. The little girl twisted in her chair in the kitchen's breakfast nook where she'd been having a mid-morning snack of "pig" newtons and milk, nearly falling off her booster seat.

"Lily, stay still. I just want to make sure you're not getting sick."

"Not sick." Lily bent down and rested her cheek on the bleached oak surface of the table. Her eyes had tears in them. "I want my daddy," she said. "And I don't want any milk. I hate milk."

"Okay, but we don't say 'hate,'" Karen said. "Remember what I told you? Why don't you and I go outside and play in the garden and wait for Daddy to come home. You can be the first to see his car coming up the street. He's driving the big white one that you and Bear like to ride in."

Lily jumped out of her chair and ran to the front door while Karen followed behind, having tossed away the offending milk. "Let's put on your jacket first in case it starts getting cooler."

Lily submitted to her mother's ministrations, then the two of them stepped outside. Bear was already there, sprawled on the grass and snoozing in the sun. An "invisible fence" kept him from wandering away from his own property, and Lily had been told not to stray too close to the electrical field lest Bear follow her and hurt himself. The warning had the added benefit of keeping the little girl from running into the road. She would never allow her dog to be harmed.

"I don't see Daddy," Lily now said. Her expression was at its most serious, and the sight of the small, angelic body holding itself in imperious judgment brought a quick smile to Karen's face.

"We have to wait, Lily."

Bear stood groggily, turned his head to glance at mother and daughter, then flopped back down on the grass.

"We have to wait, Bear," Lily told his languid back. Then she also plopped herself onto the grass, where she stretched her bare legs before her.

"Oh, sweetheart, don't sit on the damp ground. Let's walk around back to the deck and you can sit in your special chair."

"I want to see Daddy come."

"Okay, we'll both get your chair, and you can sit out here in front."

"I want to wait and see Daddy come."

Karen sighed. "If I leave you and go to the back of the house, you have to promise me not to move from this spot."

"Okay . . ." The sound was bored and a little superior.

"You have to say you promise."

"I promise."

"I'm trusting you to stay right where you are and not go anywhere near the street, Lily-bet."

"Promise."

But when Karen returned less than two minutes later her daughter was nowhere to be seen. It was if she had evaporated.

For the first split second, the mother's reaction was disbelief; her eyes rapidly scanned the spot where Lily had been sitting then jumped to Bear, who was still lying inert as a stone.

Then immediately followed irritation. "Lily Tacete, you come here immediately!"

No Lily; not even a reaction from the dog, who ordinarily would have been affected by the harshness of the words.

"Lily?" Karen's tone had become perplexed. "Where are you . . . ? Come on . . . this isn't a good time to play hide and seek. You want to be the first to see Daddy coming home, don't you?" By now the sound of her voice vacillated between cajoling and pleading. "Lily?"

But Lily neither responded nor appeared.

"Oh, wait, here he comes now," Karen lied. "I see his car turning the corner." The gambit failed to work. There was still no sign of her daughter.

After that, panic ensued. It was the terror that lies beside every parent's heart, just waiting for the most opportune moment to strike. Karen's face turned ashen, and her lips clenched in a bloodless line. *What did Dan say about someone following him home two nights ago? Or the mysterious caller who hung up? What was all that crazy stuff about? Maybe Dan wasn't simply tired and inventing scary scenarios. Maybe someone had actually been stalking him. Or . . .*

Karen shut her eyes, then as swiftly opened them and stared fiercely ahead. *No one would take my Lily away,* she promised herself. *No one in the world would consider such a cruel and terrible thing. Besides . . . besides, this is a safe neighborhood. Everyone knows one another. Nothing bad could happen in a place like this.*

But even as these arguments flooded Karen's brain she realized the reverse was by far the truer argument. *It was precisely neighborhoods like Halcyon Estates that were targets for criminals. And the children of wealthy parents were their favorite* . . . She couldn't bring herself to finish the thought.

Karen turned on her heel and walked toward the front door, but before she'd gone more than two steps, she spun back toward the lawn and garden again. "You stupid dog," she all but shouted. "Can't you even bark or—?" A sob shook her chest. "Just lying there while my baby is . . . What good are you?" The accusation ended in a low wail. She shut her eyes again, even while warning herself that she had to get a grip, had to to focus and concentrate, had to figure out what to do next.

"Don't be mad at Bear, Mommy."

The voice was worried and flutey. While Karen steeled herself, her eyes closed, her lungs trying simply to breathe in and out, the words swam into her ears as if they'd come from a great distance.

"I'm sorry, Mommy. I shouldn't have hided from you. Where's Daddy's car?"

Karen opened her eyes. There stood her daughter, her jacket dusted with torn leaves and shards of twigs, her knees muddy, a look of penitence and apprehension on her face.

Karen's lips formed an O, as if she were about to speak, but instead of words came tears, and she bent down and swept Lily into her arms.

"I shouldn't have hided from you, Mommy . . ."

"No, you shouldn't have," Karen wept.

"Where's Daddy?"

"It . . . it was a different car. One just like Daddy's."

"Don't be mad at Bear, Mommy."

"I won't. I won't. I won't."

After that, they settled down to wait for Dan.

CHAPTER

8

"It's Karen." Belle held her hand over the receiver as she turned to speak to Rosco. "She wants to talk to you. She sounds very upset."

Rosco took the phone from his wife, blew her a small kiss, and then concentrated on the caller, "Karen. Hi. What's wrong?"

The sobs on the other end of the telephone made it difficult for Rosco to piece together the story, and his own brief and disjointed responses and questions made it well nigh impossible for Belle to do anything but guess at what the problem might be.

"I see . . . I see . . . And then what . . . ?" He drew in a long breath. "Mm hm . . . okay . . . and when did you last see or hear—?" He nodded in silent reply as another torrent of words poured forth. When the voice at the other end of the line ceased, he asked a quiet, "Did you call the police?"

Belle couldn't hear the reply, although she stood close to her husband.

"And what was *their* suggestion . . . ? Mm hm . . . Yes, that sounds about right. Not what you wanted to hear, I know. . . .

But you don't know that something horrible's happened. You've got to remind yourself of that fact. . . ." As Rosco stood, listening, he glanced at Belle, who made obvious hand and facial gestures indicating that she wanted to know what was going on. He ignored the pleas, but his face had assumed such a grave expression that Belle forgave him completely.

She moved away a step or two to give her husband some breathing room and looked past him into the rest of the kitchen, where they'd been in the midst of preparing a spaghetti supper. The soft light of a late spring evening washed the walls and ceiling with a honey pink; and the old fixtures, the painted wood cabinetry, and the linoleum countertops that had stood proudly for more than fifty years had taken on a timeless placidity and an almost maternal warmth. It was hard to imagine the world having direr problems than fallen angel food cakes or hand-beaten biscuits that refused to rise. Belle found herself sighing in nostalgic regret as she turned back to face Rosco, who was now staring at the blank wall above the phone.

"No, I guess there really *isn't* anything they can do at this juncture. . . . Not until . . . Look, why don't I drive over and pick you up. You two can have supper with Belle and me. . . . No, it's no imposition at all. We can hash this out, and then I can handle the other issue—"

A muffled crackling of noise interrupted him.

"You're sure? I don't mind coming over there, Karen. Because you sound—"

Again, Rosco's suggestion was cut short.

"You're positive you're okay to drive? Okay . . . okay. . . . We'll be waiting for you, then." Rosco hung up. He looked at Belle, but didn't yet speak.

"Well?"

"Dan hasn't come home."

Belle frowned slightly and waited for her husband to continue.

"He was supposed to take the afternoon off from work

and return home in time for lunch. Then all three of them were going to take Bear to the park."

"I was wondering why Karen didn't show up this afternoon. She's always there on Thursdays. Not that what you're saying isn't potentially serious . . . but I was afraid . . . well, that it was Lily who was missing." Belle cocked her head; her lips were pursed, her gray eyes dark with worry. Then her expression brightened slightly. "Does he have relatives he could have decided to visit? Maybe there was a family emergency and he simply forgot to beam in—"

"He's got one brother. Karen called his number, but there was no answer. She said she doubted he'd be there anyway. The parents are deceased."

"That's right. . . . Karen had told me he was an orphan." Belle hunched her shoulders. "I take it you discussed contacting NPD?"

"Yes, but a missing person isn't deemed a police problem after only six or seven hours."

"What about the state police? Or the hospitals?" The question was posed with a good deal of hesitation; Belle winced as she said the words.

"I told her I'd make those calls with her when she got here. She's really shaken. She said that Lily had disappeared for a little while earlier in the day, and she totally freaked. Apparently, Dan believed he was being followed home the day before yesterday, and it made her jump to all sorts of nasty conclusions."

"Whew," was all Belle could say in reply. She reached out her fingers and touched her husband's arm. It was a gesture of both need and love.

Dinner was postponed until Rosco—with Karen at his side—made the necessary calls to area hospitals and the state police while Belle fed Lily then took the little girl into her office to play games and read stories. A good deal of Karen's panicked state had rubbed off on her daughter, causing Lily to waiver between pleased attention in the activities Belle provided and vacant and petulant distraction. "I want to go home and wait for Daddy," she insisted several times until fatigue finally overwhelmed her, and she allowed Belle to put her down for a nap. But then only if it was in "Gabby and Kitty's bed"—meaning the four-poster the dogs occasionally shared with the human residents of the house on Captain's Walk.

After that, Belle rejoined her husband and Karen downstairs, and the three sat down to a morose supper.

"I just can't understand it," Karen said. "It's so unlike Dan not to let me know where he is." She paused and shook her head. "He'd never do anything to upset Lily, and this . . . it's just so bizarre . . . so out of character . . ."

"I assume you've got your cell phone with you in case he needed to . . ." Belle left the question unfinished as Karen nodded in silent assent.

"Should we try his brother's number again?"

"I did before driving over here. This time I got a recorded message saying he's in San Francisco on business. Actually, I've never met the guy, even though he only lives down in Connecticut. He's a good deal older than Dan." Karen left the rest of her explanation unfinished, and neither Belle nor Rosco felt it appropriate to push for additional information.

"And the folks at his office confirmed that he left at noon?"

"Yes."

"And didn't return?"

"No."

Rosco took a deep breath. "I've got to ask some hard questions, Karen."

She glanced down at the table. The spaghettini with marinara sauce had congealed on her plate, almost untouched. "I'm sorry, Belle. I just wasn't that hungry."

Belle stretched out her hand toward her friend's. "It's okay."

Karen sighed, looked up, and took a steadying breath. Her face looked as vulnerable as a child's. "Okay, Rosco. Shoot."

"Well, for starters, the good sign is that the state police have no accidents involving Ford Explorers to report, and the hospitals haven't admitted him."

"I know . . . that's something," Karen voiced weakly.

"On the other hand, Rhode Island isn't far, and Connecticut not much farther, and we haven't checked there. . . ." He paused for a moment before continuing. "In my experience, people don't intentionally disappear without having a strong motive . . . and a place to go. That sounds simple to say and understand, but sometimes families can be the last ones to notice telltale signs that might have been observed weeks or even months before—signs that would have revealed the person's intention before the act was committed." Rosco hesitated again. "So what I'm going to lay out for you will be a couple of tough scenarios to imagine— especially when a couple is as close as you and Dan are—but here goes. One: Could Dan have been seeing someone else? And two: Was he depressed?"

Karen shook her head. "He loves me, Rosco! We have a wonderful life together. Everything he always wanted and dreamed about—that's what he keeps telling me—the best of everything! Why would he want to give that up? Either for some other woman or—" Karen broke down and sobbed, and Belle stood, walked around the table and put her arm around the convulsing shoulders.

"Do you want to stay here tonight?" Belle said. "You and Lily can have the guest room."

Karen shook her head. "No. I need to be home. Besides, there's poor Bear. He's been acting unusually groggy all day. . . . No, I should get back. It will be easier on Lily if she's in her own bed. . . . But thank you. Thank you both for being such good pals."

Rosco glanced at his watch. "It's only nine thirty. I know

he's been missing quite a while, but it's still early. I'm certain he'll be home before long . . . and with a logical explanation."

Karen wiped the last tear from her eye and said, "I wish I could share your optimism."

CHAPTER

9

When morning came, one of the first things Belle did was telephone Karen Tacete. It wasn't a task she relished or felt especially well-equipped for, but her friend's obvious needs overcame Belle's hesitation.

Rosco stood beside his wife in the kitchen as she asked the all-important question and received the leaden response of, "No, Dan hasn't returned yet." In the background, Belle could hear Lily begin shouting with mirth. Karen had told her daughter that her father was away on business and that he'd bring her a "big present" when he came back. Lily was celebrating what she anticipated would be a very happy reunion.

Belle felt her heart fly up into her throat. She was afraid if she tried to speak she'd start crying. She motioned to Rosco, who walked into her office and picked up the phone on her desk.

"What would you like me to do, Karen?" he said. "I'm happy to help."

"Do?" Either distracted by Lily's noise or too befuddled to think clearly, Karen sounded strangely spaced-out and incommunicative. "I don't know. . . . What does someone usually 'do' in situations like these?"

"Well, I can begin by checking on any auto accidents with the out-of-state police, in Rhode Island and Connecticut. Vermont and New Hampshire, for that matter. If Dan decided to—"

"But why would he go to any of those places without telling me? It doesn't makes any sense."

On her extension in the kitchen, Belle heard her husband drawing in a slow breath.

"Well, for the time being, let's just suppose that he had a compelling reason, whatever it might be, and forgot to—"

"Oh . . ." The word was a sigh only. It sounded to Belle as though Karen were falling asleep.

"And I should check on credit cards, gas company cards . . . see if there's any movement there—"

"Yeah . . . sure . . . I see . . ."

"I'll want to talk to Dan's partner, as well. Sometimes a business colleague has a different understanding of a situation, sees things that—"

"They didn't like each other; there were increasing problems where work was concerned."

"Well, that's helpful to know, Karen."

"No, no . . . Lily honey . . . come here to Mommy and stop bothering Bear. . . . He's not feeling too well. He's still Mr. Snoozy, like he was yesterday. . . ." Then Karen returned to Rosco and Belle. "Yeah . . . I guess . . . whatever you think best, Rosco. You're the pro—"

"Karen," Belle broke in. Rosco could hear the forced cheer in her tone. "I just got an idea. Why don't I come over and spend the day with you while Rosco does his thing? I'd love to spend more time with Lily, and if the weather's as nice as it was yesterday, we can take Bear to the park—"

"No, I should wait here for Dan."

"Well, I'd be happy to wait with you."

"I couldn't impose . . ." Karen's voice began to fade away.

"It's not an imposition if I get to spend time with Lily-bet. . . . Let's just say it's settled. I'll stop at the deli on the way over and buy us a bunch of sinful nibblies. We'll have an all-girls day. Okay?"

"Okay . . ." Then the phone on Karen's end dropped back into its cradle with what sounded like a crash.

Rosco's face, when he returned to the kitchen, was lined; a clear indication he was thinking the worst. "Not good," is all he said.

"No," agreed Belle. She dumped granola into two bowls, sliced bananas, and tossed them haphazardly on top while Rosco refilled their mugs with coffee. Neither paid much attention to the act of making breakfast, and neither spoke as they consumed their brief meal. They perched on two stools nearest the coffee machine rather than sit at the table facing the bay window as they usually did.

"All set?" Rosco asked as he cleared away the crockery and put it in the dishwasher.

Belle nodded, rose, pushed the stool back under the countertop, and began to walk toward the coat closet to fetch her purse. Then she turned back to face Rosco. "Can you take this much time off from working on your other case?"

"I guess I'll have to," was her husband's resolute response. "Right now we're in the middle of a waiting game. Oddly, no news is good news, and Karen needs all the help she can get, both emotionally and physically."

Belle nodded again. Her eyes were now the color of charcoal. "She doesn't sound good. Did you notice her voice seemed off?"

"Well . . . don't forget that her husband's a doctor."

"What's that supposed to mean?"

"It wouldn't be the first time a doctor prescribed 'comfort drugs' for his wife."

"That's not Karen," Belle said emphatically.

Rosco shrugged. "Nothing surprises me anymore. . . . Why don't you check on Dan's credit card activity when you get to their house. I'm sure Karen has all the numbers. All

54 ■ NERO BLANC

you'll need is his Social Security number, mother's maiden name, and zip code to access the accounts by phone. Write down the dates and times if anything shows up after he disappeared. I'll run down the merchants if you find anything. I'm going to start with the partner. Maybe Dan confided something to Jack Wagner that he couldn't tell his wife."

"Karen already said they didn't get along."

"I'd like to get Wagner's perspective on that." He kissed his wife lovingly. "Let me know if anything jumps out on those credit cards."

R osco was in luck when he rang the buzzer of Smile! at quarter to nine. Appointments weren't scheduled to begin for another fifteen minutes, but Jack, Bonnie, and Ginny—the hygienist who worked Monday, Wednesday, and Friday mornings—were already gearing up for the day. Fortunately, as yet the waiting room was devoid of patients.

"I'd like to speak to Doctor Wagner if I could," Rosco told Bonnie.

She gave him her professional smile. "If it's an appointment you need, I can—"

"It's a personal matter, I'm afraid. It'll only take a minute."

"Oh!" Bonnie looked momentarily perturbed, and Rosco sensed her scrutinizing him in an effort to ascertain what the issue might be. "You're not with the police, are you?"

"No. Are you expecting the police for some reason? Have they stopped by or called?"

"Er . . . no, but Doctor—" She stopped and glanced down at the appointment book, although it was plain that she wasn't really focusing on anything. "I'm sorry." She then reached for the intercom button. "Let me buzz Doctor Wagner for you, Mr. . . . ?"

"Polycrates. Rosco Polycrates. My wife is a friend of Karen Tacete's."

But before Bonnie could convey this information, Jack Wagner himself came barreling through the door that led to the examining rooms in the back.

"Where the hell is Dan?" he barked. He then glanced briefly at Rosco before leveling an indignant gaze on Bonnie, as if blaming her for his partner's tardiness. Wagner's perfect teeth were clenched, and the jaw that looked surgically enhanced quivered. It was clear that the dentist was barely containing a considerable amount of anger. Rosco studied the man—his hair was black and wavy, his eyes almost as dark, and his complexion the color of opals. As a Greek American in a city full of people of Portuguese, Italian, Russian, and Armenian descent, Rosco wondered if "Jack Wagner" was the name he'd been born with; in fact, Wagner looked a lot like Rosco's second cousin Ari.

"Doctor Wagner, this is Mr. Polycrates. His wife is a friend of Mrs. Tacete's."

Jack Wagner didn't extend his hand. A look of something approximating outrage passed briefly across his face, then it morphed into what Rosco assumed was an effort at empathy. "Is Dan all right? I mean, he hasn't been in a car accident or anything like that, has he?"

"Is there somewhere private we can talk, Doctor Wagner?"

The co-owner of Smile! turned without speaking and led Rosco back to his office.

What do you mean, 'missing'?" Wagner demanded, flipping Rosco's business card back and forth between his manicured fingers. He was seated at a mahogany desk whose surface was so meticulously ordered it looked as though every object on it had been lined up with a ruler. Three life-size replicas of the human jaw, pink gums and pearly white teeth gleaming, rested on a Plexiglass shelf on the wall behind him. Above them were picture frames displaying the requisite medical degrees and scholarly accolades from Harvard and the University of Pennsylvania medical school. Ensconced in one of the two chairs reserved for patients, Rosco let his eyes drift to the signatures of the university big-wigs. He was having a difficult time overcoming his initial dislike of Dan Tacete's partner.

"Missing means missing. That's the word we're using at the moment."

"What do you mean, *we're?*"

"His family. The police. Doctor Tacete has been officially listed as a missing person. Maybe there's another word that you feel might better apply to the situation?"

Wagner eyed Rosco coldly. "What are you trying to imply?"

"I'm implying that you, as Doctor Tacete's partner, may have been privy to information he might not have wished to share with his wife. In circumstances like these, there are generally three probable scenarios. One: there's another woman or man; two: the person in question may have manifested signs of depression—not being able to work, showing up late, and so forth. As a result—"

"Oh, yeah, he's showed up late, all right. But that's because he's such a damn goody-two-shoes. It had nothing to do with depression." Wagner leaned forward and rested his elbows on his desk. "So, my partner's flown the coop, is that what you're telling me?"

"Well, there's the third option, which is foul play." Rosco watched Wagner's face to see what secrets it might reveal. The doctor only clenched his chiseled jaw.

"Look, I don't know what you're suspecting me of, or why you're poking your nose around here—"

"I don't suspect you of anything. I'm simply asking if you've noticed anything unusual. I'm trying to locate a missing person. That's it."

"Dan does his work; I do mine. End of story. If he's missing, I'm sorry. It doubles my case load, all right? He'll turn up. But when he does, he won't be getting any red carpet treatment from yours truly."

"What can you tell me about his work at the Bay Clinic?"

"I never go down there."

Rosco waited for Wagner to continue, but instead he stared belligerently ahead. "I take it you didn't approve of his donating his time?"

"Look, Polycrates, we're a small but busy practice—just the two of us. If Dan gets stuck helping a bunch of ne'er-do-wells and leaves me hanging, then what am I supposed to feel? Pride that he's such a terrific and generous guy? Or ticked off because the folks who pay our rent—and who let Dan indulge his taste for expensive cars—are breathing fire down my neck? This is a profession, not a charity. And, for the record, I didn't approve of his bringing those undesirables into our office here. This is a nice place, and I've worked hard to establish it within a certain social strata of the city. . . . Now, if you'll excuse me, I've got to prepare for my first patient." Jack Wagner didn't stand and walk Rosco to the door; instead, he depressed a button on his intercom and leaned into the speaker. "Bonnie, cancel Dan's patients for today, will you? Try to set them up for next week sometime. And try to squeeze in any emergency cases there might be into my schedule."

B onnie O'Connell's eyes were huge and anxious when Rosco reappeared at her reception counter. "Is Doctor Dan okay?" she asked in a near-whisper. "When his wife called yesterday to ask if he'd left yet, I had a feeling she was upset about something. And not just the usual work-related stuff." Although Bonnie's voice was full of worry, Rosco detected an underpinning of strength. Looking at her face, he noted the same traces of determination and resolve. He imagined she was a person who'd weathered a good many difficulties in her short life.

"Doctor Tacete never returned home; no one's heard from him since he left here yesterday."

Bonnie drew in a rapid breath. "Oh . . . but . . . I mean, where could he have gone?" She seemed far more upset over the news than Jack Wagner had been.

"We have no idea. Did he have any relationships with patients that seemed odd to you? Either overly hostile, or overly friendly? Or did he seemed depressed at all?"

"Well . . . I mean," she said uneasily, "we're not all that close. I mean, he's always pleasant when he arrives here, but he usually goes straight to the back and gets to work. I'm not saying he's not a nice guy to work for and everything, because he is. But he *is* my boss; well, he and Jack are *both* my bosses. . . ." A tear formed in her eye. "This is horrible. Doctor Tacete can't just disappear. I mean, where could he be?"

"That's what I'm trying to find out." Rosco placed his card on the counter. "If he there's anything you think I should know, give me a call, okay?"

Father Thomas Witwicki was in his fifties, stood six-feet-five, and weighed close to three hundred pounds. His short-cropped hair was a fiery red, and he had a slight limp and a nose that had been broken three times. Rosco always felt that Father Tom, as he was affectionately called by the men residing at the Saint Augustine Mission, looked more like a former pugilist than a man of the cloth.

The mission itself was housed in what once had been a boot factory in the section of Newcastle that had formerly been strictly industrial and that was now undergoing a steady transformation. Trendy lofts were sprouting up in buildings that had been warehouses and manufacturing plants during the late nineteenth and early twentieth centuries, and the spaces were now deemed "hot properties" on the residential market. At least once a year some new neighbor would make it his or her *raison d'etre* to try to force Father Tom and his "clients" to move to a less hip area.

Rosco's path had crossed Father Tom's on several occasions in the past, and they'd developed a mutual fondness and respect for one another. Upon seeing Rosco, the priest gave him his habitual ironclad handshake and followed it with a bone-crushing bear hug. "Long time, no see," Father Tom bellowed. "I don't suppose you'd like to step into the kitchen and give us a hand fixing up today's lunch?"

Rosco raised his hands, regained his breath, and smiled. "No can do, Padre. I'm up to my ears."

"Yeah? What's shakin'?"

"I'm working on a little missing persons problem."

Father Tom sighed. "Okay, shoot. Give me a description, I'll let you know if he's checked into the mission. But I've gotta tell you, Rosco, I haven't seen any new faces down here for the past few weeks."

"No, I doubt if this guy would be checking into the mission." Rosco stopped and gave Tom's notion some thought. "But then again, you never know who's got a secret passion for the demon rum, causing him to slip off the deep end one day."

"Happens all the time, my friend."

"No, I'm looking for the dentist who works with your men."

"Dan Tacete?"

"Yep. He left work yesterday noontime and hasn't been seen since. I gather he was at the Bay Clinic on Tuesday?"

Tom tilted his head toward the mission's kitchen door. "Come on, I'll buy you a cup of coffee. I need to make sure things are going smoothly back there. Don't worry, I won't put you to work baking bread like I did the last time you drifted in here."

The men entered the kitchen, walked over to a standing urn, and filled two porcelain mugs with coffee. Three other men were busily making sandwiches while another was dumping commercial-size cans of soup into a large steel pot on a gas range.

"Twenty-four hours," Father Tom said after he'd sampled the coffee. "That's a little early to start calling out the Marines, isn't it?"

"Tacete's a family man, Padre. No, I don't think it's too early to start looking. His wife's very concerned."

The priest nodded toward the men toiling in the kitchen. "They're all family men, too. I guess the difference is, nobody's looking for them." He sighed and leaned his big frame against a work table. "Dan's a good person. He started the dental branch of the Bay Clinic, and he's the only reason it's kept going. The few other dentists he persuaded to get involved haven't lasted. There's no Medicare money floating his way—it's all pro bono stuff. A lot of people aren't into that, or simply don't have the time, or devote the time they do have to golf . . . but I have to tell you . . ." He stopped and took another swig of coffee.

"Tell me what?" Rosco prodded.

Father Tom considered his answer for a moment longer, then said, "I've watched Dan work. He has a real affinity with these men. They get along very well. They have a lot of laughs together. Believe it or not, these guys actually look forward to going to the dentist."

"So, what are you saying? Dan Tacete's a sorcerer? I have a lot of laughs with my dentist, but that doesn't make his drill a sight for sore eyes."

"No. What I'm saying is, he's got a lot in common with the kind of men who end up here. In an odd way, they seem cut from the same cloth. I've spent half my life around men who've dropped out. There's a through-line in most of their stories. . . . I guess I'm saying that it wouldn't surprise me if Dan just took off. It's not something I would have suspected or predicted, but now that it's happened . . ."

"No, no," Rosco objected, "we don't know anything's 'happened'."

"I understand; and I may be wrong. As I said, it's a little early to start sending up flares. But—."

"But it wouldn't surprise you if Tacete turned up three sheets to the wind in a homeless shelter in Toledo by Monday morning," Rosco said facetiously.

Father Tom nodded at the man opening cans. "You see

that fellow handling the soup? He's been here about seven months now. Does he look familiar?"

Rosco shook his head. "No. I don't think I've ever seen him before."

"That's because twenty-two months ago he was a federal judge in Broward County, Florida."

CHAPTER

10

Rosco walked into his office, draped his windbreaker over a wire coat hanger, and then wedged the garment onto the wooden rod in his overly crowded corner closet. The closet was home to a serious collection of thrift-store clothing—items that came in handy when he needed to convince someone he was something other than what he really was: a PI.

There was a designer three-piece, charcoal-gray suit—that he detested wearing—but nonetheless made him look every inch the high-priced attorney or stock broker. There was a pair of distressed work boots; four pairs of blue jeans in various stages of deterioration; white painter's pants; a scuffed, black leather motorcycle jacket; a construction hardhat; green hospital scrubs; a tweed sports jacket with leather patches on the elbows; a pair of cowboy boots; as well as a spectrum of sports caps that were designed to persuade folks that he was either a local—and therefore a rabid Red Sox or Pats fan—or that he came from as far away as California and Florida. The Lakers and Marlins were represented; Washington D.C. was covered with a *Go Skins!* hat. Though, given his Massachusetts accent, these out-of-town ruses were never quite as successful as he hoped.

After marrying Belle, Rosco had relocated his office from a low-rent neighborhood to a newer building not far from

Lawson's Coffee Shop—which many considered one of the hubs of downtown life. The reasons for Rosco's move had been threefold. One: his business had improved steadily, and he could now afford a raise in rent; two: Belle had developed a habit of dropping by unannounced every now and then to add some "great find" of hers to his undercover clothing collection, and he didn't like the idea of her having to search for a parking place in the raunchy section of town he'd originally inhabited; and three: he liked Lawson's. Beside being a favored haunt of his old NPD pals and allowing him pick up all sorts of useful information, it was also the scene of the Saturday morning "Breakfast Bunch"—a convivial crew that formed the basis of many of the friendships he and his wife shared.

Maybe it was the fact that the restaurant had seen its last major renovation sometime during the Eisenhower admin-istration, or that its resolutely pink decor couldn't help but produce a smile, or that the waitresses and kitchen staff treated everyone like family. Whatever the cause, stepping inside the glass-paneled front door was to return to an easier era in American life. In the heart of a big, modern city, Law-son's was its own small and quirky village.

A normal Saturday gathering at the eatery consisted of too much food and too many laughs, which meant that everyone involved in the "Bunch" would waddle out the door at nine thirty or ten A.M. with their midsections in cramps. The participants varied from week to week depending on schedules, but this Saturday varied in another way: NPD had leaked a photograph of Dan Tacete to the evening news, and his disappearance was now general knowledge. Naturally, everyone in the Breakfast Bunch had an opinion, even though only one of them had actually met the missing man.

Martha, the fifty-something-year-old waitress whose hair, makeup, and attitude made her seem as if she'd just stepped out of a 1957 T-Bird ad—blonde beehive and American Beauty–pink lipstick startlingly intact—analyzed the situation with her customary grain of salt. "And you say he owned six cars, Rosco? That spells one thing to me; P-L-A-Y-B-O-Y. Tacete's found himself a younger chickie and flown the proverbial coop!"

But Abe Jones, the African American with the movie-star looks, who happened to be NPD's forensic expert and was no slouch in the playboy category, didn't buy Martha's scenario. "No way, Marth. Nobody walks away from all those goodies. Rich people like their S-T-U-F-F, and men like their trinkets. Especially car guys. Sure, he might take a powder on his wife, but there's no way he leaves a Porsche 911 behind."

"There's a loving comment, gorgeous," Martha wise-cracked, and Abe responded with an equally droll: "And 'flying the coop's' supposed to be sympathetic, Marth?"

"You want T.L.C, how's about a B.L.T. with extra mayo, Dr. J?"

Al Lever was also there, and his offering was a habitually jaded "Not my department, Missing Persons, but nine times out of ten, it turns out these guys scooted up to Boston for a little hanky-panky. When they creep home, they've got their tails between their legs, and a dozen roses clenched in their sorry fists."

Sara Crane Briephs, the grand old lady who traced her ancestry back to the first settlers of Massachusetts, and who had become Belle's surrogate grandmother, offered a more genteel and empathetic version. "Well, I've only met Dan Tacete a few times at charity fund raisers, but I can attest that he seems a most upright and wholesome young man. A thorough professional, I would imagine, beside being very pleasant . . . which leads me, I'm afraid, to fear the worst. I don't mean to be a pessimist, but I don't foresee a happy ending to this situation."

"What *situation* would that be, Mrs. B?" Al asked her as he forked up his order of French toast with a double side of bacon—extra crispy, as usual.

"You're in charge of our city's homicide investigations, Albert dear," was Sara's smooth response after she'd dabbed daintily at her lips with a still-clean paper napkin. "Perhaps, you should be telling me."

* * *

Later on, remembering those ominous words, Rosco slumped into his office chair and rubbed his stomach. Once again, he'd overeaten. He released a groan as he scanned his cluttered desk. Dedicating a full day in an effort to help Karen locate her husband had left him behind with his investigation into the Porto Ristorante valet parking scam. On top of that, his answering machine was blinking rapidly. He tapped the play button, and an automated voice announced, "Friday, one twenty-seven P.M." This was immediately followed by a human, but also staccato, "Rosco, it's Elaine Vogel. I was hoping to catch you in. I'd like to work with you on the Snyder case, but if I need to get someone else, let me know ASAP." She then left a string of numbers for work, home, and cell. She was a person who left nothing to chance.

Rosco released a second groan, although this one was full of self-criticism. He'd promised to call Elaine on Friday, but with the Tacete mess it had completely slipped his mind. He punched in her first contact number and reached a voice mailbox. "Elaine, it's Rosco Polycrates. Sorry about yesterday. Listen, I know you're not making a dime on this one, so let's just say I'll help you out where I can. I'm really too busy to take on something else right now . . . but I've been in and out of a lot of body shops lately working on another situation. If anything looks fishy or seems like it might have bearing on the Snyder case, I'll get back to you, but if you need a full-timer I'll understand."

He left identical messages at Elaine Vogel's other mailboxes then replaced the phone in the cradle. It rang within seconds.

"Polycrates Agency."

A grave voice responded with, "Yeah, this is Phil Gronski. You left me a message earlier in the week."

Rosco pushed through some papers on his desk until he found the one he wanted. "Yes. Right. Mr. Gronski. I understand you had your BMW stolen in front of Porto Ristorante on the evening of March fifteenth."

"Yeah, right, a Z-8."

"I've been hired by Northern Mutual to look into—"

"I'm not insured by Northern. My company's G.I.A."

"Yes sir, I know that. There are a number of companies handling the claims. I'm trying to talk with everyone who had a vehicle stolen regardless of their insurer. We're looking for any thread, anything that can help us piece together who the perpetrator might be. I was wondering if you—"

Again Gronski interrupted Rosco. "It's sleazeballs like you who make life miserable for the rest of us."

"Pardon me?"

"All I want is my damn money. I could care less if you catch the jerks who lifted my Z-8."

"Northern Mutual's paid off their claims, Mr. Gronski. What they're looking for is criminal prosecution and the opportunity to reclaim some of their losses if they can."

"Yeah, well, G.I.A. hasn't paid off jack," Gronski growled into the phone. "And you know why? Because they're waiting for you people to get your act together. All I get from my agent is, 'That case is still pending criminal investigation.'"

Rosco shook his head. G.I.A. Insurance was one of the worst companies in America, notorious for stringing customers along for months, even years, before settling claims, in the hopes that eventually clients would give up or just fade away.

"Well, sir, I can't answer for G.I.A., since I've been hired by Northern, but if that's their position, perhaps it would be in your best interest to answer a few questions? Get the ball rolling?"

"Yeah? Says you. Why don't you just go to hell."

Instinctively, Rosco pulled the receiver away from his ear, knowing full well that Gronski's next move would be to smash the phone down into its cradle. And like clockwork, that's exactly what he did.

Rosco leaned forward and drew a narrow line through Phil Gronski's name, moved his pen down to the next name on his list, and reached for the telephone. Once again it rang before he had the opportunity to lift the receiver, and he answered with his normal "Polycrates Agency."

"Rosco, thank goodness you're there," Karen sobbed into the phone. "Dan didn't disappear. Someone has him. Someone's kidnapped him! They just called!"

Across

1. Part of S.P.C.A.
4. Nap spot
7. Virginia's specialty
10. Tam
13. Cable network; abbr.
14. Theater worker; abbr.
15. Yalie
16. Fuss
17. Sea eagle
18. Map abbr.
19. Kitty Fisher, e.g.
21. Nursery rhyme
24. Remove, in trips
25. Pepper's pal
29. Nab
30. A Tucker
32. Hare's adjective
33. British Air, once
35. Tempe campus; abbr.
37. Airport info
38. "The Grasshopper & the__"
41. Vol/time fig.
42. Mythical bird
43. Cobra kin
44. Ghostly sound
45. British honor; abbr.
46. Gals' dates
48. Puss in__
50. Fish eggs
52. With 20-Down, Tibetan terrier
55. Against
56. Wood preservative
59. Nursery rhyme
63. Marvelettes hit
66. Cartoonist Browne
67. Fall back
68. "The Mind Benders" actress
69. Pitcher's stat.
70. ". . . little girls__made of."
71. WNW counterpart

72. Mr. Beatty
73. Steal
74. Buddhist temple
75 Morning shakes

Down

1. Book support
2. Hugh, Pat, or Edmond
3. Nicaragua fighter
4. Nursery rhyme
5. Bone; comb. form
6. A man in a tub
7. Beatles hit
8. Lotion ingredient
9. "Three Blind__"
10. 48-Across, e.g.
11. Orange or lemon add-on
12. __favor
20. See 52-Across
22. Newspaper, informally
23. Siouan
26. Like the Owl & the Pussy Cat
27. "__Hang On!", 4 Seasons hit
28. Snare
31. Nursery rhyme
32. Nursery rhyme
34. Edwards or Andrews; abbr.
36. Old French coin
38. "Dancing Queen" group
39. Twelve
40. Blow one's horn
47. Tie back
49. "Once upon a__"
51. Wood sorrel
53. Like Polly Flinders
54. "Finally!"
57. City in Madagascar
58. Rims
60. "The cow jumped__the moon"
61. Roman fiddler
62. Lackluster

"SUGAR AND SPICE"

1	2	3		4	5	6		7	8	9		10	11	12
13				14				15				16		
17				18				19		20				
21			22			23								
24										25	26	27	28	
	29					30	31		32					
		33		34			35	36			37			
38	39	40		41			42				43			
44				45			46		47					
48		49			50	51			52		53	54		
55					56		57					58		
			59	60	61	62								
63	64	65					66				67			
68				69			70				71			
72				73			74				75			

63. Good times
64. Mine find
65. Little__Riding Hood

CHAPTER

11

Unaware of Karen's calamitous news, Belle pulled into the small driveway in front of her house on Captain's Walk. After leaving Rosco to catch up on work following their weekly rendezvous with the Breakfast Bunch, she'd decided to give the dogs a brief run in the cliff-side park before settling down to an afternoon of crossword editing. The morning was simply too pleasant to resist; and she'd found the surprisingly visitor-free park a welcome relief after the emotional roller coaster of the previous forty-eight hours— as well the equally impassioned or trenchant comments Dan Tacete's disappearance had elicited from the crowd at Lawson's.

Reflecting on Sara's kindly concern, on Martha's joking skepticism, on Abe Jones and Al Lever's seen-it-all world-weariness, Belle realized how nice it was to toss a Frisbee or a stick while gazing at the salt waves of the bay and feeling the heat of the sun beating through the cooler ocean air. It felt good to clear her brain.

Watching Gabby and Kit bounding along, tearing after squirrels and each other, Belle considered how much humans could learn from studying the behavior of their canine friends. Joy was immediate; worry and fear became issues only when the need arose. Dogs didn't have sleepless nights fretting over mortgages or leaking roofs or roving spouses; they didn't torture themselves over past mistakes or un-kindnesses or those many sins of omission. They existed to give love, receive love—and eat. Which wasn't a bad notion as long as someone else was paying the bills.

It was in this reflective frame of mind that Belle—along with Kit and Gabby—had finally returned home. As the three climbed the stairs to the porch, Belle noticed that the front door was slightly ajar and that there was an envelope wedged in the crack. Pulling it out, she noted that her name and street number were handwritten, that the script appeared feminine in shape, and that there was no return address.

Belle walked inside as she opened the flap and extracted a crossword with a Post-it providing the constructor's name, Randy E. Isaacs, and email address. "Oh . . . ," she mur-mured, scanning the puzzle, " *'Sugar and Spice.'* This looks like another nursery rhyme theme. . . ." Her brow creased in thought as she walked into her office and retrieved the "Baby Steps" puzzle Artie had delivered on Wednesday morning. Either these are constructed by the same person using different names for authorship, Belle decided, or there's some weird kind of *zietgeist* going on.

She spread the crossword on her desk, muttering aloud as she scanned the solutions and clues. "4-Down: CURLY LOCKS . . . 21-Across is LITTLE BO BEEP . . . MARGERY DAW is the answer to 31-Down . . . We've got Kitty Fisher's nemesis at 32-Down, and *Like Polly Flinders* at 53-Down. . . . Good . . . good . . . Those references work well with the 'What are little girls made of?' theme." Then she sighed as she realized she couldn't put two puzzles into the same col-lection that were so similar in message and intent.

She set the crosswords side by side, but as she scrutinized them, Rosco burst in through the front door. "I didn't want to phone you with the news," she heard him call out as he hurried through the living room. She turned toward her office door. Only rarely did her husband come home without announcing himself with a cheery "Hiya Belle!" Something was wrong.

"You found Dan," she said. Her tone was level, but fearful. "He was in an accident, after all—"

"No." Rosco shook his head. "He's been kidnapped. Karen called me at the office. I came home to get you. I thought you'd want go over there with me. The kidnappers contacted her a half an hour ago."

Belle stared at her husband as she tried to process this news. "What . . . ? How . . . ?"

"That's all I know. She said she needed to speak with me in person. We'll bring the dogs and the picnic hamper as if we're were all going out together—in case the house is being watched. Whoever got him may not know I'm a PI; I want to make it look like a social call." He hurried down to the basement and returned a moment later carrying the wicker basket from which he removed the thermos, replacing it with a box containing electronics equipment. Then he crossed to the hall closet, reached behind an overcoat, and retrieved his .32-caliber automatic. This he nestled in among the floral-patterned plastic plates and glasses.

"Oh, Rosco," Belle half-whispered as she watched him.

He put his arms around her and held her close. "All I could think when Karen called with the news was how lucky I was to have you waiting for me at home."

Belle shut her eyes. "Don't ever leave me," is all she said.

"I was going to make you promise the same thing."

"I promise." When Belle opened her eyes, there were tears in them.

T̲he ride to Halcyon Estates was spent in near silence. Rosco said very little while Belle only murmured variations on a worried "Poor Karen . . ." and a quieter but no less anxious "How's she going to help Lily weather this . . . ?" By the time husband and wife arrived at the Tacete home, two black storm clouds rife with questions and concerns roiled through their unhappy brains.

"What else did the caller say?" Rosco sat across from Karen as he spoke. The three adults were in the breakfast nook. Easily visible, Lily was scampering around in apparent unconcern on the deck. Bear and Kit and Gabby were with her, and both Rosco and Belle were dividing their time between watching Lily playing with the dogs and gauging the expressions on Karen's face.

"Only that he had Dan. And that I couldn't go to the police or FBI. He said Dan wouldn't 'survive' if I did."

"And there was no mention of money?" Rosco prompted.

Karen shook her head. "He said he'd call back—that I was to 'sit tight' because he'd be 'waiting and watching.' Those were his exact words."

"And then he put your husband on the phone?" Rosco continued. "And all Dan said was, 'Don't cooperate'?"

"That's all he had time for. They yanked the phone away from him the moment he said that, and I heard a thud and Dan groan."

"They?"

Karen trembled. " 'They.' 'He.' I don't know. I guess I just assumed it was a 'they.' . . . What I mean is: How could only one person do this? Dan's not a small man."

"And you're certain it was Dan's voice."

"Yes. Absolutely."

"And did you recognize the kidnapper's voice?"

"No."

Rosco breathed in deeply. "I'd feel a heck of a lot more comfortable if you'd let me inform the Newcastle police and the FBI. They're the folks who can best handle—"

"No!" Karen all but cried out. "The guy was really clear on that issue. 'No cops, no Feds'; that's what he said. I can't let you do that. They'll kill Dan."

"If they've taken your husband out of state it's a federal

crime, Karen," Belle said as gently as she could. "We all have a duty to report it."

"I don't care!" she almost screamed.

Rosco rubbed at his forehead. "Look, I know Al Lever as well as I know the members of my own family. I'd trust him with my life—or with Belle's. He can be discreet, and he'll find people at the federal level who are, as well. They've handled these situations before. They can tap your phone and never come anywhere near your house. They can trace calls in a matter of seconds; even cell phones are—"

"No! I won't risk it, Rosco. When the guy calls back and tells me what he wants, I'll give it to him. He can have the entire house and everything in it as far as I'm concerned. I didn't come from money, and neither did Dan. We don't need big bucks to survive. I just want to do what I'm told and make this awful situation go away."

"But people like this can—"

"No, Rosco! I'm not bringing the police into this!"

Rosco studied Karen's impassioned face. Then he stood. "With your permission, I'd like to, at least, put one of my own recording devices on your phone—"

"But that's the same as calling the cops, isn't it?"

"No. It's not a police unit. It transmits nothing. It only records at the source. What I'm suggesting is for my use only. Nothing will be given to the police without your permission. I'll give you the same confidentiality I would a client." He continued to hold Karen's gaze. "I'll be the only person monitoring the device. Assuming there will be multiple contacts, I'll need to review each telephone call carefully, listen to the voices, listen for background noises, try to determine a location."

"But won't this guy be able to tell the phone is tapped?"

"No. You can only detect it if you're actually using the extension that's being monitored—which quite clearly isn't going to happen unless the criminal enters your home."

Karen shook her head in anguished ambivalence. "All I

want is to give whoever it is what they want and get Dan
back."

"I promise Karen. I won't jeopardize the situation—or
Dan's safety in any way." Sensing she was in no condition to
make rational decisions, Rosco opted to push forward.
"Now, I'm guessing the kitchen extension is a logical
choice . . . or maybe upstairs in your bedroom?" He removed a small digital voice recorder from the wicker basket.
"This will only monitor one unit, as the receiver must be off
the hook before it begins recording."

"The bedroom's best, I suppose, because Lily's room is
right next door. . . ." Karen's words trailed off. At length,
she stood wearily and led the way upstairs while Belle remained below to watch the little girl.

When Rosco and Karen returned, she huddled back into
her chair, then drew her feet up to the chair's seat and
hugged her bent legs. She looked as though she were trying
to keep warm. "I just can't imagine what Dan's going
through right now . . . how frightened he must be . . ."

Neither Rosco nor Belle said anything. They simply let
Karen speak.

"Dan saved my life, you know. . . . Well, not literally,
but, well, almost. . . ." The words trailed off. "What am I
going to do? What am I *supposed* to do?" She looked be-
seechingly at Belle, who reached out her hand in comfort.

But Rosco knew he had important questions that
wouldn't wait any longer. He walked to the door leading to
the deck, then turned and faced Karen, crossing his arms in
a compassionate but urgent manner. "Has Dan exhibited
any unusual behavior in the last few months?" he asked.

She shook her head. "Except for growing that mustache,
which I like and Lily doesn't." She giggled suddenly. "I
think it's sexy, but—"

"No, I mean, has he changed his schedule in some way?
Did he have time periods that were unaccounted for, or had
he seemed edgy for no reason?"

Again, she shook her head, but didn't otherwise reply.

Rosco continued to gaze down at her. He didn't speak for several moments. "If we're going to play it your way, Karen, we'll have nothing but a waiting game on our hands. I'd be less than honest if I said you were making the right decision. And if the kidnapper is watching this house, he won't make a move as long as Belle's car is parked out front— picnic basket and dogs or not. Which means we're going to have to leave."

"I know," Karen said softly. "I thought of that. I'll be all right."

"These types of crimes take a lot of planning, and the people who commit them follow their own set of rules. . . . What I'm trying to say is that no matter what you'll be told in the next hours or days, you have no guarantees Dan will be returned unharmed. I'm sorry, but those are the realities. So, before we leave, let me ask you again: Has Dan mentioned anything odd? New people in his life? Or was he quarreling with anyone? Does anyone hold a grudge against him?"

Karen didn't reply for a long moment. When she did, her voice dragged uncertainly. "No . . . nothing that I can think of."

"Everything fine at work?"

She shrugged. "It's okay. . . . Well, no . . . it's not that great. Not always."

" 'Not that great'? Can you be more specific?"

Karen forced a laugh. "Jack would never kidnap his partner, if that's what you're suggesting."

Rosco continued to regard her, but it seemed that no further information was forthcoming. "The reason I ask is this: Often a kidnapping is an inside job. The perpetrators know the victim and feel certain they can judge how the mark— which is you—is going to respond. Do you have any domestic employees?"

"A cleaning woman and a gardener. But they're both very nice people. They wouldn't dream of—"

"I'm sure they're very nice," Rosco interrupted. "But can

you give me their phone numbers? It wouldn't hurt to have a talk with them. Maybe they've noticed something unusual."

Karen wiped the tears from her cheeks once more. Her voice remained distracted and unfocused. "Dan put the numbers on the auto-dial. I don't remember them. I'll look around and see if I can find them in his address book."

Rosco nodded to Belle and stood. "Okay. We're going to leave now, but you have my cell phone number. You can reach me at any moment—day or night. Call me as soon as you locate your help's contact numbers. . . . and if you think of anything else that might be important. And until this is resolved, use only your bedroom telephone; or be sure it's off the hook if you're on one of the extensions. That's the only way the device will pick anything up. I want every call that comes in or out of your house to be recorded. That's imperative."

There was no response from Karen, so Rosco added, "Karen? Do you understand what I'm asking you?"

"Yes," she said weakly as Lily came charging back inside followed by the three dogs.

"When's Daddy coming home? When's Daddy coming home?"

CHAPTER

12

When Bonnie O'Connell returned to her apartment at six that evening she could already feel the soreness in her muscles. She'd spent nearly three hours at the gym, doubling her normal exercise routine in the hopes that the strenuous workout would take her mind off the problems that seemed to be spinning quickly out of control. But in the end she was just plain worn out, and her anxiety hadn't been relieved in the slightest.

She tossed her gym bag onto her couch and flopped down on the cushion next to it, putting her feet up on the armrest. Then she hugged one of the pillows, burying her face in its soft and comforting depths. She could feel tears welling in her eyes. As she reached for a tissue from the box on the coffee table, her telephone rang out. The noise startled her, causing her to sit bolt upright and drop the pillow; her heart was beating faster than it had during her entire workout session. Then she forced herself to stand and walk into the kitchen to answer it, although she squinted her eyes in fear as she did so. "Yes? Hello?"

"Hey, Bonnie, what's up? It's Carlos." Carlos Quintero was the lead singer for The Ravens. He was Bonnie's age, a

little younger than the rest of the band, and a real nice guy—
at least as far as Bonnie was concerned. She'd dated him
when they were in high school together; he was one of the
reasons The Ravens had taken on her brother Frank as a
drummer.

"Oh, hi . . ." Bonnie made no effort to disguise the fact
that she was both emotionally and physically drained.

"You okay? You sound like you're stoned."

"I'm not. It's just been one of those weeks."

"Tell me about it," was Carlos's dramatic reply. He was
clearly more concerned with his own problems than Bonnie's. "Actually, that's why I'm calling. I've been trying to
get a hold of Frank all day. He's not answering his phone, or
it ain't paid up; I don't know which. I've been trying since
nine o'clock this morning. Know where he is?"

"I thought you guys fired him."

"Well . . . yeah . . . we sorta did. . . . Sorry, Bonnie, but
you know he's got a problem with the Oxy-C, as well as
some other junk he's been getting into lately. I know I'm
not tellin' you anything you don't already know, but I mean,
we couldn't have him showin' up to rehearsals and floatin'
higher than the trees. We weren't gettin' anything done. I
mean, like, he couldn't even hold a beat."

Bonnie sighed into the phone. "So what do you need him
for now?"

"Turns out this dude we snagged last week couldn't keep
up with us. Needed more breaks than my granny. We had to
tell him to take a hike, too. . . . But we've got a gig at Oasis
tonight, so now we're up a creek without a drummer.
Frank's the only guy around who knows our stuff. I was
hoping he might be at your place."

"I haven't seen Frank in weeks," Bonnie lied, although
she wasn't certain why.

"Ahh, man, that's a bummer. . . . I don't suppose you feel
like doin' me a favor and drivin' over to his place and lookin'
for him?"

Bonnie sat heavily on a kitchen stool; her shoulders

sagged and her head dropped in worry. "Don't ask me to do that, Carlos. You guys have to work this out on your own."

"Ah, come on, Bonnie. It'll take you ten minutes. We're all down at Oasis setting up. We can't go. They've got a drum set here, so Frank doesn't even have to load his stuff up or nothing. Just get him here, with his sticks, in an hour so's we can go over a few things. Come on, Bonnie, for me? For old time's sake? I'll love ya forever, ya do this for me."

Despite her own worries, she found herself smiling wanly. Carlos Quintero could charm anybody. She groaned and said, "I could just kill you, you know that?"

"Thanks, babe, I owe you one. . . . Look, if Frank's high, pump some java into him, will you? And call me at Oasis if you can't find him. We'll have to move onto plan B."

Although Frank's apartment was only a few minutes by car from Bonnie's, the neighborhoods were like night and day. Unlike her own self-contained complex, the buildings in this section of Newcastle had been constructed as large and comfortable middle-class homes during the early 1900s. In the intervening years the owners had come to view their spacious habitats as albatrosses: dormer windows that never stopped leaking, wide verandas replete with rotting floorboards, vast expanses of shingles that seemed to require continuous repair and paint—to say nothing of the ever-escalating cost of heating such huge living spaces. The single-family tenants decamped to the suburbs, and the houses were split into rental apartments whose landlords either took minimal care of the units or abandoned them altogether. Trash littered the barren front lawns and sidewalks, and the street lighting ranged from poor to nonexistent. Bonnie was thankful that the sun hadn't yet set.

She parked in front of her brother's building behind a rusted-out Camaro and stepped from her car. Frank's truck was nowhere in sight, and she found herself thinking there was little point in climbing the porch steps and ringing the bell. But when three large, tough-looking teenage boys rounded the corner and sauntered toward her, she marched up the stairs and stood by the front door. The boys stopped at the foot of the steps, where one whistled at her while the other two made off-color comments.

Bonnie pressed Frank's buzzer. She realized it was a futile effort, but she now felt trapped by the boys as they stood between her and her car. Again, she pushed the buzzer, but as she did so she spotted her brother's pickup truck rolling down the street. She waved to him, and he tapped his horn twice. The exchange was enough to get the teenagers to move off. Bonnie walked down to the curb and waited as Frank parked his truck.

"What's up, babe?" he said as he stepped from the cab. "You look like you just lost a wrestling match." He was surprisingly lucid and sober.

"Carlos called me. The new drummer didn't work out. They want you to play their set at Oasis tonight."

"Cool." Frank began to walk toward the house.

"You don't need your drums, just your sticks."

He turned to face her. "Yeah, but I gotta change my clothes." He studied his sister for a long moment. "You all right? You're shaking."

"Where have you been? Carlos said he couldn't reach you; your answering machine isn't hooked up. He's been trying to get in touch with you all day. And so have I."

"So? I've been out. Maybe I was lookin' for a job?"

"Oh, please . . ."

"Look, where I've been ain't nobody's business but my own, okay? I had things to do, people to see."

Bonnie's response was to fold her arms across her chest and turn away from him.

"What? What's that mean? I can't have a private life around here without my kid sister stickin' her nose into it?"

She gazed at the sidewalk, then raised her head and stared hard at her brother, "Dan Tacete has disappeared."

"Disappeared?" He laughed. "You mean like gone up in smoke?"

"No one's seen him since he left the office at noon on Thursday. Yesterday, a PI named Rosco something came to the office to talk to Jack." She paused, although she continued to eye her brother, who avoided her glance, instead looking up the street toward the corner. The lighted Pepsi sign from a convenience store was just blinking on.

"We could be in big trouble here, Frank. We could go to jail—"

"Hey. Hey. Hold it right there. No one's going to jail." Frank lit a cigarette and took a minute to ponder the situation. "Are the cops lookin' for him—or just the private dick?"

"There's a missing persons report out, that's all I know. Didn't you see it on the news?"

"My TV's busted. Besides, I never watch the news," Frank said in answer. Then he inhaled deeply from his cigarette. "So, that's it, huh? Just a missing person?"

Bonnie nodded, but didn't speak.

Frank flipped what was left of his cigarette out into the street. "I'm going down to Oasis and make like nothing's goin' on. I suggest you do the same thing. Just play it cool."

Bonnie repeated the words in a barely audible voice. "Play it cool. . . ."

"No one's goin' to jail, sis, okay? No way, José. You and me, we're gonna be fine. We're gonna be okay."

CHAPTER

13

"*Jack and Jill went up the hill to fetch a pail of water . . . ,*" Lily recited. Her voice was a sing-song chant, and her blonde head bobbed from side to side in rhythmic unison as she continued the nursery rhyme. "*. . . Jack fell down and broke his crown, and Jill came tumbling after . . .*" She drew a breath, hummed tonelessly, then began her invented melody all over again. This time she added a skipping motion as she circled the foyer, then continued in a rambling loop into the kitchen where Karen was preparing their lunch.

"Lily, honey . . . I bet we can find some other songs for you to sing." Karen cut the crusts off her daughter's peanut butter and jelly sandwich.

"*Jack and Jill . . .*" Lily started for the sixth time, then stopped herself. "*Jack Sprat could eat no fat; his wife could eat no lean. . . .* What's 'lean,' Mommy?"

" 'Lean' means meat that has had the fat cut off."

"And what's 'fat'?"

"Fat is the part of bacon you don't like."

Lily frowned as she looked up at her mother's hands moving across the work island. "I don't want peanut butter," she announced.

"But you just told me you did." Karen's voice had a resigned but edgy tone. She drew in a frustrated breath and then compensated with what she hoped was a coaxing smile.

"It's fat. Daddy says so."

"No, it's not, honey. Peanut butter is made of peanuts. They're legumes." Karen sighed again. She realized she was merely asking for additional questions by providing more information than Lily needed. "You love peanut butter! You know you do. And so does Bear."

Lily's small face had now darkened in stubborn petulance; her hand darted out and grabbed one of the sandwiches from the cutting board, then shoved it toward Bear's face. Naturally, the big brown dog consumed the offering in a single gulp.

"Lily! That's a very naughty girl. You know your daddy doesn't like you feeding Bear—"

"I want my daddy," Lily fought back. "I want my daddy."

Karen gripped the countertop and lowered her head. "We just have to be patient, sweetheart. Daddy's coming home soon, but we have to be good until he gets here."

"I want Rock," Lily countered indignantly. "I want Cookie."

"Well, we can't have Rock and Cookie visit us right now, Lily-bet."

"I want to go to the park with Rock and Cookie and Gabby and Kitty."

"We can't do that either, because we have to eat our lunch. Besides, it's Sunday, and you know how crowded the park can be on Sundays. Remember the time those two German shepherds knocked you down?" Karen's voice had taken on a strangled tone.

"I don't care! I want to go to the park, and I don't want legumes."

Despite her anxiety, Karen laughed. "You didn't even know what they were until this minute."

"I do so!" She pointed to Bear. "I won't eat legs or feets or hands." Then Lily began another rhyming song. *"Humpty-Dumpty went up a hill to fetch a pail of water—"*

"Lily-bet, let's stop now and eat—"

"Humpty-Dumpty broke his crown . . . Humpty-Dumpty broke his crown . . ."

"Lily! Stop!" Karen's voice had turned strident. "I mean it!"

"I want my daddy!" Lily wailed, and she threw herself down on the floor in despair.

The telephone rang at that moment, and Karen grabbed it. Distracted by her daughter's temper tantrum, she totally forgot Rosco's instructions. "Hello . . . ? Hello . . . ? Yes, I'm listening. . . . Dan! No, she's just a little cranky; it turns out that peanut butter—Hello . . . ? Dan . . . ? Dan . . . ? Are you there . . . ? Please, whoever this is, put my husband back on the phone . . . !" Karen's eyes remained glued to her daughter's writhing form as she spoke. "No, I told you I wouldn't go to the police, and I haven't! I swear it! . . . But they're friends of mine! That's all! Just friends! They won't talk to anyone—!" But the line was already dead.

Returning the receiver to the cradle, Karen recognized her error. Her cheekbones quivered as if she were warding off a blow. "Oh, no. . . . Oh, your mommy's made such a big mistake, Lily-bet."

The sound of her mother's sorrow caused the little girl to cease her protestations, and she pulled herself into a sitting position as Karen looked at the clock and again picked up the phone and purposely dialed Belle and Rosco's home phone. When the expected answering machine picked up, she stated a breathless, "I know you're at the park. Don't try to contact me. Ever. They're watching the house. They told me that Lily—" Karen didn't finish the sentence; instead she forcibly returned the receiver to its cradle.

"Lily, what, Mommy?"

"Lily won't eat her peanut butter and jelly sandwich."

CHAPTER

14

A t seven forty-five Monday morning, Belle and Rosco were sitting in abject silence in the midst of Lawson's convivial weekday bustle. Karen's message, which they'd retrieved from their answering machine late the previous afternoon, and her refusal to speak with them when they'd return the call, had been so disconcerting that even fourteen hours later the couple felt the need for more companionship than was offered by their two-human, two-canine household. Comfort food, the familiar clank of knives and forks scraping plates, and the joking banter between Martha and Kenny, the fry cook—or between Martha and anyone else—was what they wanted before heading into the day's work.

"What's up with you two sad sacks today?" Martha teased as she sloshed hot coffee into their cups. "You didn't get more bad news on the Dangerous Dan front, did you?"

Belle's eyes widened in surprise. "Why do you ask that?"

"Hey, like I wasn't here on Saturday when you all were palavering about Tacete taking a hike?" she demanded facetiously.

"Oh, yes . . ." Belle forced a smile while her peripheral vision took in the jaunty flamingo-and-bubblegum hues of the coffee shop's decor and the color-coordinated uniforms worn by Martha, Lorraine, and the other waitress. "In the pink" seemed a term invented for Lawson's, although, at the moment, Belle felt the global aspects of the expression had failed her.

"So, any updates in the wayward-husband scenario?" Martha asked.

"No," Belle and Rosco responded in unison and too quickly.

"You two are a piece of work this morning, that's for sure. Maybe I should ask King Kenny to fry you a couple of steaks instead of the French toast and flapjacks you always order. You look like you could use a little iron."

"Well, we are kind of tired," Belle admitted.

"Haven't you lovebirds learned what weekends are for?" Martha chortled loudly, then shook her buxom body in delight. "Never mind. I take that back. Maybe you should try to spend more time *outside* on your days off. Possibly you need *less* time in bed instead of more?" With that, she flounced away, bellowing greetings and wisecracks to other regular patrons who returned the comments with equal verve and gusto. Any stranger entering Lawson's time-warp linoleum-and-chrome world would have decided that Newcastle was a joyous city indeed.

"So, what do we do next?" Belle asked after another leaden moment had passed between the couple.

"There's nothing we can do, Belle. Karen all but told us to take a hike and now is refusing to speak to us."

"But that seems so wrong, Rosco. . . . So . . . I don't know . . . so *irresponsible* on our part. If Dan were hurt, or Lily—" Belle left the thought unfinished.

"We'll have to hope Karen comes to her senses and contacts the police. Which she may still do. This is an extremely volatile time for her, and she may be taking out her anger on us simply because she can't place it where it should be."

"But what about Lily?" Belle asked. "And whatever Karen failed to explain in her message last night . . ."

Rosco remained in silent deliberation while his wife continued, "Because if this person has started threatening a child—"

"Unless we can talk to Karen, Belle, we have no idea what she was told."

Belle took a deep breath. "I feel awful, Rosco—"

At that moment, two plates piled high with sugar and caloric-hell were slid in front of them by Martha. "Watch out, the maple syrup pitcher's real hot. . . . You want extra whipped cream on those flapjacks, Cute-buns?"

This time Rosco didn't even wince at the waitress' favorite nickname for him. "Sure, why not?" The tone wasn't one of his more chipper efforts, but Martha failed to notice Rosco's distracted state.

"I don't know how he does it, Belle. I swear. If Big Al were to even *look* at one of the platters your hubby regularly puts away, he wouldn't be able to squeeze into this seat."

"Are you talking about me, Marth? Behind my back, no less?"

Martha, Rosco, and Belle swung around. Standing alongside the next banquette was Al Lever, himself.

"Well, if it isn't the big man, himself," Martha cackled. "And larger than life, to boot! I thought you had a court date in Beantown this morning."

"What? You've taken to hacking into the NPD computers in your spare time? You have our phones tapped? And I'll take some java while you're at it—if it's not too much trouble for her highness to find the carafe."

"The bunch of you have communal memory loss this morning or what? You and Abe were grousing about the Boston situation on Saturday, Big Al—in between yakking about a certain missing male." Martha walked away and returned with the coffee and a cup and saucer, as well as a paper placemat, napkin, and silverware. "I take it you're going to horn in on your buddy's *tête-à-tête* with his adorable wife."

"They had all weekend for canoodling," was Al's blithe reply as he slid into the banquette opposite Rosco and Belle.

"And from the looks of them, they used up every lovin' minute," the waitress joked.

Al glanced at his former partner, and then at Belle. "What gives? Martha's right; you two *are* awfully quiet this morning. You didn't have a fight, did you?" Lever looked genuinely worried as he asked this question.

But Rosco and Belle were saved from an immediate answer because Martha pulled out her order pad and retrieved the pencil she kept stuck into the shellacked waves of her blonde beehive. "So, what'll it be, Big Al? By the way, is this breakfast number two or number three . . . ?"

"Yuk, yuk . . . And it's my first, for your information."

Martha arched an eyebrow, an action she'd perfected during her many years as Lawson's queen bee. "Helen's finally put you on that diet, has she?"

"If you knew my wife's cooking, you wouldn't bother to ask."

"Save it, Big Al. I know the routine already. The only danger Helen ever encounters in your kitchen is the risk of freezer burn, right?"

"Well, it's true. A cook she definitely ain't." Al didn't bother to reach for the menu as he spoke. None of Lawson's regulars did; just as Martha didn't really need to write down their orders. "A couple of eggs over easy—"

"And a double order of hash browns . . . and extra bacon, extra crispy, and a large O.J." Martha finished the words for him.

"Only if you twist my arm, Marth."

"Since when have you needed persuasion when it came to chow, Al?"

"Ho, ho." Al stirred cream into his coffee, then turned toward Belle. "How's your friend, Karen, doing?"

"Karen?" she said too quickly, wondering if Al could now read her mind.

"Oh, boy . . ."

"Oh, that Karen!" Belle pasted on a smile. "She's okay, I guess."

"No word from the Doc, I take it?"

"Not that I know of."

Lever frowned. "You mean she wouldn't call you if he suddenly reappeared? Or Missing Persons? I hope the heck she'd notify NPD so we could call off our search for the Explorer."

"Sure . . . of course, she would. Certainly. Yes." Belle's words tumbled over each other, and Al Lever's scowl deepened.

"You lovebirds *did* have a fight, didn't you?"

"No, Al. Honest!" Belle smiled brightened in order to prove her point, but the effort failed to convince Al that she was telling the truth.

"Something's wrong, and I know it." He looked at Rosco. "Aren't you going to ask me if we've had any luck at all in chasing down Tacete's Explorer?"

"I thought I'd let you eat your breakfast in peace before hammering you with questions, Al."

"Since when do you allow me any kind of peace, Poly—crates?"

Rosco laughed. The sound was relaxed and jocular enough to fool Lever. "So, what's the word on the Explorer?"

"Obviously nada. Zilch. Zip. I guess the guy's serious about hiding himself from the little missus. Or maybe he's just evaporated?"

Martha appeared with Al's orange juice and toast. "Leave him alone and he'll come home, dragging his tail behind him," she misquoted. "Or not." She laughed and moved away again, and Al concentrated on covering his toast with strawberry jam. After a moment, he sat back. "I guess we'll be sending one of our officers out to the Tacete household today—"

"That's not a good idea, Al," Rosco interrupted.

Lever gazed at his former partner. A look of annoyance crossed his face. "Maybe you'd like to tell the boys and girls over at Missing Persons why it isn't."

"Karen's at sixes and sevens," Belle interjected too hastily. "I think an official visit would push her over the edge. . . . Right now, anyway."

"Why don't I act as a liaison, Al," Rosco offered. "Just until Karen's over this initial emotional hump. It's the least I could do."

Lever finished his toast, pushed the plate away, and looked for Martha. "Where the heck's my eggs?" He turned back to Rosco. "If I didn't know you two as well as I do, I'd say something fishy was going on."

"Well, fortunately, you do know us." Rosco grinned as he spoke.

"Yeah, that's what worries me even more." Al stood. "I gotta get back to the rat race. . . ." He slid a tip for Martha beneath his saucer. "I'm gonna have to ask her to put my breakfast in some Styro so I can take it back to the station. When do you want me to finish up hunting for that new car, Poly—crates?"

"Actually, Al, I'm a little swamped at the moment."

Lever gave Rosco a quizzical look. "On the other hand, maybe you could borrow one of Dan Tacete's rides for the time being. I can definitely see you cruising around in a Bentley."

Rosco's smile remained stuck to his face as Lever made his way toward the cashier, grabbed his eggs from Martha, and then ambled out the door.

But Belle's own bright expression wobbled, and her lips twitched in worry. "I hate this, Rosco," she murmured. "I feel like *we're* the criminals. Or that we're abetting the crime."

"We'll give the situation another twenty-four hours—max. And then that's it. Karen's wishes or not, the Feds need to be brought in on this."

"A lot can happen in twenty-four hours."

Across
1. Resistance units
5. Tennis org.
8. Cheat
12. A time to___, Ecclesiastes
13. A time to___, Ecclesiastes
14. A time of___, Ecclesiastes
15. Mr. Mason
16. Rascal
17. Like Miss Muffet's curds
18. Baseball stat.
19. Garden tool
20. Ms. la Douce
21. Jack Be Nimble prop
25. Hitchcockian vane reading
28. "Exodus" author
29. Lyric poems
30. Buck's partner
31. October birthstone
32. ". . . and put them to___"
33. See 9-Down
34. City in Texas
35. Suit piece
36. Cookie ingredient
37. Suffix for red, white, or blue
38. Runner Sebastian
39. Mr. Huntley
40. Fib
41. Ms. Lanchester
42. Blunder
43. Lincoln model
44. Suggestion for 21-Across hurdler
48. MGM founder
50. Iota
51. Half MCII
52. It's often busted
54. Finished first
55. Takes___
57. Side
58. Shock
59. Mr. Gardner and namesakes
60. Questions
61. Docs' aides
62. Seven days

Down
1. "Hänsel und Gretel," e.g.
2. Where did that mouse go?
3. Scratch
4. "The___is falling!"
5. "Hasta luego!"
6. A time to heal; a___, Ecclesiastes
7. Energy
8. Meeting spot?
9. With 33-Across, rhyme line
10. High card
11. All the king's___
12. Dimension; abbr.
14. Makes coffee
19. "For___a jolly good fellow!"
20. Chilled
22. Cart
23. ___Abner
24. Thought
26. Pitcher's goal
27. A time to___Ecclesiastes
31. Watering hole
34. A time to___Ecclesiastes
35. Pear selection
36. Chinese dynasty
38. Paw part
39. ___au vin
41. Throw out
42. A time to___, Ecclesiastes
45. "I'll grind his___to make . . ."
46. Wall hook
47. Smooch
49. Mind—P's & Q's
52. Arts deg.
53. Indian dance
54. A time of___, Ecclesiastes
55. A time of___, Ecclesiastes

"AS TIME GOES BY"

	1	2	3	4		5	6	7			8	9	10	11
12						13				14				
15						16				17				
18					19				20					
21			22	23			24				25	26	27	
	28					29					30			
	31					32					33			
34					35					36				
37				38					39					
40			41					42						
43			44			45						46	47	
	48	49			50					51				
52	53				54			55	56					
57				58			59							
60			61			62								

56. Anger

CHAPTER

15

As Belle stood waiting for the elevator that would carry her from the *Evening Crier*'s busy lobby up to her cubicle-size office, she had no idea what lay in store for her. Although she did experience a keen sense of premonition, almost of doom. The fact that her brain kept repeating its complaint that she and Rosco were withholding information didn't alleviate the feelings of hopelessness and fear. Nor did her surroundings help; in the seven years Belle had called the *Crier* her professional home, she'd never warmed to its post-modern architecture or the ambience that seemed to have all the luster and fizz of a high school cafeteria after the home team had lost a deciding game. The word "bleak" had found a special niche in the newspaper's physical plant.

The smeary steel doors of one of the four elevators opened. A few men and women hurriedly strode off; many more walked on; some words of greeting were exchanged but not many, as the doors closed and the metal box creaked upward. Monday morning, even Monday morning at almost nine thirty, wasn't the cheeriest hour at the *Crier*.

Belle rode to the third floor, where she and some equally silent colleagues exited. Then she walked down the lackluster corridor with its tired beige paint and its scuffed beige floors and turned the key in her, yes, *beige* office door. She was in the midst of condemning the designer who'd created such an impersonal space—something she did on a regular basis—and wondering whether the intention was to prove the superiority of cerebral activity over visual stimuli, when a manila envelope lying on the floor caught her eye. Someone had slid it beneath the door, which was not how mail was delivered at the *Crier.*

Her instantaneous reaction was a double dose of the apprehension than she'd felt in the lobby. Belle sensed the missive related to Dan Tacete—which then immediately led her to a more powerful response, which was panic. Although without basis and completely inexplicable, Belle felt as though *she* were the crime's mastermind and was now in danger of being caught. *I'd never make a good crook,* she decided, bending down to pick up the envelope. *I just don't have the cool nerves required for the job. One strange look from any of my co-workers out there on the elevator would cause me to blurt out the truth.*

She closed the door behind her and locked it—another bizarre nod to the clandestine mission she felt she'd embarked upon.

Seated at her desk, which was a rectangular piece of dark beige laminate covering a pressed-wood core, and facing a built-in bookcase constructed of the same attractive stuff, Belle opened the envelope and pulled out a crossword. Her breathing had grown fast and shallow; her eyes crossed in recognition as she read the title, "As Time Goes By," and the constructor's name, "Sal D. Anderson."

She quickly scanned the Across and Down clues. Sure enough, the theme was not only time but the actions that accompanied it. At 12-Across was a reference to the Biblical book of Ecclesiastes in *A time to* SPEAK; 13-Across was *A time to* DIE. *A time to* WEEP was at 27-Down; 34-Down was *A time to* KILL.

SPEAK, Belle thought. *If Rosco and I—or Karen—share*

what we know with the police, does Dan Tacete DIE? But even as Belle pondered this horrific possibility, her brain made the next leap. Like the two seemingly innocent puzzles she'd received at home, and had assumed were intended as submissions for her crossword compendium, this creation was full of clues based on childhood tales. *Like Miss Muffet's curds; Jack Be Nimble prop; Hänsel und Gretel.* . . . Belle actually felt herself begin to pant, and her stomach churned in distress. What if the other puzzles had contained clues that she'd missed? What if the situation with Dan could have been prevented? What if the constructor had been trying to warn her that something evil was afoot? And Sal, the mystery constructor? Is that a man or a woman? Is it short for Sally or Salvatore?

A knock on her door made Belle spin in her chair; she shoved the crossword under a pile of papers before moving to twist open the locked knob.

"Goodness, *mia Bella,* you look as though you've seen a ghost! You're as white as a sheet of empty newsprint. Or should I say, as gray." Bartholomew Kerr tipped upward on his toes as he spoke, his enormous glasses enlarging his myopic eyes and making him appear insectlike in his intensity. He looked like a praying mantis cloned with a particularly frail specimen of the human race. Despite the *Crier*'s gossip columnist's disconcerting appearance, however, he was the soul of kindness where his friends were concerned; and Belle was numbered in that elite group. "What are you doing, hiding in here, my dear? Not constructing a ransom note in crosswords, perchance?" Bartholomew chortled at what he intended as a witticism, but Belle continued to gape down at him in distress.

"A ransom note?"

"Or a message concerning a heinous heist. . . . Although the latter might be unwieldy, given the amount of time required to ink in the answers, and the probable intervention by the constabulary before the crime could be considered a *fait accompli,* and so forth."

"Time?" Belle murmured. She was trying to focus her thoughts on this conversation but wasn't having much success.

"Oh, dear me, I see I've disturbed you when deep in lexical mode. . . . I'm like that nasty man from Porlock."

" 'Porlock'?" Belle echoed.

"Now, *Bellisima,* don't tell me that you, our resident maven of *ars poetica* could possibly have forgotten the wretched fellow from the hamlet of Porlock who disturbed the young Mr. S. T. Coleridge in his Somersetshire snuggery when he was in the throes of penning *Kubla Khan?* Of course, our famed wordsmith was high as a kite on laudanum. Not terribly laudatory, but there you are. . . . 'Beware! Beware!' as he himself wrote before going on to extol the benefits of drinking 'the milk of Paradise' . . ."

Belle remained mute, but Bartholomew was now on a roll and didn't notice. "A terrible husband, though, by all accounts was our beloved Samuel T. . . . Kept disappearing from his dear wife and kiddies and washing up in the fleshpots of the Mediterranean. . . ."

Belle nodded, although the action was halfhearted.

"Different days, back in the early eighteen-hundreds. I would imagine a clever person could do a most credible vanishing act, as opposed to nowadays with our myriad electronic minders: cell phones and autos equipped with satelite-enchanced tracking devices, and so on. . . . A pity, really. I suppose Coleridge and all those other naughty writer laddies who snuck away for a little fun on the side would not have produced their extraordinary bodies of work if they'd been within beeping range of home and hearth. Rather spoils the pleasure if your phone transmits a digital photograph of your insalubrious surrounds back to the mother ship. . . . Speaking of which, any word on our latest dust-up? The tooth-man gone to earth . . . ? You're acquainted with the wife, I believe—"

"No," was Belle's too-rapid reply.

"Oh! I was misinformed, then. I thought I saw you two having a confab in the dog park."

"Oh, yes . . . yes, I'm a friend of Karen's," Belle said with what she hoped was a candid smile. "But, no, she hasn't shared her concerns about Dan with me."

"Well, that's an oddity in itself, isn't it? Aren't gal-pals traditionally prone to divulge *all,* as opposed to their tight-lipped masculine counterparts who would sooner die than 'breathe a word about their loss'—to slightly misquote R. Kipling?"

Belle became aware that Bartholomew's professional manner was asserting itself. He was clearly on the scent of a story for his column.

"Maybe the lovely lady's hiding something," he added.

"Oh, I don't think so," was Belle's airy answer.

"Hmmmm . . ." Bartholomew cocked his big head to one side.

"Besides, I'm trying to give Karen a little space right now. The last thing she needs is a curious friend pestering her."

"Hmmmm . . ." Kerr repeated. "And this from our nationally acclaimed 'crossword sleuth.'" Then he eased back from his search mode. Belle was a friend, not a "contact," after all. "Well, let me know if there's anything juicy in the works, *Bella mia.* I'll be the soul of discretion. . . . Well, perhaps not the *sole,* when so many of my detractors refer to me as a *shark* circling the waters of celebrity. But I do promise to sheathe your illustrious name in the deepest secrecy. . . ." With that, Bartholomew began to toddle away, but he turned to face Belle once more. "Remember what I said about Coleridge's unfortunate troubles, dear girl. Physicians and other practitioners of the healing arts can also develop an overfondness for doses of their own medicines."

"Smile! Good morning. May I help you?" Bonnie said into the office phone. She was doing her level best to appear as cheery as the practice's name, but was finding the effort taxing indeed. "No, that's correct, Mrs. Harris, Doctor Tacete isn't currently scheduling patients. . . . I'm afraid I can't answer that question. . . . No ma'am, I mean 'can't,' not 'won't.' " Bonnie's lips pulled back to show her teeth, but the effect was more threatening than warm. "If you'd care to speak with Doctor Wagner about the situation, I can have him return your call. . . ." She pulled the receiver away from her ear and winced at the loudness of the voice on the other end of the connection. "No, ma'am, I can't say when he'll have the opportunity—"

But the line was dead. Bonnie sighed, then glanced at her wristwatch: 11:42 A.M. It was going to be a long day.

She replaced the receiver, but no sooner had she done so than the button indicating the internal line lit up. "Yes, Doctor Wagner. . . . ? Yes, sir, I canceled all of Doctor Tacete's appointments"—Bonnie glanced at the scheduling book lying open in front of her—"except for Mr. Rossi, who's supposed to come in for another check-up this afternoon at four forty-five. . . . Yes, sir, I called his home and left a message, but he hasn't bothered to return the call." She gritted her teeth at the harsh words that next assailed her ear, but tried to mask her discomfort for the sake of the patients waiting there.

"I understand your feelings, Doctor Wagner, but—" Bonnie stifled a second troubled sigh while another irate directive poured forth. "I'll call his place of employment and see if I can head him off. . . ."

Hanging up, her left hand remained on the receiver while her right began scrolling down the computer screen until she came to Rob Rossi's entry. Her fingers tapped the numbers for the Black Sheep into the phone. "I'd like to speak to Rob Rossi, please. . . . Oh, I see. . . . Well, when do you expect him? Oh!" Bonnie frowned as the response was given, then she replaced the receiver and sat for a moment, thinking. Her eyes were becoming dangerously brimful of tears, and the fingers of her right hand, which were still resting on the computer keypad, trembled. Her mind was not on Rob Rossi's whereabouts, but on Frank.

Finally, she took up the phone again and placed a brief

and furtive call to her brother's answering machine. "It's me, Frankie. I'm at work. Don't call me back here. Rob hasn't been at the Sheep since Thursday. . . . If you've done something stupid and gotten him involved in this mess, you'd better let me know. I don't know how much longer I can play dumb."

CHAPTER

16

Al Lever had never warmed to the notion of disposable plastic cigarette lighters, which meant that for the past twenty-plus years he'd lit his Camels with matches—which, in turn, kept him ever mindful of the proper disposal of used matchsticks when it came investigating crime scenes. Al's routine was simple. He struck a match, waited for its sulfur tip to cool, then stuffed the remaining sliver of cardboard into his pants pocket. His dry cleaners had picked up on this eccentricity and were careful to check for matches before running his trousers through the process. The same was true of the chinos his wife, Helen, washed and ironed for him. Early on she'd learned it was better to personally search his pockets than to suggest he might want to get rid of the burned stubs himself. That is, if she wanted her laundry to remain stain-free.

Standing on the brambly hillside, as he stared grimly down at a still-smoldering car lying at the bottom of the ravine, Lever repeated this well-documented procedure. His reasoning was what it always was at a crime scene—or even a *potential* crime scene: If Abe Jones's forensic team or the fire inspectors or anyone else investigating the site decided to scour the area, things like a discarded matchstick could play a significant role. And Al had no desire to confuse the issue.

He took a long drag on his cigarette while the hand with the discarded match still rested as though forgotten in his pocket. He didn't like the sight below him; and at three thirty in the morning, the black of night only made it that much more disturbing. A charred body in a burned-out automobile was one thing, and notifying next of kin, another, but this scenario was different; it was too close to home. Dan Tacete's death would effect more than his immediate family; the ripples of loss would be felt in people Al counted as good friends. The situation would require delicate and personalized attention.

Thoughtfully, he nudged the rear license plate with his foot. It had been torn loose during the car's descent and now lay on the ground nearby. Al inhaled deeply once again, then sat on the end of the galvanized steel guardrail that the automobile had missed by less than two feet. He almost wished the plate hadn't been discovered—not yet, anyway.

Newcastle County's medical examiner, Herb Carlyle, struggled up through the underbrush that covered the hillside, and Al watched the man tear at the vines and saplings as if he believed they'd been put there on purpose to hinder his progress. As long as Lever had known him, the M.E. had regarded any such difficulty as a personal affront.

A thin man in his late fifties with albino-white shoulder-length hair, unhip, black-framed glasses, and purplish shadows lurking under his deep-set eyes, Herb Carlyle could look ghoulish in the best of lights. And this was not the best of lights; in fact, the flickering of the red, white, and blue emergency vehicle strobes made the M.E. look positively otherworldly.

Carlyle grasped at the thick ground cover and swore loudly. Below him, the fire department was finishing their work of extinguishing the last of the small brush fires that had been byproducts of the crash. The vehicle itself, a 1995 Corvette, was no longer burning, but much of it had been reduced to a mass of molten fiberglass and metal. Tacete's remains were still strapped into the driver's seat.

"What brings you out at this hour, lieutenant?" Carlyle huffed and puffed as he finally reached the pavement and approached Al. "This is hardly a homicide."

The detective only shrugged, so Carlyle continued with an aggrieved "I can't get close enough to make any preliminary judgments, but from a distance things seem pretty cut and dried. The ground's still hotter than blazes down there." He stared at Lever's stoic face for a moment, then added, "You wouldn't have another smoke, would you?"

Lever offered him a cigarette, let him light it from his own, but still said nothing. The medical examiner also sat on the railing, and the two men watched as the firemen began to roll up their hoses. The silence between them was not a companionable one. Carlyle had been working in the Newcastle morgue for thirty ears. He'd known Lever since the lieutenant had been a rookie cop, and the two had never hit it off. In fact, the only person Carlyle had less use for was a former NPD detective by the name of Rosco Polycrates.

Carlyle looked around the area in an exaggerated fashion, craning his neck first to the left, then to the right; and finally added a facetious, "What? No Abe Jones here to check up on my work? Mr. *C.S.I.* can't get out of bed at three in the morning? Entertaining yet another hot-patootie no doubt."

Al shook his head; the gesture was more out of frustration with Carlyle's flippant attitude than in response to his query. "Busy night. Robbery's got Jones over at Papyrus, the office superstore on the other side of the Interstate. Someone knocked off their safe to the tune of an unbelievable sixty grand. Jones and his wizards are dusting for prints. He'll be here later." Lever's solemn stare returned to the ravine.

Carlyle also studied the wreckage. After a minute he said, "I'm gathering you're unwilling to accept the obvious, lieutenant—that this was an accident? Drunk driver? Sleepy driver?" He didn't roll his eyes, but his caustic intent was audible in his voice.

"I don't know what to make of it . . . but the tire marks bother me. They're too . . . I don't know, ordinary. Bing: the car's making the turn, and then bang: it's slipping past the guardrail and plummeting over the edge. The guy barely taps his brakes? Even a drunk has a moment of panic when he spots something like this curve looming ahead of him—"

"Hold on there, Lieutenant. First off—"

Sensing that one of Carlyle's lengthy and exceptionally dull dissertations was about to be forthcoming, Lever held up his hand, then reached for the dislocated plate. He tilted it toward the headlights of a police cruiser for the M.E. to read.

"T-U-T-H D-O-C," Carlyle spelled out. "What's that supposed to mean?"

"It means that half your work's done. Our dead man is Dan Tacete, DDS. Sergeant Gonzalez found the tag torn off, halfway down the slope. Tacete was his dentist. Gonzalez recognized the tags and what's left of the car—which he just happened to pull over for speeding two months ago."

"You mean the same Tacete who disappeared last week?"

Lever nodded.

"I thought he was supposed to be driving a white Explorer when he vanished."

"That's what we were told."

Carlyle puffed on his cigarette. If Al had been looking at him, he might have noticed the M.E.'s eyes beginning to glow with a morbid pleasure. "So . . . the guy creeps home with his tail between his legs, tries to smooch it up with the missus but she's not buying his apologies . . . then he storms off in a rage, takes the babe-magnet LT-5 'Vette instead of the SUV family-man-mobile, gets tanked trying to drown his domestic sorrows, or hook up with some cutie at a local watering hole . . ." Carlyle was obviously relishing his theory. He glanced at his watch for effect.

"The 'Vette crashed around two thirty or three AM, a normal hour for a D.U.I. . . . Hey, maybe it wasn't booze; maybe your doc was high on some other nifty substance courtesy of the pharmaceutical industry. After all, who else has such easy access to all those nice, little pills except those of us in the medical profession? Then again, he could also have committed suicide, or as I suggested, simply fallen asleep at the wheel. . . . But my guess is drugs or alcohol; I'll test for both. Nine times out of ten, those are the culprits in situations like this. That 'moment of panic' of yours can take a very delayed form according to the mix of substances. . . . Hell, remember the case of the woman in Ohio who swore she didn't know she'd hit a homeless man . . . ? She drove home with the guy still kicking and screaming in her windshield, and left him to die overnight in her attached garage while she went inside to sleep it off."

Carlyle's stock in trade were stories like these; Lever merely nodded his response, hoping the end was in sight. There was no point in eliciting the M.E.'s lugubrious tales of death and disaster if they could be avoided.

A uniformed police sergeant approached the two men; in his right hand was a navy blue nylon-and-mesh bag. "Looks like Tacete's gym bag, lieutenant." Gonzalez handed it to Lever. "It's got the usual equipment, plus photo ID from the BodyWorks Gym on Ninth Street. . . . I guess the bag must have been stowed in the trunk, then bounced out when the car hit the slope and the latch opened."

Lever took the bag in silence while Carlyle wrapped this newest piece of information into his proposed scenario. "Okay . . . okay . . . Doc walks out on the missus . . . hits the *treadmill*, where he's surrounded by a bunch of happy-go-lucky hardbodies . . . *then* he decides to get tanked, because no one's looking his way. . . ." Carlyle glanced at both Gonzalez and Lever for confirmation that they found the notion credible, but neither said a word.

"I'm wondering when he traded the Explorer for the Corvette?" Lever finally pondered aloud while Carlyle shrugged.

"What's that got to do with the price of eggs?" He smiled and stood. Like his other facial expressions, this also bore a trace of the spectral. "Hell, since he's a local, we sure won't have to have to hunt high and low for dental records, will we? Makes my job a lot easier. Where was his office?"

"Smile! is the name of the practice," Gonzalez said. "It's on South Charleton Street."

Carlyle chortled. "Oh, yeah, I've heard a lot about that sleazeball. My sister went to see him a while back. She said he was a real crook. Tried to talk her into a few thousand dollars worth of work; all sorts of cosmetic rebuilding, implants, bonding, orthodontics, crowns: you name it. He even had the gall to offer her his own payment plan with *special* interest rates. I mean, my sister's sixty-two years old; what's she need all that bunk for? She told him to take a leap. . . . But, I thought his name was something else, like Wagner, or something?"

"That's the partner," Gonzalez replied. He cocked his head toward the ravine. "You had to make sure you got Tacete and not Wagner. Dan wasn't into jacking up the bill."

"Jacking . . . That's the one, *Jack* Wagner." Carlyle dropped his cigarette onto the asphalt and crushed it with his shoe. "Leave it, lieutenant; this isn't a crime scene. Your wandering dentist was either flying high or it was a suicide . . . maybe both; it's less painful that way." The M.E. began to move away. "I'm going to bag this baby up. As soon I can reach the folks at Smile!, I'll confirm your boy's ID."

"Good. I'd rather not have to ask the wife to come down to the morgue and look at this. It's going to be hard enough as it is." Despite the medical examiner's injunction, Lever tamped his own cigarette out on the guardrail and slipped the butt into his pocket alongside the match and grudgingly picked up the M.E.'s butt as well. Then he looked at his own watch. "What are we talking about, Herb? Five? Six hours?"

"Max." Carlyle walked toward his morgue wagon, where he retrieved his tool satchel and a black plastic body bag. He and his assistant then worked their way back down the ravine to the Corvette.

Lever looked at Gonzalez and folded his arms across his

broad chest. "I just can't figure out why Tacete was driving the Corvette and not the Explorer. If he returned, why didn't his wife call us and have him taken off the missing persons list?"

"Maybe Polycrates knows," Gonzalez offered. "He was friendly with the wife, right?"

Out of habit, Lever glanced his watch again. "It's tempting to call him, three forty-five or not. I was getting some strange vibes from him and Belle yesterday morning at Lawson's. I had a feeling they knew more about our missing dentist than they were letting on."

"So, call him, lieutenant. You're into hour number twenty, and now you've got to be back at it at seven. Let someone else lose a little sleep. And to be honest with you, I don't think Rosco would mind. . . . Besides, like you said, someone's going to have to notify Dan's wife, right? Why not let Rosco do it?"

Lever seemed to give it all some serious thought, but in the end he said, "No. I've got to do it. But I'll get Carlyle's report in my hands first." Then he paused and stared into the night. "It's all part of the job, isn't it?"

CHAPTER
17

Breaking bad news to loved ones: Despite what Lever had told Gonzalez about the task being part of a homicide detective's job description, it wasn't one Al relished. In fact, he downright hated it. Dealing with the investigatory aspect of a murder was one thing—unraveling clues, searching blind alleys for leads, even dealing with recalcitrant and often dangerous suspects had a certain cerebral methodology—but "method" and "process" were of no use when it came to meeting with the victim's next of kin.

Every time Al was called upon to sit down and talk with the bereaved, he thought of the men and women of the armed forces who had to inform families of their losses, who had to put on their dress uniforms and present themselves at unfamiliar front doors and explain to the parents or wives or husbands that the person they dearly loved and took such pride in would never be coming home. Al simply didn't know how anyone could face such heartbreaking duty.

Which is why he ultimately opted to leave urgent messages on both Rosco's and Belle's answering machines the moment Herb Carlyle had made a positive ID on Dan

Tacete's body. Al wanted Karen's friends close at hand when he told her about the wreck. *At least Tacete went quickly,* he reminded himself as he drove out to Halcyon Estates. *There's some consolation in that fact. Not much, but some.*

Pulling up just short of the Tacetes' driveway, Al was dismayed to see that neither Rosco nor Belle had preceded him. He made two more hurried calls, but was still greeted by recorded messages. For a split second, the seemingly callous and cantankerous detective considered slinking away, hightailing it back to the station house until he could muster sufficient backup for the unwelcome job at hand. He lit a cigarette for moral support, but the nicotine and smoke didn't help; he stubbed it out and left it crumpled and bent in the ashtray.

Then duty won out—as it always had, and always would—and Al turned into the drive. As he parked, unfastened his shoulder belt, and prepared to take his first heavy steps toward the house, both Belle and Rosco came roaring into sight: Belle in her own car, Rosco in the leased sedan that was currently replacing his dearly departed Jeep. In Lever's estimation, the only thing the car had going for it was its color: an opalescent white that made it look so much like an airport rental that Al was certain Rosco could effect any number of out-of-towner disguises while driving it.

Rosco's face, as he approached his former partner, was grim. Belle looked close to tears. Al noted that both were wearing dark clothes; the civvies he'd chosen for this particular mission were equally austere, making the trio appear almost threatening amidst the abundant morning sunshine. Without a sound of acknowledgment or greeting, they stepped up onto the Tacete porch and rang the bell.

The first words Karen uttered after she opened the door were "I told you not the call the cops! And not to come back here, either! They've been watching the house!" But the brief diatribe was uttered after she'd turned dangerously white and shaky. She stared at Al with eyes gone terrified and huge.

"May I come in, Mrs. Tacete?" Lever's tone was hushed and formal. He didn't ask how she'd pegged him as NPD, and he was so intent on his prepared speech of sympathy that it took a moment for him to recognize the importance of what Karen had just said. Then he looked at Rosco and Belle before returning his concentration to the new widow. "No one called me, Mrs. Tacete—"

"They're probably watching the house right now!" Karen all but shrieked.

"Let's go inside," Belle suggested, moving forward as she did so. "Is Lily around?"

"No. She has playschool on Tuesday mornings. . . ." Then Karen gasped. "Oh, my God! They got her, too, didn't they?" She glared at Al. "That's why you're here, isn't it? To tell me those creeps took my baby! The school has security guards. We pay a lot for that!"

"Is there someplace we can sit, Mrs. Tacete?" Lever asked, but Karen was no longer paying attention to him.

"I shouldn't have listened to you, Rosco! The guy told me if I screwed up, he'd hurt Lily!" She opened her mouth as if to scream, but instead clamped her hand over her lips. "I did everything they said . . . drove the Corvette to Gilbert's Groceries . . . put the twenty-five thousand dollars in Dan's gym bag. I left it in the trunk like they said—"

Lever interrupted, his gaze taking in both Karen and Rosco. "Are we talking about kidnapping, Mrs. Tacete? Your telling me your husband had been kidnapped?"

Karen spun back to Al. She opened her lips, but no sound came.

"And you knew about this, Polycrates?" Lever was so per-turbed he didn't bother to use Rosco's butchered nickname. "You knew the doctor had been kidnapped?"

"Lily's fine, Karen," Belle interjected as she put her arm around the distraught woman's shoulders. "Why don't we phone the playschool so you can talk to her yourself?" Even as she uttered this soothing suggestion, Belle was praying that what she said was true.

She steered Karen toward the kitchen, where they made the necessary phone call, after which Karen burst into tears of unconstrained relief. "I couldn't stand it if they took her, too!" she wailed. "At least with Dan . . . well, he's an adult, he can look after himself. . . . But my little girl . . ." Finally, she refocused on Al Lever, and then on Rosco. Her brow was furrowed in concentration. "They told me not to call the cops," she repeated in a leaden voice. "You shouldn't be here."

Al took a breath. "No one called me, Mrs. Tacete, but I'm afraid I have some unfortunate news. . . . Your husband's body was found this morning. It looks like his Corvette didn't make that sharp turn out on East Farm Lane. Death was instantaneous."

Karen's eyes fluttered across Lever's face before moving to Rosco's, to Belle's, and then back to Al's.

"He can't be dead. I did everything they told me to. . . . Why would they kill him when they had the money? Why would they do that? They wouldn't do that, would they?"

But Karen's queries were answered by the grave expressions that continued to regard her. "You're not telling me those creeps killed Dan, are you?" Anger and disbelief burned in her eyes. "You're not telling me that, are you?"

"I'm afraid I am, Mrs. Tacete."

Karen sagged, then steadied herself, and at length allowed Belle and Rosco to lead her to the table in the breakfast nook, where Belle kept a consoling hand on her arm while Rosco made her a cup of tea and Lever posed the gentlest questions he could. Karen's recitation rambled, punctuated by grief, confusion, and denial; and it took several retellings of the story before Al felt appropriately apprised of the necessary facts.

"But what made you decide not to use the recording device Rosco put on your phone?" Al asked during a break in Karen's anguished monologue. "It would have been much better if . . . A voice recognition expert could have—"

"I didn't *decide!* . . . I just . . . I just forgot. . . . I was making lunch for Lily . . . and she was having a hissy fit over how she wasn't going to eat peanut butter ever again. She'd gotten all mixed up over something Dan had told her about 'fat' versus 'lean.' . . . When the phone rang, I . . . I just answered it. I didn't think about going upstairs . . . because Lily was . . ." Karen looked at Belle for emotional support. "That's when they put Dan on the line. That's when the guy threatened my Lily."

"And the next call?" Al prompted.

"I wasn't expecting it so soon. . . . I wasn't in my bedroom. . . . I know I thought that would be the best place for you to install the thing, Rosco, but . . . well, I guess I imagined they'd be calling at night, and I'd be . . ." She hung her head and stared sightlessly into her untouched cup of tea.

"So we have no recordings of the kidnapper's voice." Rosco commented to no one but himself.

"I'd recognize that creep anywhere!" Karen spat out. Then she glowered at Al. "He told me no cops, and look what's happened!" Finally, her rage turned on Rosco. "You're all alike!" she hissed. "This is nothing more than a game for big boys to play, isn't it? . . . Catch the crook . . . who cares what you use for bait—?!"

"Karen," Belle interrupted. "Rosco's not to blame, and Al's not to blame—"

"Get out of my house!" Karen raged. "If it weren't for you, my Dan would still be alive! Get out! All of you!"

Standing in the driveway, Al and Belle and Rosco didn't speak for several moments. An air of gloom mingled with a disconcerting level of mistrust had settled around them.

"You should have persuaded her to call us, Poly—crates," Lever finally offered. The use of the nickname removed some of the edge of harshness from his tone.

Rosco shook his head. "You heard her, Al. There's no persuading Karen Tacete. I was caught between a rock and a hard place. I was treating her like a client. She deserved the kind of confidentiality I'd give anyone else—"

"We were going to give the situation another day and then tell you, Al," Belle interjected. "Rosco and I felt like total heels keeping this a secret. . . . When we saw you at Lawson's yesterday morning—"

"So, that's what was eating you both. I assumed you guys had had a fight—"

"Karen phoned us. Told us to butt out after she got the first ransom call," Rosco added. "That was Sunday afternoon; almost evening really, by the time we picked up the message. Apparently, the kidnapper was quite clear in his threats to harm Lily, as well and insistent we stay away from NPD or the FBI. When we saw you on Monday, we knew nothing about the Corvette and the drop at Gilbert's . . ."

Lever laid a hand on Rosco's shoulder. "It's not your fault that Tacete's dead, Poly—crates. Historically, the lower the ransom demands, the more brutal the perps. It's almost as if they're doing the job for kicks. And leaving witnesses behind is rare."

Rosco shrugged but didn't otherwise answer.

"Look, buddy, we don't know how this thing went down. Maybe whoever was holding the doc *did* release him. . . . Maybe this was an accident, pure and simple. A high-powered car and a notorious curve. Or maybe Dan escaped and was being pursued. . . . Who knows? The goons could have drugged him, too. . . . Carlyle will be able to make that assessment in a day or so. But whatever happened, you can't go around blaming yourself. You didn't send Tacete into that ravine."

Rosco nodded. "Yeah, I know . . . but I still don't like to see innocent people get raked over the coals on account of what I did or *didn't* do."

"That's law enforcement, pal—as you well know. It comes with the territory."

"Which is why I prefer dealing with situations like hoods doing simple things like swiping pricey cars from swanky eateries."

"Yeah, but some of those jerks are into more than grand

larceny, Poly—crates. It's not hard to graduate to homicide."

Throughout this exchange, Belle had remained silent. "There's something else you should know, Al. Yesterday, I received a peculiar crossword. It had been hand-delivered to my office at the *Crier.*" She paused in thought before continuing. "What made it unusual was that it was the third I've received that employed a nursery rhyme theme. The other two came to the house—which is also strange, although I didn't think much about it at the time . . . only that the coincidence of receiving two puzzles submitted by two constructors who both used Mother Goose is noteworthy."

"And you're certain there were two separate constructors?"

"One submission used a P.O. box for a return address; the other constructor had an email address."

Al nodded. "Which doesn't necessarily prove anything. Both permit a degree of anonymity. What about the one you got yesterday?"

"There was a street address . . . I think . . ." Belle frowned. "To tell you the truth, Al, I didn't pay much attention. I was too focused on what I believed might be a sinister message. . . . Karen's phone call had gotten me worried about Lily's safety, too; and the weird similarity of crossword clues and solutions only heightened my concern. . . . Then Bartholomew interrupted me—"

"Where are the puzzles now?"

"At home."

"I'll tell you what; why don't you bring them down to the station house, and we'll have them scanned for prints. Then I'd like you two to talk to Carlyle, and tell him everything you've told me."

Rosco groaned.

"I know . . . I know, Poly—crates. Mr. Personality, he ain't."

"It's not that, Al. I can handle rude and overbearing when someone's good at their job. But Carlyle's sloppy—you know that. He's made too many mistakes in the past."

Lever sighed. "I'm not going to disagree with you, but as long as his brother remains mayor of our fair city . . . well, what can I say?"

"What time do you want us, Al?" Belle asked. She touched Rosco's arm as she spoke. It was a gentle, wifely warning. Carlyle's reputed errors were no longer her husband's responsibility or concern.

"Let's say noon? Right now, I'm heading over to Smile! to talk to Jack Wagner."

"*Jack Be Nimble*," Belle mused aloud. "That was one of the clues in yesterday's puzzle.

"I'll keep my eye out for candlesticks while I'm there."

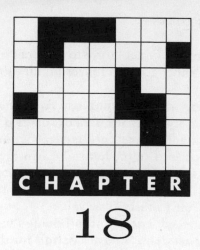

CHAPTER
18

When the electronic buzzer of Smile! rang announcing that the practice's front door had opened, Bonnie O'Connell's reaction was one of startled fright. She jerked upward in her office chair and made a sound that was half-whimper and half-sob. Her eyes were already red and swollen from crying, and the tissue in her hand was saturated. With blurred vision, she watched a heavy-set, balding man—one she didn't recognize—cross the waiting area and approach the reception desk. He had an intense expression and a purposeful stride, both of which she mistook for anger.

Believing that the visitor was a potentially violent person and that the situation could turn dangerous, she depressed an under-counter button that sent a silent alarm back to Dr. Wagner's office, alerting him that there was an unexpected and unwanted visitor who was clearly not there for dental work. When the man reached Bonnie, he placed his right hand under his jacket as if he were reaching for a gun. She was so shaken that she let out with a small scream—a noise that in turn startled the single patient already ensconced in the waiting area.

"My name is Lieutenant Al Lever. I'm with the Newcastle

Police Department. I'd like to speak to Doctor Wagner." Al removed his identification and placed it on the counter as he spoke.

Bonnie's response was to begin weeping afresh. She yanked additional tissues from a box, daubed her eyes, and inclined her head toward the desktop while the alerted Wagner hurried into sight, his right arm held awkwardly down at his side, a small caliber semi-automatic pistol clenched in his hand. Lever lifted his ID into the air and uttered a level "Police officer!"

Wagner marched irritably into Bonnie's work space and set the gun on her desk. "I have a permit for that. It's in my office. We've had two burglaries." He wrapped his arms over Bonnie's slumping shoulders. "It's okay, Bon, relax . . . take some deep breaths. In and out, slowly. C'mon, there . . . nice and slow. . . . Now, let's lower your head. . . . I know it's been a terrible morning. . . ."He looked at Lever and growled, "What is it you people want? Can't you see that she's been upset enough for one morning?"

Al returned his ID to his jacket. "My name is Lieutenant Lever. I take it you're Doctor Wagner?"

"What right do you have coming barging in here?" Wagner snapped. "I already sent everything over to Doctor Carlyle."

Lever turned and glanced at the waiting patient, who was giving the situation his full attention. "Is there a place we can talk privately?"

Bonnie was now trembling uncontrollably. Wagner brought her to her feet and steadied her. "It's okay, Bon; take deep breaths." He looked toward his patient. "This is going to take a few moments, Mr. Parsons, but I'll be with you as soon as I can." Then Wagner returned his antagonistic stare to Lever. "We can talk in Dan's examining room. I believe my receptionist needs to lie down for a little while." Wagner guided Bonnie down the hallway to Tacete's dental office and helped her into the examination chair while Lever followed in silence.

"Suffice it to say that your medical examiner's phone call came as a terrible shock," Wagner said as he slid a metal stool next to Bonnie's prone form and sat. "It was also delivered in a most callous and inhumane manner. Surely, there are better methods for requesting dental records than announcing a brusque 'We think we found your partner's charred remains.'"

Al's response was a stifled sigh. *Not if you're Herb Carlyle, it isn't,* he thought.

"I gather you're here to confirm that the body in that car crash *was* Dan's?" Wagner continued.

Al leaned against the formica counter top and folded his arms across his chest. "Yes, I'm afraid that's true. I'm sorry."

A fresh wave of tears filled Bonnie's eyes, and she began to tremble once more. Wagner reached for a box of tissues and handed it to her. He then stood, opened a wall cabinet, and removed a jar of pills. He shook a number of them into his palm and handed them to Bonnie. "Why don't you take these? They'll relax you."

At first, Al had assumed that Bonnie and Jack were husband and wife. Despite an age difference, which he estimated was close to twenty years, the relationship seemed far more intimate than boss and office staff; and Wagner had no compunction about comforting the young woman physically. But Lever now noticed that while Wagner wore a wedding ring, Bonnie did not. He watched the dentist fill a paper cup with water and gently touch it to her mouth. Jack Wagner appeared a great deal more concerned with her well-being than with his partner's death.

After Bonnie swallowed the pills, Wagner turned to Lever. "Okay, you've delivered your bad news. Now if you don't mind, I think we could use some time alone. Feel free to let yourself out."

"There have been other developments you should know about." As Lever spoke, he tried to observe the reactions of Bonnie and her boss, but both seemed wholly perplexed at the news.

"Developments?" Wagner asked.

"We have just learned that Doctor Tacete's disappearance was the result of an abduction." Again, Lever took a moment to watch for a reaction, but confusion was still the only emotion he read on the two faces. "We suspect that Dan Tacete was attempting to flee his captors when he drove off the road. Either that, or he was drugged when they released him and he blacked out or lost control of his vehicle. Whichever the case, I intend to pursue this as a homicide until I learn differently."

"Certainly, you can't suspect that we're involved!" Wagner stated indignantly.

"When you say, 'we,' Doctor, you're referring to yourself and—?"

"Ms. O'Connell, here."

"I see," Lever said. "And why would the police department suspect such a thing, Doctor?" Al paused a moment. "May I ask what your relationship is?"

"I've already told you. Bonnie is the receptionist at Smile! I would think that's rather obvious."

"Which means your relationship is of a professional nature only?"

Wagner's jaw tightened. "What do you mean by that question?"

"I just wasn't certain if you were married or not—"

"Lieutenant, I'm a busy man and seriously understaffed at the moment. I'm going to have to ask you to leave now."

Al held up his hand. "I don't want to get off on the wrong foot with you, Doctor Wagner. You're a respected professional in this community, and I can't imagine you being involved in a fairly penny-ante kidnapping. However, your business partner is dead, and someone has made off with a bundle of cash. Time is of the essence if we intend to catch the people responsible. That's why I would like your full cooperation."

Wagner pondered what Lever had said, and after a moment he seemed to settle down. Whatever he had given

Bonnie had worked like a charm, and she was now in another world, humming softly and seemingly unaware that there were other people in the room.

"All right," Wagner said, "what do you want to know?"

"For starters, do you have any idea who might have decided to kidnap Dan Tacete? Clearly, it was someone who was familiar with his routine."

"How much money did they get?"

"Twenty-five thousand dollars."

Wagner smiled briefly and shook his head. "Whew, that *is* penny-ante stuff. I can get that much money out of a single mouth if I can find enough problems." He rubbed his chin as though in thought, but Al felt the gesture was superficial and insincere. "Dan did pro bono work down at the Bay Clinic. Many of his patients were the men at the Saint Augustine Mission. Twenty-five grand would be an enormous amount to those low-lifes. The people who walk through this door? Hell, they run up that much on their VISA cards each month."

"I intend to visit the Saint Augustine Mission, Doctor Wagner, but I find it difficult to imagine that someone who is homeless would have the wherewithal to accomplish a crime of this scope."

"Well, I have no intention of grilling my patients, if that's what you're suggesting."

"I'm not suggest—"

"Rob," Bonnie interrupted in a dreamy voice. "Where has Rob gone to?"

"Who's Rob?" Al asked.

"Just calm yourself, dear," Wagner said to her. "Don't try to speak." He then looked at Lever. "She's been sedated, Lieutenant. I don't think you should take anything she says seriously."

"Do you know who this Rob is?"

Wagner suppressed an irritable sigh. "Dan had a patient by the name of Rob Rossi. Another one of his charity cases. Or close to."

Lever looked past the dentist. "What can you tell me about Rob, Ms. O'Connell?"

"Lieutenant, she's in no condition—"

"Bartender . . . kinda cute. . . . He didn't . . ." Bonnie giggled lightly, then dozed off, allowing Wagner to speak for her.

"Rossi failed to appear for a scheduled appointment with Dan. There's no more to the story than that. And it's behavior that's not uncommon within a certain element of Dan's clientele. . . . Now, if you'll excuse me, I've kept Mr. Parsons waiting long enough—"

"I'd like to get a list of all of Doctor Tacete's patients, if I can."

"Now?" Wagner's veneer of politeness was rapidly eroding.

"The longer we wait, the colder the trail gets. The kidnapper has already had enough time to put a lot of distance between himself and that Corvette."

"I'll fax you a printout this afternoon." Wagner stood and began striding to the door while Lever scrawled the NPD fax number on a prescription chit.

"I'd like that list in an hour, Doctor. You don't want to see Al Lever turn into an unhappy cop. . . . Nobody does."

CHAPTER

19

Few people actually enjoyed being in Newcastle's dank basement morgue, but Herb Carlyle and his assistant Estelle were the exceptions to the rule. Both seemed to thrive on the frigid temperatures while the similar and ashen hue of their skin made a disconcerting complement to the bluish color of the stainless steel examining tables, the gray linoleum floors, the metal drawers of the refrigerated body compartments, and the institutional green of the pallid walls. And they both maintained a devoted—some might say, unhealthy—fascination with the dearly, or not so dearly, departed.

But where Estelle was meticulous in her observations and almost fanatical about neatness and cleanliness, Carlyle was lackadaisical. He treated the morgue as an extension of home, often eating take-out burgers and fries in the midst of examining a corpse, or chain-smoking cigarettes until the Petri dish that served as an ashtray reached the point of overflowing. How these two had managed to work so well together for so long caused other members of the NPD to scratch their heads in puzzlement, although there was one thing everyone agreed upon: Herb and Estelle believed the morgue to be their private sanctuary.

Neither the medical examiner nor his assistant enjoyed visits from outsiders—particularly detectives, whom they deemed to have little or no understanding of basic human anatomy. Carlyle considered himself the ultimate expert, though few others did, and he greeted queries or dissent with his pronouncements with an almost pathological defensiveness.

So, when he spotted Al Lever through the large windows that separated his inner office from the morgue proper, Carlyle sighed and turned off the computer game that had been holding his attention for the last half hour. Lever was accompanied by Rosco and Belle, a fact that made Herb's groan take on exaggerated and put-upon proportions.

The detective tapped on Carlyle's glass door twice, stepped into the office, and said, "Herb," in a manner that was intended to be a pleasant salutation but that fell just short of the mark.

The M.E. looked at his watch and responded with a surly "I thought we agreed on noon? That was twenty minutes ago."

"Right. We got delayed."

Carlyle cocked his head toward Rosco. "What's with him? The department can't handle this on their own? Or is the NPD handing out *Second Guessing* awards this week?"

"Mind if we sit?" Al asked, purposely ignoring Carlyle's hostility toward Rosco.

Carlyle shrugged, and the three settled into folding metal chairs that faced his desk.

"Rosco and Belle were apprised of Tacete's abduction at an early stage," Lever explained. "I feel there's a certain advantage in keeping them up to speed. I'm not opposed to asking for help, Herb. You know that. I take it where I can get it." The tone made it clear that Al planned to conduct the investigation by his own rules and that he had no intention of being strong-armed by Carlyle—mayor's brother or not.

"The situation's personal this time," Rosco added. "Karen Tacete's a friend of ours. I intend to help out wherever I can."

"Before I get into any particulars," Carlyle told Lever while he leveled his gaze at Rosco, "maybe your former partner can bring *me* up to speed. How *did* this all shake down?"

Al gave Rosco a be-my-guest nod, so he took a large breath and began. "Dan Tacete was last seen leaving his office Thursday at noon. His wife phoned Belle that evening in a panic. On Saturday morning, Karen received a call from a man claiming to hold Dan hostage. Ransom particulars were to follow. The kidnapper was adamant that Karen not contact the authorities, causing her to decide to distance herself from Belle and me, as well.

"Yesterday morning, following new demands on the part of the kidnapper, Karen Tacete placed twenty-five thousand dollars in cash in Dan's gym bag, which she secured in the trunk of his Corvette as per her instructions. She then drove the car to the Gilbert's Groceries parking lot, where she left the keys under the front seat—again as instructed—and took a cab home. Nobody heard anything else until last night when the 'Vette ended up in the ravine off East Farm Lane. The gym bag had been emptied."

"Well, like I pointed out last night," Carlyle said as he lit a cigarette, "the situation is cut and dried. The good news for your doc is he was most likely dead before the Corvette turned to toast."

"How do you know that?" Lever asked.

"His forehead was caved in, which was almost certainly the result of hitting the windshield frame . . . kinda like cracking an egg. I'm guessing—more than *guessing,* I'm guaranteeing that he was dead before the car came to a stop and before the gas tank blew."

"So there was no smoke in his lungs." Rosco's comment was more statement than question.

Carlyle stiffened. "Cause of death is acute cranial trauma.

Period. Our boy was dead before the fire broke out. So, no. There would be no smoke in his lungs."

Rosco felt sure that the M.E. hadn't checked the victim's lungs, but opted not to verbally disagree. Besides, if the skull was crushed, the likelihood of smoke in the lungs was indeed remote. "Is it possible that he was killed some time before the crash? Say, an hour or even a day?"

"Sure. But it would be the first time a dead man drove a car off a cliff." Carlyle all but sneered. He looked at Lever. "Whose investigation is this, Lieutenant?"

"Mine. But Polycrates has a good point. Isn't it possible that someone could have killed him, strapped him into the driver's seat, and ran the 'Vette over the edge?"

"I'm placing time of death at the same time as the accident."

"I'm sorry," Belle interjected, "but if Dan had his shoulder harness buckled, how could his forehead have reached the windshield frame?"

"He's tall, and the windshield is low." Carlyle's response was snippy and dismissive. "Hardly a physical impossibility for a big man like him." He took a long drag from his cigarette and refocused on Lever. "There's something else. Your boy was loaded up on OxyContin. He was in no condition to drive. He should never have gotten into that car in the first place. Whether your kidnappers fed it to him or he was a doper, I don't know, but there's my theory: He was higher than a kite and drove into the ravine all by his little lonesome."

"Maybe he was being chased?" Belle pondered aloud.

"Why? You just told me they got their money. Maybe the perps figured they'd live up to their part of the bargain and simply let him go."

Al's reply was a terse. "Anything else I should know, Herb?"

"Nope. That's it: crushed skull and doped up. Cut and dried, like I said."

"You wouldn't mind if Abe Jones takes a look at the

remains, would you?" Rosco asked, knowing full well the suggestion would push every one of Carlyle's buttons.

The M.E. stood and pointed at Rosco while again speaking to Lever. "I don't need to put up with this crap from him. That's why your buddy couldn't hack police work; he never had any regard for procedure; he always thought he knew more than the experts. Jones doesn't go anywhere near that body unless it comes straight from the captain. Got it? He can play forensics whiz kid anywhere else—and *with* anything else, except my corpse. Now, if we're finished here, I've got work to do."

"Really?" Rosco looked at the computer screen. "Still stuck on Pac-Man, Herb, or have you moved up to Tomb Raider?"

"All right . . . all right," Al said. He stood and placed himself between Rosco and Carlyle before their animosity could escalate into a show of physical force. "Let's take this discussion to my office, Poly—crates." He waited for Belle and Rosco to step out, then added, "Thanks, Herb, I'll keep you posted."

"You do that." Carlyle's face was turned toward the computer screen, but his eyes were unmoving.

B elle and Rosco and Al refrained from talking about the case until they reached Lever's office. The decision wasn't based on concerns about being overheard, but because each was wrapped up in speculation as to what might have occurred on East Farm Lane.

"Do you think the captain will let Abe take a look at Dan's body? To corroborate Carlyle's findings, I mean?" Belle asked as she sat in the battered wooden ladder-back chair that lay opposite Lever's desk. Al had flopped down in his swiveling office chair, his body tilting backward and his feet itching to settle on the desktop—where they would have been, were it not for Belle's presence. Rosco found himself a perch on the corner of the desk's scarred surface. The positions were similar to ones the three had taken up many times before; and they carried with them an odd sense of deja vu, and a certain kind of comfort in familiarity.

"That's a tough call." Al reached for a cigarette but then tossed the pack back onto the blotter. "Sorry, I forgot that you health-nuts aren't into secondhand smoke. . . . No, I don't think the captain will want to go mano-a-mano against the mayor's brother; i.e., the mayor. I'll have Abe look over Carlyle's report. If he has problems with it, I can push for a forensic examination, but I'm not optimistic it'll wash."

"I can't imagine that Dan Tacete would get high on drugs if they'd just released him," she mused, "but maybe the kidnappers had already doped him up . . ."

"And then let him drive away?" Rosco asked.

"Why would they care what state he was in?" Belle countered. She turned to regard her husband. "In fact, wouldn't it have been better if Dan had been kept in a perpetual, drug-induced haze? That way, he wouldn't have been able to identify his captives."

"The scene on East Farm Lane revealed no evidence of panic," Lever interjected. "No tire marks indicating Tacete saw the guardrail and attempted to stop—which lends credence to Carlyle's OxyContin discovery." Rosco was shaking his head slowly, so Al added, "What? You don't like that scenario? Too simple for you, Poly—crates?"

"My gut tells me that Dan was murdered, Al. Someone bashed in his head, put him in the Corvette, and drove it into the ravine. That's why I'd like to see Abe confirm the time of death."

"That's not his job," was Lever's brief answer.

Rosco snorted a short laugh. "Well, don't tell me Abe can't pinpoint time of death. We've both seen him do it in the past."

This time it was Al who shook his head. "Look, I know I agreed with that notion earlier, but the more I think about it, the less it works for me. The 'Vette was a stick-shift, Poly—crates. It would have been next to impossible to put it in gear, pop the clutch, and get it rolling fast enough; not to mention guiding it around the guardrail, and then jumping out without having it stall; or, seriously, maybe even mortally, injuring the perp who was playing Hollywood stuntman. To say nothing of attempting all that while sitting on the lap of the dead man who was strapped into the driver's seat. . . . Can't be done. Besides, how Tacete died is neither here nor there. Right now, I'm only concerned with catching a kidnapper or kidnappers. I'll worry about cause of death if and when I've got someone to prosecute."

"So, where do you start?" Belle asked.

"The first thing I do is get over to Gilbert's Groceries and see if anyone saw who might have driven the Corvette out of their lot." Lever pulled a sheet of paper from his inbox and set it on the desk next to where Rosco was perched. "Jack Wagner faxed that to me a half an hour ago. It's a list of all Tacete's patients. Wagner marked five names that he considered to be 'shifty characters'—his words, not mine. But it's a place to start. I'll also have Abe scour the 'Vette for fingerprints . . ." He shrugged. "Who knows? Something might turn up."

Rosco picked up the list of names and perused it. "Nobody here I recognize." He handed the list to Belle.

Lever said, "No. Me neither. . . . The one guy," he reached across the desk and pointed at a name near the bottom of the page, "Rob Rossi?"

"Yes?" Belle said.

"Wagner's receptionist, Bonnie O'Connell, mentioned he was a bartender somewhere, but that's it. At least Wagner printed out their home phone numbers and addresses. They shouldn't be too hard to dig up."

Belle read down the list of names. "Ed Trawler, Hank Unger, Rob Rossi, Carlos Quintero, and Terry Friend. . . . Huh, Terry? Could be a man or a woman, right?"

CHAPTER

20

Knowing someone—or even knowing *of* someone—who died violently produces odd and unsettling reactions among the living. Time is warped; thoughts become dream-like in intensity as well as maddeningly obscure; the mind visits and revisits the scene of death, imagining it from different vantage points with differing outcomes, replaying the invented pictures until they begin to lose all resemblance to the perceived truth. The question *Why did this have to happen?* is the only constant, and it jabs at the brain continuously.

Leaving the NPD and driving home while Rosco proceeded to his own office and a late start on his day's work, Belle couldn't have described where the hours went after she returned to the house on Captain's Walk—or even how she got there. When she came to her senses, she felt the same as when she'd almost fallen asleep at the wheel during one particularly arduous all-night excursion back in her college days. Her body jounced into alertness; her head snapped upward; her eyes widened while her startled glance took in the empty plate on her cluttered desk, the crumbs of bread that indicated she'd made and eaten a sandwich, the mug containing the dregs of tea, and a gnawed apple core. All spoke to her of time vanishing without her being aware of having lived it.

"Yikes!" she murmured, stretching forward in her chair as if she'd truly dozed off. Her eyes continued to rake the desktop before dropping to the floor, where she spotted Kit and Gabby; the dogs had found two sun spots and curled themselves into separate havens. Their human companion's behavior obviously hadn't been a cause for canine alarm.

Belle's gaze returned to the papers lying beside the plate. There were Xerox copies of the crosswords she'd given Al, and she'd arranged them in order of when she'd received them: "Baby Steps," "Sugar and Spice," "As Time Goes By."

She read, or more accurately, reread, the step-quote in the first of the puzzles: A MAN OF WORDS AND NOT OF DEEDS IS LIKE A GARDEN FULL OF WEEDS. If that had been intended to be a reference to Dan Tacete's kidnapping and death, Belle couldn't find it. The second crossword contained a number of feminine names from nursery rhymes: Kitty, Polly, Lucy, Margery, as well as Bo Peep and Curly Locks. But there again, they seemed to have no bearing the case. The "Time . . ." crossword, however, listed *Jack* twice, once as a clue and once as a solution.

And that single name was enough to hurtle Belle out of her chair, out of her office, out of her house and into her car. Jack, as in Jack Wagner, had to be able to fill in some answers. Even as she drove toward downtown Newcastle and the Smile! office she knew how tenuous this clue might be; but Rosco had taught her that "coincidences" were rare when it came to criminal investigations.

" Ms. O'Connell?" Belle asked the woman sitting at the dental office reception desk. The nameplate indicated she was Bonnie O'Connell, but "bonny" wasn't a word Belle would have used to describe the austere matron facing her. "Dour," "glum," "testy" would have seemed a better fit—but those weren't appellations parents supplied to infant girls.

"I am not O'Connell," was the receptionist's stern reply. "She was sent home early. I'm filling in. What may I do for you? If you're Mrs."—she peered down through her bifocals at the appointment book—"Mrs. Schultz, just have a seat, your appointment isn't for fifteen minutes."

This brief speech sounded like an unhelpful "Why are you bothering me?" rather than an expression of professional assistance, but Belle pasted on her most endearing smile. Then she touched her left hand to her cheek as though in sudden physical pain. "No, I'm not Mrs. Schultz. I have a bit of a toothache, I'm afraid . . . and I was wondering if Doctor Wagner could squeeze me in?"

"Are you a regular patient?" The nameless receptionist consulted the appointments book on her desk once more.

"Well, no . . . but I've heard such wonderful things about Doctor Wagner, and I—"

"He's completely booked this week." A basilisk stare challenged Belle to refute this piece of information.

"Ohhh . . ." Belle's brain flew through a number of clever and winning responses while also providing a running critique of her lack of preparation for this interview. *Dummy! You don't just waltz into a doctor's office and expect to be seen that very minute, do you? Especially when you're not a patient.* "Oh, of course he is! I should have realized that, given the accolades I've heard about his work. . . . I was only driving by when this pain developed, and I was hoping—"

"I wouldn't know about that. I'm temping for the afternoon only. My sister owns the employment agency, or I wouldn't be here. I do legal, not dental. And only part-time." Bonnie's replacement continued to fix Belle with her critical gaze. "So I don't *improvise* on a scheduling policy I'm not familiar with."

The intensity of the scrutiny was unnerving; Belle took a leap of faith and concluded the sometime "legal" assistant must be a crossword fiend who had seen Belle's byline photo and was trying to recall where she'd spotted this would-be

patient's face before. "I'm Belle Graham . . . from the *Crier.*
I'm afraid this toothache has produced some swelling and
distorted my features, so you may not—"

"I don't read the *Crier.* Too many damn words if you ask
me; same as all newspapers. That, and the ads. A lot of
wasted ink and paper. Besides, I get all the news I need on
TV. I only use newspapers to line the bottom of the bird
cage. My neighbor gives them to me."

"Ah . . ." Belle found herself at a sudden loss. Someone
who wasn't a fan of words was not likely to be won over by
a person whose livelihood involved puttering about with
language.

But Belle need not have fretted over this quandary, because the temporary receptionist suddenly lowered her fierce
brow and flipped the appointments book. "Nope. Nothing.
The doctor's booked into next week, too. You can call back
tomorrow when the regular girl's here. Or leave me your
number, and I'll make a note to have her contact you if
there's a cancellation."

"Thank you, I'll do that . . ."

"But if I were you, I'd just head over to the Emergency
Room at the hospital. These fancy dentists don't come
cheap. And if you're in pain, why wait?"

Belle expected further commentary, but instead a note
pad and pen were thrust in front of her. Then the phone
rang and the woman filling in for Bonnie O'Connell dis-
missed Belle with a curt nod and directed her attention to
one of Smile!'s genuine patients.

*W*ell, *that was a total bust,* Belle thought as she returned
to her car. She sat motionless for a moment, considering her next step. She was not a person who enjoyed being
thwarted; in fact, frustration only caused her stubborn
streak to become more tenacious.

*So, no "Jack," her brain recited, and no "Bonnie," either, be-
cause she's been "sent home"—which was probably necessary given*

how upset Al told us she was. . . . Hmmm . . . Almost before
Belle was aware of having made another decision, she was
turning the key in the ignition and preparing to pull into
traffic. She'd drive to her *Crier* office and check to see if Bonnie O'Connell was in the phone directory. . . . No, she'd go
home first and don the auburn wig and retro Harlequin
glasses she'd worn at the *Crier*'s New Year's Eve costume
party, then she'd find Bonnie. *And why would Ms. O'Connell
wish to speak to you?* Belle's thoughts demanded, to which
the reply was an equally swift and obstinate: *I'll cross that
bridge when I come to it.*

It hadn't required even the simplest of sleuthing skills to
find Bonnie O'Connell's apartment complex. The Newcastle phone book had been the only tool necessary, and
Belle found herself walking up a nicely landscaped and art-
fully meandering path toward her quarry's front door a mere
fifty minutes after leaving Smile! The ease with which she'd
accomplished her task was slightly disappointing, but her
rueful attitude was tempered when she realized she hadn't
yet prepared a convincing alias with which to chat up her
prey. Then Belle noticed a discreet "Units Available" sign,
and the fictional tale she decided to offer Bonnie all but created itself. *A would-be renter questioning a current tenant about
facilities and the like . . . woman to woman, discussing issues of security, convenience, and the landlord's responsiveness if and when
problems arose. The leasing agent would have provided Ms. O'Connell's name as an excellent source of information.* Of course, Belle
was counting on the fact that Bonnie wouldn't phone the
rental office for corroboration.

But not one single part of that easy scenario would materi-
alize. Her most hopeful and innocent smile glued on her lips,
Belle knocked on Bonnie's front door. There was no reply.
Belle waited a minute and tapped again; after another minute
or two had elapsed, she rang the bell—not once but twice. In
the intervals of silence between her efforts at admittance, she

was certain she heard noise inside the apartment—not merely a TV or radio left playing, but footsteps as if a person, presumably Bonnie, were peering at her through the peep-hole then retreating from sight.

So much for worming myself into the confidences of Ms. O'Connell, Belle thought with some bitterness. She was about to leave a note detailing her bogus mission but suddenly decided it wasn't necessary. If Bonnie was indeed inside and spying on her unwelcome visitor, she could invent her own story about the red-headed woman with the odd-looking glasses.

Belle recrossed the tree-lined walkway and wandered slowly back to her car, where she slumped in the seat, yanked off her wig and glasses, and tossed them unceremoniously into the glove compartment. She felt irked and frustrated, but above all her competitive spirit was experiencing an unwelcome sense of defeat. She sat for some long moments pondering what a dearth of information there was on Dan Tacete's kidnapping and death. And then the corner of her eye caught sight of a taxi stopping near Bonnie's unit, and a woman's body lurching unsteadily out the front door, fumbling with keys, dropping and retrieving them, then almost running toward the cab. Instinctively, Belle started her engine and began to follow the driver and his fare.

The cabbie's destination was The Black Sheep Tavern. Belle watched as the person she assumed was Bonnie hurried inside. Giving herself the briefest of seconds to consider what her next step would be, Belle also walked toward the entrance. She ran her fingers through her hair, creating some fluffy bangs and hoping that no elastic marks from her false hairdo remained.

"But he's gone!" Belle heard Bonnie wailing the moment she stepped into the bar's dark interior. "And his phone is dead."

"He's not gone, babe. He's probably just missing for a little while is all. Layin' low. You know how Frank gets. And this isn't the first time he hasn't kept his phone paid up, is it? Let's think about that, why don't we?"

"Well, I need him here! I need him here now!"

"What can I say, Bon? Frank's never been Mr. Reliable."

Bonnie burst into a fresh spate of tears, although Belle intuited they were not from grief.

"C'mon, Bon, let's you and me sit down and—"

"I don't want to sit!"

"Okay, we'll stand, then. We'll stand at the bar and—"

"And where's Rob gotten himself to?"

"How would I know? I don't own this place, in case you forgot."

"Well, you act like you do."

"Act, and *action* ain't the same thing. Walt owns the Black Sheep—always has, always will."

"Both of them! Both of them gone!"

"Hey, Bon . . . it's okay. . . . Let's be a happy lady, why don't we . . . ?" By now, the man with whom Bonnie was so urgently speaking was gently but insistently steering her toward two stools at the bar's farthest end. Like a magnet, Belle moved after them, until a giant of a man stepped in front of her. He had russet-colored hair, a tawny, freckled face, and the kind of forearms that looked as though they hoisted yearling calves for a hobby. "Lookin' for someone, honey?" The smile that accompanied the question was not accusatory or unkind, but it seemed threatening to Belle because the person—and his face—loomed so tall against the age-blackened ceiling.

"Actually, I am. . . . I'm looking for . . . a waitressing job and wondered . . . I think I read somewhere, in the newspaper maybe, that you were hiring waitresses. . . ."

"That so?" The giant gave Belle what she could only interpret as a leering grin, although she now noticed that the voice that accompanied the question had a curiously high-pitched tone, as if his vocal chords were straining within all that muscle-bound flesh. "I never seen no waitresses hereabouts. Walt's tryin' something new, is he?"

"Oh . . . well, I couldn't have gotten the name of the restaurant wrong. . . ." Belle fumbled through her purse. "I should have brought the ad with me. This is the Black Sheep, isn't it?"

"None other."

"Maybe I should talk to Walt?"

"Ain't here." Belle's would-be friend lowered his lofty head and looked down the bar toward Bonnie and her companion. "Yo, Carlos, you know anything about old Walt hirin' waitresses for this dump?"

Belle's ears pricked up. *One of Dan Tacete's patients was a Carlos. . . . Of course, the chance of this being—*

"Hey, yo, Quintero, I'm talkin' to you, buddy!"

Ahhh, Belle thought while the object of Jack Wagner's professional censure swore a disgruntled curse. Then Bonnie released her own unintelligible oaths and began to cry loudly. A split-second later, she was hurtling past Belle and hurrying toward the door.

"Hey, Bon . . . calm down. I didn't mean that the way it sounded. I'll drive you home."

"Just stuff it, Carlos!"

"Bon . . . come on . . . Frank'll show up—"

"And Rob? What about him?"

"Lighten up, sweetpea. They're both big boys. Besides, what's the worry? They'll be back—"

"Just like Dan Tacete, huh? Just like that?" With that final question, Bonnie rammed her shoulder into the door and ran outside before Carlos had time to suggest phoning for a cab—which seemed to be the words on his lips as the door slammed shut behind her.

"Sugar and spice and everything nice." He shrugged as he turned back to the room in general. "I'd say Ms. O'Connell forgot to stir in that sweet, little *sugar* part today." Then

Carlos caught sight of Belle. "Well, hello there. . . . Look what the cat dragged in."

"The lady's lookin' for a waitress gig, Quintero. I ain't seen hide nor hair of Walt today. He didn't mention nothin' about puttin' on a waitress to you, did he?"

"Here?" A good deal of disbelief echoed in the tone.

"What she says. Maybe Rossi knows somethin' about it."

"Rob hasn't been around for a while, in case you hadn't noticed." Carlos focused again on Belle. "How about you, blondie? Can you tend bar? 'Cause it's beginning to look like Walt's gonna need to replace the Rob-man."

Belle couldn't believe her good fortune. "Would that be Rob *Rossi,* the bartender here?" She hoped her expression looked as naive as she believed her words sounded.

"You know the Rob-man?" It was Carlos who responded. He hitched up his pants. There was a swagger in his movement and a peacocking challenge in his eyes. "He surely does get around."

"No . . . ahh . . . the ad mentioned his name. Applicants were to ask for Rob Rossi."

Carlos looked at Ed and the big man shrugged. The handful of Black Sheep afternoon drinkers paid little attention to Belle or the two men; they were too intent on nursing their beers.

"You got some real pretty hair, blondie," Carlos said as he returned his gaze to Belle. "Don't she, Big Ed?"

"I guess I should be speaking to Mr. Rossi, then," Belle persisted. She maintained her smile, but it wasn't easy. Providing ample personal space didn't appear to be one of Carlos Quintero's priorities.

"I guess you didn't hear me tellin' my little friend there that he wasn't around."

"Oh, was that your ladyfriend?"

Carlos chuckled and looked up at Ed. "What do you say to that, Mr. Trawler? Is Bonnie my squeeze?"

Ed Trawler, Belle thought. *Boy oh boy, have I hit the jackpot tonight!* But finding three of the names on Jack Wagner's list of questionable patients seemed minor in comparison to what she next discovered.

"Not as long as Mr. Big-Bucks is in the picture, you ain't."

Belle felt one eyelid twitch and a corner of her lips flicker. It was all she could do not to shout out loud. So, Al had been correct in questioning Bonnie's relationship to her boss. Belle took a steadying breath and returned her focus to Carlos. "Well, I really need the work, so if you could tell me when Mr. Rossi—"

"I already told ya. He's not around."

"Well, when he comes in then. The newspaper ad said—"

"I don't know nothin' about no ad, sweetpea. What I *can* tell ya is that Rob ain't here. You can come back tomorrow if ya want to try your luck again. Walt should be in tomorrow. Maybe Rob'll be puttin' in an appearance, too; who knows."

Belle frowned. "But I don't know why this Rossi person was mentioned if he's not here. Maybe I got the name wrong."

"Hey, it's a mystery to me, too. Rob's got a good gig goin' here, and he's makin' a big mistake thinkin' Walt's gonna hold it for him forever. Guaranteed income, which means nice digs and a good-lookin' ride. Why louse it all up by doin' a disappearin' act? But hey, maybe he's got himself another job?"

It was only after Belle had extricated herself from the Black Sheep and was driving home that a phrase Carlos Quintero had used returned to her.

"Sugar and spice": It seemed impossible that his use of the nursery rhyme words was coincidental.

CHAPTER
21

Despite Dan Tacete's death and the turmoil of the last few days, Rosco was still in the employment of Northern Mutual Insurance, which meant that he felt obligated to keep an appointment he'd scheduled the previous week with Sonny of Sonny's Autobody. The shop was on Clawson Street in the industrial zone, which sprawled along the coastline at the northeastern end of the city and featured a polyglot assortment of businesses: distributors specializing in reinforced concrete, manufacturers of steel beams and bars, residential and commercial storage facilities, trucking depots, used car lots, and a gigantic wholesale food mart.

Sonny's Autobody was the sixth such establishment on Rosco's list of potential accomplices in the disappearance—and possible dismantling—of twenty-two luxury automobiles from Porto Ristorante on March 15. To this point, the investigation had come up dry. The previous five body shop owners he'd spoken with had appeared to be running legitimate concerns; although, to a man, they'd maintained that there were no assurances that the auto parts they used were "factory fresh." The rule of thumb seemed to be that as long as wholesalers guaranteed the parts, the shop owners asked no questions.

Adjusting the blue ABC-TV baseball cap that had been a souvenir from a recent trip to Los Angeles, Rosco ambled through the broad double garage doors that led into the airplane-hanger-like expanse of Sonny's Autobody. As with the previous repair shops, his "cover" involved being a location scout for the Boston-based TV program, *Back Bay D.A.,* and the necessity of finding a place to shoot an upcoming episode about a sting operation.

Initially, Rosco had wondered if his chop-shop description of the storyline might deter the owners, but as a Hollywood producer had once told him, "Hey, it's TV. Nobody says no to TV." Rosco had found the maxim to be one hundred percent correct. In fact, as Sonny extended his muscular hand in greeting, the first words out of his mouth were an enthusiastic "Hey, great hat. ABC-TV. Yeah, that's cool. Can you get me one of those?"

Physically, Sonny was a clear departure from the previous autobody shop owners. Where the others had been roundish, meat and potatoes, hands-on sorts of men with soiled mechanics' jumpsuits and black fingernails, Sonny was trim and tall, six-two at least; judging by his weightlifter's forearms and biceps, he appeared to spend a good deal of his time working out at a gym. His stylishly faded blue jeans were pressed and spotless; his apple-green polo shirt was form-fitting with *Sonny* embroidered in the spot where others might display an alligator or little man on a horse. His sandy blond hair was salon-tinted and blow-dried, his mustache neatly trimmed. There wasn't the slightest evidence of grease and grime anywhere on him, least of all under his fingernails.

Rosco pulled the cap from his head and looked at the logo. "These babies are hard to come by. ABC changed their colors a while back, but I'll see what I can do for you. . . . I'm Rick Richards, from the *Back Bay D.A.* production office."

"Yeah, I figured," Sonny responded with a genuine smile.

He cocked his head toward the open garage door and Rosco's parked car. "I mean, who else drives those low-end leases these days besides middle-management types and salesmen? No offense meant, Rick. But, hey, that's what keeps the Big Three going, right?"

"Big Three?"

"GM, Ford, and Chrysler."

"Ahh. . . . And you knew it was a lease? Just by looking at it?" Rosco glanced back at the car. "I don't see anything wrong with it myself."

"Hey, Rick, wake up. It screams *corporate lease.* You need something that says you're your own boss if you want to turn some heads. That's what a BMW says—'I'm hip, I'm cool, and I got money to burn.'" He looked quickly at Rosco's left hand and his wedding ring. "But, what the heck, you're a married man, same as me. Which means our babe-magnet days are over. Besides, you take what the boss gives you, right? It's a freebie, so go for it."

Knowing that he really *was* in the market for a new car, Rosco said, "Actually, ABC has been trying to phase out the leases. They're looking into having employees buy our own cars, then providing a mileage allowance. Cost-cutting obviously, but I'll be losing that sedan soon, and I'll need to purchase something of my own. Anyway, I'm not here to yak about what I'm driving; or what I might or might not be buying in—"

"No, no," Sonny interrupted, holding his large paw up toward Rosco's chest. "I get my hands on some very nice— and I mean *very* nice—low-mileage vehicles here. Sure, they've been nicked . . . door-panel or bumper crunched, so the original owners don't want them anymore. That's how these Beamer-boys are. As soon as the vehicle gets a scratch, they trade it in, or go back on the lease. So I'm the guy who has the first look-see if some hot-shot wants to dump his car. . . . And they're clean as a whistle when my shop's done with them; you'll save yourself a bundle over new car sticker prices. You let me know when you're ready to make a move,

Rick. I'll hook you up with something really nice." Sonny
pointed at an SUV sitting out in the lot near Rosco's lease.
"Take that red Explorer out there. It's got a ding—that's all,
just a ding. The babe who dumped it is moving up to a newer
model. Just came in this morning. The gal didn't even smoke,
so it's sweet as a rose inside and out."

"I don't know," Rosco said, "My last car was red. Somehow
it seems as if I'd be unfaithful if I bought another red car."

Sonny laughed. "Hey, we're not talkin' about your wife
here, Rick. . . . But you don't like red? No problem. My
guys can make it L.A.-style aqua-blue. Detail it with a couple of tiny palm trees, too. Real discreet. Just say the word
and people'll think you're Brad Litt."

"I'll think it over." Rosco looked around Sonny's shop.
Unlike other places he'd visited that specialized in body
work, Sonny's was also equipped to handle any and all mechanical repairs. There were six hydraulic lifts, each with a
vehicle in place and a technician performing some type of
mechanical magic. The shop walls displayed handsomely
lettered signs that outlined hourly wages and the spectrum
of available services, from simple oil changes to brake jobs
to complete engine overhauls. Beyond the lifts was the autobody shop itself, where half a dozen men were working on
dented automobiles; and beyond that were four dust-proof
paint stalls, two of which were aglow with amber heating el-
ements used for drying fresh paint. Rosco noted that nearly
every car in the shop was European or a high-priced SUV.

"This is some operation you have here," he observed. And
he meant it; Sonny's was easily three times larger than any
of the previous shops he'd seen.

"Yeah, well, my dad started it all. He named it after me,
Sonny, but he did all the dirty work. He kicked the bucket
a while back, but my mom still runs the books and everything. Me? Hell, I don't know jack about mechanics or
knocking dents out cars, but I'm a good front man and I've
got an eye for what sells, know how to talk to different types
of customers, too. . . . That's what four years at Yale will do

for you. Got a lotta actor in me, if you know what I mean? I'd be great on *Back Bay D.A.* People look at me and say to themselves, 'Heck, if my car comes back lookin' half as good as Sonny-boy, I'm in Fat City.' " He laughed, exposing all thirty-two of his perfect white teeth.

Rosco strolled halfway down the mechanic's area, taking in as much as he could. He pointed up to the steel I-beams that supported the roof. "Can we hang some of our lighting equipment from there if we need to? Will it support the weight?"

"You can hang a tank from there, Rick. My dad built this place himself."

"So if this was really a chop-shop—as our script requires— how would a situation like that work in a place like yours?" The question was posed casually while Rosco continued observing the space as though envisioning camera angles and the positioning of the booms and dollies necessary to shoot an interior scene. "Would someone bring the stolen vehicles in at night, and then—"

"Nah, nah, you got it all wrong, Rick. First off, this part of Clawson Street never shuts down. They're unloading vegetables—carrots, garlic, radishes, and whatnot—across the street all night long. Too many witnesses. You'd have to bring the cars in through a back door. On the alley, where no one would see what you're doing."

"Do you have a rear door here? One we could use for the shoot, I mean? Make it look like the genuine article?"

Sonny thought for a second, glanced once toward the office door, then said, "Yeah, it's in the back."

Rosco refrained from saying, *That's a good place for a back door,* and instead opted for "Can we take a look at it? Just for sight lines and so forth. I'm not certain yet how the director wants to approach that aspect of the storyline, but I need to see everything I can."

"You bet."

As they worked their way past the mechanics, body shop workers, and paint specialists, Rosco became aware that many of the men had stopped work. The glances they gave him appeared less than friendly. "You seem to get a lot of German cars in here," Rosco said as the walked toward the rear garage entrance. "Mercedes, BMWs, . . ."

"Yeah, that's our specialty. And SUVs. See, it takes just as long to knock a dent out of a Honda as it does to clean up a Mercedes Benz. So why mess around with the small stuff, right? Plus our turnaround time is faster than anyone around. These big-money guys like that. If they plan to hang onto the car, they want it back in jig time." Sonny pressed a button on the wall and a large rear door silently rolled off to one side. "Quiet as a church mouse . . ." Sonny laughed again. "That's what my dad used to say every time he opened this door."

"If your turnaround time is quicker than other shops, then you must be able to get your parts faster than your competitors."

"Not really. . . . It's our staff that makes the difference." He cocked his thumb over his shoulder toward the men working on the cars. "I don't order parts; my mom does that. But we have more employees than the other dudes. They're more dedicated, too. That's the reason we work faster. Plus, my mom's figured out some good incentive deals for the guys."

"Got it. . . . So, let's see, a stolen vehicle—or vehicles—would enter through this door. . . . then what happens? You cut them up for parts on the spot?"

"If this was a real chop-shop?" Sonny asked in a slow and cautious tone.

"If this was the genuine article . . . right. Which it isn't, of course."

"It would depend on how big the operation in your storyline is. I've heard of some syndicates taking direct orders from Mexico and South America; they're looking for specific makes and models, and colors, too. They're not after parts, at all; they just ship those babies right out of the country. ASAP."

Rosco stepped into the alley and looked up and down. "Pretty quiet back here. Of course, we'll need to get a permit from the city to shoot in the street." He glanced at the bright afternoon sky. "Speaking of Newcastle, didn't you guys have a big auto theft back in March, was it? A lot of high-end cars stolen from some local restaurant?"

Sonny barked out a big laugh. "Oh, yeah, that was a real howl. Now that's something you should put on *Back Bay D.A.* That heist was really slick."

Rosco watched as Sonny continued to laugh. He was either completely innocent of wrong-doing or he was one of the best actors in the world. Rosco couldn't figure out which. "From what I heard, the crooks got away with twenty-plus cars? Wouldn't the shop need to be at least as big as yours to handle an operation like that?"

"Oh, yeah, easy." Sonny stopped laughing abruptly. "What? You think I pinched those vehicles? Hey, Rick, come on, this is a legit deal I'm running here."

"And the place would have to be fairly close to the restaurant, right? I mean, you can't be driving a convoy of BMWs and Porsches up Route 140 toward Boston. Plus, you'd need to have a bunch of drivers in on it."

"Hey, what is this?" Sonny demanded. "You accusing me of running a chop-shop? Is that it?"

Rosco held up his hands and chuckled. "No, no, hold on. *Back Bay D.A.* is a detective show, right? Well, it's got lawyers, too, but this is the kind of detail they're going to ask me about as soon as I get back to Boston. I've gotta have some answers for them."

"Why don't they shoot it in Boston, then? There's gotta be body shops up there they can use."

"It's a union thing," Rosco said, knowing that the relationship between television networks and their unions was a subject that no one fully understood. Sonny nodded knowingly, so Rosco added, "Who do you think did snap up all those cars last March? Local guy?"

"No telling."

"It'd be great if the *Back Bay D.A.* research team could have a sit-down with the perpetrators. Talk about realism!

You didn't hear any rumors? It'd be a feather in my cap to
go back to Boston with that kind of stuff. There must be chat
that goes around—"

"Even if I did hear something, I wouldn't be dumb
enough to talk about it. A job that big? Had to have mob-
sters mixed up with it. . . . Nobody I'm gonna fool with."

Rosco nodded while he continued to study Sonny, trying
to determine if he was being truthful or not, but the man's
face remained remarkably unreadable.

"Sonny!" a female voice shouted out from the front of the
shop.

Sonny sighed and said, "My mom. . . . I'll be right back."
He trotted toward the office.

Rosco also ambled back to the front of the building, stopping every now and then to chat with an employee. None
were remotely talkative. Instead, they seemed unusually
tight-lipped, apparently unwilling to discuss anything: the
cars they were working on, the Red Sox, the Pats, even the
weather. Rosco reached the front of the shop just as Sonny
was emerging from the office.

"Listen, Rick," he said. "My mom doesn't think it's a good
idea for your show to use the shop as a location. Sorry, I
shoulda cleared it with her first, I guess. Like I said, she's really the boss. Like the gal-behind-the-throne kind of thing."

"What's the problem?"

"She just thinks it wouldn't look good, you know, for
the business." Sonny shrugged; he appeared genuinely
disappointed.

"We'd cover up all your signs. We'd rename the business.
We're not going to splash 'Sonny's Autobody' all over na-
tional TV if that's what she's worried about."

"Nope." Sonny reached out his hand. "When my mom
says no, she means no. I'll see ya around. Sorry about this."

"Do you still want me to get you one of these ABC hats?"

"Nah, that's okay."

Rosco shook Sonny's hand and took five or six steps toward his car. He then turned back and said, "You know,

Sonny, we have an episode coming up later on in the sea-
son . . . It's about a hit-and-run accident. . . . A young kid
gets killed, and the driver finds a body shop that repairs
the dent produced by the collision, and then keeps quiet
about it. . . . Everything'll be interior shots, so there's no
way anyone's going to recognize your place. . . . In fact,"
Rosco paused. "In fact, there's a part in the script you might
be perfect for. Would you like me to mention you to my
producer?"

Sonny perked up. "Yeah. That'd be cool. I'll check with
my mom and let you know."

"Have you ever heard of a situation like that? Someone
asking you to do that kinda work on the sly?"

Sonny gave Rosco another toothy laugh. "What? A guy
bringing in a car with blood all over it? And he doesn't
know us from Adam?"

"I see your point. . . . He'd need to clean off the vehicle
first, right?"

"Sure. Then he'd tell us he hit a deer or a tree or a road
barrier or something. He'd even report it to his insurance
company in order to collect the dough. And who's gonna
question an owner who describes what sounds like a legit
accident? Not us. We're not in that business; we leave it to
the private detectives. As long as our customers pay their
bills, we're happy. And don't think that every other body
shop in the country doesn't operate in the exact same way."

Rosco nodded slowly and walked over to his car. "What
are you asking for the red Explorer here?" he called back.

"Ninteen five."

"Ouch."

CHAPTER

22

"We're not discussing the case with Sara," Belle announced as she and her husband drove to that august lady's noble home for dinner. "I just don't think it's professional. Al Lever wouldn't, Abe wouldn't." Belle's tone had taken on a finicky, some might even say "bossy," ring. "What I mean is, we've been given information that's highly sensitive, and we shouldn't allow ourselves to indulge in idle conjecture or gossip. . . ."

Rosco didn't respond; from long experience he knew it best not to interrupt when his wife embarked upon one of her more serious monologues. Besides, nine times out of ten, she would amend her statement long before she finished it.

". . . Not that Sara's a gossip, mind you. In fact, she's the farthest thing from such a person. But I don't like the notion of talking out of school. . . . Of course, Sara would never stoop to prying, so we don't have to worry about deflecting a lot of indelicate questions . . ."

It took all of Rosco's concentration not to disagree with what Belle was saying. If there was someone on this earth with as much mule-headed curiosity as his wife, it was Sara

Crane Briephs, Newcastle's octogenarian dowager empress.

". . . I don't mean that she's *in*curious, because someone as quick-witted and bright as Sara is naturally full of intellectual inquisitiveness . . ."

By now the car was climbing Patriot Hill, the habitat of the city's old money and even older lineages. The driveway leading to White Caps, which was Sara's ancestral home, would be on their left in less than two minutes.

". . . Well, I guess what I'm saying, Rosco, is that we should try to keep the evening on a strictly social level—"

"What do you mean 'try'?" Rosco finally asked as the drive appeared between two magnificent stands of rhododendron, whose blossoms lit the dusky twilight with a dazzling display of mauve and white.

"Attempt . . . strive . . . endeavor . . . undertake . . . essay—"

"I know what the word means, Belle." Rosco laughed.

"Both of us should," was her airy reply as White Caps' former carriage house came into view. Parked in front, as if just returning from a spin, was Sara's ancient black Cadillac, its surface shiny with polish, its chrome as glossy as silver. Standing a few feet from the spotless vehicle, her walking stick in hand, was the owner in person. Ramrod-straight, her white coiffure impeccable, and her lilac linen dinner suit a stirring reminder of a more genteel era, Sara appeared as out of sync with the hustle and bustle of the twenty-first century as did her 1956 Cadillac. Looking at the scene, Belle had the feeling of being transported back to a golden age of courteousness and ease when the universe was at peace with itself.

Then she opened her door, calling out a joyous "Sara!" which was immediately followed by "Guess what? You're not going to believe this, but Dan Tacete was murdered! Al has officially classified the death as a homicide."

"So much for 'our' professional discretion," Rosco murmured as he gave his wife a sidelong smile.

"You know Sara would never forgive us if we kept her out of the loop."

"She might 'try' though," Rosco said, but the gibe was lost on his wife.

Dinner over, the hostess and her guests sat in White Caps' Victorian-era conservatory, where Emma, Sara's equally elderly maid, had laid out the silver coffee service and the gilt-edged porcelain cups. Over the many years of their joint occupation of the house, the two women had developed a symbiotic relationship that permitted Sara to maintain an appearance of authority while Emma's role remained one of helpmeet and confidant. In culinary matters, however, the tables were turned; the maid became the de facto ruler of the roost, and Sara's position fell to that of an apprentice admiring the expert's considerable skills.

"Thank you, Emma," the ostensible mistress of White Caps now said.

"Will you be needing anything else, madam?" was the habitual reply.

"If we do, we'll rustle it up ourselves. You've had a long day."

"Very good, madam."

"Lovely dinner, too, Emma. I don't know how you do it."

"I'm glad you were pleased, madam."

"I always am. You're a positive wizard. All our guests say so."

At this point in the familiar exchange, Belle expected Emma to forsake her formal demeanor, plop herself down in a chair, take out a bag of knitting, and join the general chat. Instead, her old knees bent in a kind of bob that in earlier years would have been a curtsy. Then she turned and began to trundle off toward her kitchen castle.

"Thanks again, Emma!" Belle called to her retreating figure.

"It cheers up the house when you and Mr. Rosco visit. And we like a cheerful home, don't we madam? And I certainly enjoy cooking for more than two people."

Then Emma was gone, and the tall glass room with its potted palms and flowing plants settled into stillness. Sipping her coffee in silence, Belle smelled the earthy scent of growing things, of humus and orchid bark and damp clay pots. It was a place of such tranquility that it was difficult to remember that criminals roved the same terrain.

"I worry about my Emma," Sara mused aloud. "She's getting old."

Belle and Rosco held their tongues. Mistress and maid had been born within a few months of one another.

"We all grow feeble eventually, I suppose," Sara continued. "Still, one doesn't appreciate witnessing the effects of time on a person one is fond of. I was fortunate in not having to watch my dear husband cope with the depredations of the passing years—or my son."

Again, Rosco and Belle kept silent. It was the murder of Sara's middle-aged son, Thompson, that had initially established their friendship.

"Ah, well," Sara mused. "*Les temps perdus,* as the poets say. . . . Although time is never quite 'lost' is it? Just as the dead are never fully gone if they live in memory." The indomitable old lady replaced her cup on the silver tray and raised her patrician chin. *The past is the past,* her expression seemed to say. *We must forgive even if we cannot forget—especially if we cannot forget.*

At length, she released a small and melancholy sigh and returned her concentration to her guests. Her astonishingly blue eyes were now focused on the present. "So . . . Albert has classified Dan Tacete's death as a homicide." It was a statement rather than a question, since the threesome—or rather, Belle and Sara—had discussed the case in detail over dinner. Rosco, alone, had tried to maintain a "professional" stance. "It's too bad the FBI won't be brought in, because something seems highly irregular in everything you've described. Not that I don't believe darling Albert is more than capable of divining the perpetrator—or perpetrators."

"There's no evidence that anyone crossed state lines," was Belle's response.

"A shame. One would imagine that with Dan Tacete's two automobiles zipping here and there, some border would have been crossed."

"A 'border,' as in the line dividing Massachusetts and New Hampshire?" It was Rosco who asked this question. He was smiling as he did so. "I gather you'd feel better if there were checkpoints?"

"Don't you get flippant with me, young man," Sara chuckled in return. "If the people of Keane and Concord wish to espouse 'Live free or die' as their motto, they obviously don't care a whit about their neighbors' well-being—"

"I don't believe the expression was intended as an insult to their fellow colonists," Rosco rejoined.

"*Humph*," Sara answered with a quick and mischievous grin. Then she turned back to Belle. "And those nursery-rhyme-themed crosswords you received . . . there's no possibility of tracking their authorship?"

Belle shrugged. "Post office boxes can be registered under false names, and the email address on the one puzzle was through one of those huge Web servers, which anyone can sign up for by presenting fraudulent information. . . . So, no, Sara, in answer to your question: The author—or authors—is anonymous."

"I don't like it," Sara said. "It makes me worry about the safety of the little Tacete girl . . . although you haven't been able to connect anything to her father except the name Jack."

"No," Belle admitted.

"Not much of a lead, other than the obvious: the partner."

"No, it isn't."

"I wish you'd brought those crosswords with you,

dear child. We could have pored over them together."

"Belle didn't intend to discuss the case with you," Rosco said with his own small chortle. "She told me so during the drive over. 'Mum's the word,' she insisted."

The old woman turned in her chair and leveled her penetrating gaze on her younger friend. "What led you to make that absurd decision?"

Belle fidgeted under Sara's scrutiny, leaving Rosco to come to his wife's rescue with a well-placed lie. "She didn't want to worry you."

"But I've been asked to reflect on nearly every crime she's helped solve," Sara asserted with some warmth. "They don't worry me in the least—unless I think one of you two might be in danger."

Belle glanced up and caught Rosco's eye. "And she also wanted to keep this evening on a purely social level," he added.

Belle turned beet-red while Sara tossed aside Rosco's statement. "What better time to discuss the workings of the criminal mind than over supper with close friends?" Then the doyenne of White Caps suddenly sat even straighter in her chair. "Rosco, I assume the attorney for the Snyder case contacted you?" But no sooner had that query been posed than Sara leapt to another. "Have I told you that I'm establishing a scholarship fund in honor of that poor boy? I know what some would say . . . that it's too late to help the child himself, but something must be done as a remembrance—and a reminder. Adults who kill children and then callously drive away must be revealed as the craven cowards they are."

"No, you didn't tell us," was Belle's reply. "But I think that's perfectly wonderful." She wanted to say more; in fact, she was on the verge of telling Sara just how fond of her she was and how very proud she felt to count her as a friend. But the old lady, as was her wont, intuited those words of praise, and so was able to forestall them with another change of subject.

"I'm wondering, Belle, dear . . . Is it possible those crosswords you received could be connected to the Snyder boy's death rather than to the Tacete's murder? Possibly the word games have nothing to do with your dentist. If indeed, these *puzzling* nursery rhymes are related to either crime."

CHAPTER

23

A t six the next morning, the sun's rays were already streaking over the oceans's horizon and gracing the peeling pink paint of the vacant Dew Drop Inn with a lively glow that temporarily banished the many unkindnesses of the decades. Except for night, when the inn was dark, it was the only time when the old structure looked halfway like it once had.

As the decrepit building reveled in its momentary return to youth, Newcastle's early risers, both human and canine, were making their way onto the expanse of lawn that had become known simply as the "dog park." The routines of the visitors were as predictable as the dawn. At a minute or two past six, Al Lever would arrive in his Plymouth sedan, open the back door, and his "big yellow mutt," Skippy, would amble forth and sit patiently beside the rear tire.

Murmuring *soto voce* endearments, Lever would then light a cigarette while almost simultaneously bending to unhook Skippy's leash. Watching the dog dart across the dewy grass at full speed was one of the highlights of the Al's day.

Abe Jones would arrive shortly thereafter. Since it was May, the canvas top of his new jet-black Thunderbird would be down. Once he came to a stop, he would reach across to the passenger's seat and unhook Buster's leash. Buster was a Lab-mix who still had a good deal of puppy energy. He always jumped from the car without waiting for the door to be opened; then he invariably went tearing after Skippy. By six fifteen on most weekday mornings, there would be at least a half dozen dogs and their corresponding people enjoying the inn's grounds. Almost all of the two-legged members of the group clutched take-out coffee containers as though the liquid were the last they'd be permitted in this life.

Belle and Rosco, with Kit and Gabby, were not part of the habitual six A.M. drill. If it weren't one of Rosco's regular jogging mornings, then sliding out of the double bed that strained to accommodate all four bodies wasn't an exercise either humans or canines looked forward to. When Rosco wasn't running, the routine worked this way: Belle would be the first up after the alarm went off. Then she'd trudge downstairs and get the coffee brewing. Kit would follow, feeling a certain amount of "watchdog" obligation, although the duties were performed with a marked lack of enthusiasm. The smell of the coffee would rouse Rosco, who would in turn inform Gabby that it was time to get her lazy bones up.

But this particular Wednesday morning was different. The conversations with Sara the previous night, combined with Belle's earlier visit to The Black Sheep Tavern, inspired her to set the alarm for five twenty so that she and Rosco— and Kit and Gabby, naturally—could join Abe and Al and their respective "canine others" for a pow-wow and update. Kit seemed game for the excursion, but Gabby needed to be carried from "her" bed all the way down to Rosco's rented car. The four arrived at the Dew Drop Inn at eight minutes past six. While the "girls" scurried off to find their friends, Belle and Rosco joined Abe and Al, who were leaning against the detective's car.

Al glanced at his watch in surprise. "What are you two lovebirds doing here at this hour?"

Rosco smiled in response, although his tone was serious. "With this Tacete mess, it doesn't look like anybody's getting too much sleep. Any developments on your end?"

"I had a man interviewing folks at Gilbert's Groceries all day yesterday. And he'll be back at it this morning. We have three people who say they saw Karen Tacete drop off the Corvette and wait for a taxi at the pick-up stand, but as of now, no one remembers seeing anyone drive *out* of the lot in the 'Vette. Which makes sense. Whoever retrieved it had to play things very cool. . . . Considering the vehicle's smoked windows, it's doubtful anyone would have been able to see who was driving anyway—unless they were looking directly through the windshield."

Abe Jones pulled a small note pad from his rear pocket and jotted something into it, prompting Lever to add a vaguely peremptory "What?"

"Nothing really . . . just another question concerning the vehicle."

"How's it going?" Rosco asked.

"Well, I've only had at it for a day," Abe said, "so I'm far from finished. I got lucky on the emergency brake handle. It was about the only place on the car that wasn't charred black. I was able to pick up a few distinctly different fingerprints. One I've been able to identify as Tacete's. I sent the others to the Feds."

"They're probably Karen's," Belle suggested.

"That was my first thought, but we've classified the prints as male by their size. For now, anyway. Interestingly, I didn't find *any* prints on the car that I would suggest they were female. But the vehicle's a total mess. Fiberglass melts and everything goes with it." Abe paused. "Another curious thing is that the shift knob is missing."

"Burnt up?" Rosco asked.

"No. Missing. It was never there. Obviously you can drive the car that way, but it's fairly uncomfortable on the palm of your hand. I phoned Karen, and she said it was in place when she left the car at Gilbert's. Apparently, it was a chrome Hurst short-shifter."

"Is that valuable?" Belle asked.

"Not really. But they're attractive."

"Maybe a kid stole it while it was sitting in the lot," Al suggested. "Karen said she left it unlocked."

"It's possible," was Abe's reply.

"Only *possible?*" Belle prodded.

"Probable . . . possible . . . All I know is that it's missing."

The four stood quietly. After a moment, Rosco addressed another question to Abe. "I don't suppose you want to go up against the captain—and city hall—and take a look a Tacete's body?"

Jones gave Rosco his signature broad and knowing smile. "You just can't leave Carlyle alone, can you?"

Rosco returned the grin. "You need to learn how to take a compliment, my friend. Is there anything wrong with my wanting The Pro to weigh in with his expert opinion?"

"Well," Abe responded, "*The Pro,* as you put it, has looked at Carlyle's report, and it's fine. Even Estelle, our ghouless-in-residence, signed off on it. Unless those two missed a bullet in Tacete's heart, which they didn't, there's no reason for me to examine the body. If it makes you feel any better, though, Rosco, I think you might have put a bit of a scare into your friend, Carlyle. He want back and retested all the fluid and tissue samples. Like I said, I've read the report. Tacete died at the time of the accident. I have no doubt about that."

"How about five minutes before the accident?"

"The only one who can pinpoint it that closely is the Man Upstairs. Even I'm not that good."

"So, anyway," Lever said as he lit his third cigarette of the morning. "We've also been chasing down Jack Wagner's five 'shifty characters' from his partner's patient list. It seems—"

"They all work at the Black Sheep," Belle announced proudly.

Al looked at her sideways. "Well, yeah, two of them do. One guy heads up a local rock band, and the other two are sometime residents of Father Tom's St. Augustine mission."

"So that would mean that Terry Friend is a man?"

"Right. We haven't tracked any of them down yet, but we'll be back on it this morning."

"I saw Ed Trawler and Carlos Quintero at the Black Sheep yesterday afternoon," Belle offered.

Lever glanced at Rosco and raised an eyebrow. "Your wife hangs out in some pretty classy joints, Poly—crates." He then looked at Belle. "I had no idea you were a regular. Somehow a spot like that doesn't seem the sort of place a renowned cruciverbalist like your honeybunch might frequent."

Belle ignored Al's gibe. "I followed Bonnie O'Connell there yesterday. Here's what I learned." She counted the items off on her fingers as she spoke. "One: Ed Trawler and Rob Rossi work as bartenders. Two: Rob Rossi hasn't shown up for work since Dan disappeared. Three: Carlos Quintero hangs out there—"

Al snapped his fingers. "He's the one in the rock band."

"That makes sense. . . . Four: There's another guy named Frank; I gather he's pulled some sort of disappearing act, too. From what I heard, he and Bonnie have some sort of relationship. . . . And five: Bonnie and Jack Wagner are having an affair."

"Okaaay . . ." Al said, dragging out the syllables. "That's what I was picking up on, too. But what makes you so sure?"

"Ed said that Bonnie was unavailable, date-wise, as long as 'Mr. Big-Bucks' was still in the picture."

"That title could refer to anyone though, Belle. Everything's relative."

"I'm just following your lead, Al. You said Wagner insisted he could earn twenty-five thousand dollars from a single mouth. Who else could the guy be?"

"Uh-huh . . ." Lever nodded. "You didn't catch a last name on this Frank fella, did you?"

Belle shook her head while Al noted the name on a slip of paper. He then added an offhanded "And, of course, we still have an APB out on that white Explorer Tacete was driving when he was nabbed. That baby seems to have dropped off the face of the earth."

Jones patted Lever on the back. "Al, it's the getaway car. It's probably in Topeka right now, out in front of an IHOP waiting for the perp to finish his cheese omelette and home fries."

"That sure seems like the logical explanation," Al agreed. "Which is exactly why I don't like it—it's too easy."

"And my guess is we should be looking for Rob Rossi," Abe replied with a shrug. "He's the only person who's skipped town."

"We've got this Frank character Belle just discovered— who also seems to have taken a powder. Plus, let's not forget that your average criminal doesn't strike and then run away. These guys are like pigeons. They're afraid to leave their own neighborhoods. You know that, Abe. A guy robs a convenience store or a liquor store, and what happens? Three days later, he ends up spending the money in the men's clothing shop around the corner. . . . The smart ones pull off a job and then amuse themselves by sitting around and watching the cops make fools of themselves. The dumb ones are their own worst enemies. Intuition tells me that the guy who killed Dan Tacete is still right here in Newcastle. I'll put money on it." Al then looked at Rosco. "You're unusually quiet today, Poly—crates."

Rosco was leaning against the NPD sedan with his arms folded across his chest, watching Gabby wrestle with Buster in an emerald-green patch of overgrown grass. He didn't turn to face Al. "I was thinking."

"Oh, boy, that's always a bad sign."

"No, I'm with you, Al; I don't think Dan's killer has left town either. Obviously Rob Rossi and this Frank guy need to be tracked down, but I'll bet they're still in the Newcastle area somewhere. What I'm wondering about is the Explorer.

If the killer's still here, then the Explorer's still here. . . . Could it have been painted? Have the windows been tinted? Has the entire vehicle been given a new look—new tires, expensive detailing? Maybe what we've been looking for is right under our noses. Maybe it's no longer white."

"Hey, you're the newfound chop-shop pro," Al said with a smile, "you tell me."

"I might just do that."

CHAPTER

24

"Back so soon?" Sonny asked as Rosco stepped from his car. It almost seemed as if he'd been waiting for "Rick" to return. "I told you. My mom doesn't like the idea of using the shop for *Back Bay D.A.*"

"Did you tell her it was thirty-five hundred a day? Plus, we'll pick up your electric tab for the month?"

"Yeah, she still nixxed it. What can I say?" Sonny gave an apologetic smile, and again Rosco was struck by the incongruity of the man's appearance with his surroundings. Sonny looked like he'd just missed a crucial putt on the country club green rather than a guy who needed to shout to be heard over the noise of half a dozen welding torches.

"No big deal. I have a back up. We'll probably go with Classic Autobody over on Airport Boulevard."

"Classic?" Sonny made no attempt to disguise his disapproval. "That's the worst shop in town. Come on, Rick, you can do better than that. Those guys couldn't repair a tricycle."

Rosco shrugged. "It's the *look* we're after. And the light. They've got a lot of north-facing windows. It works well for TV; it makes your actors look healthy."

"It's your funeral, my friend."

Rosco looked around the front parking lot of Sonny's Autobody. "That's not why I came back, though. I'm not trying to twist your arm—or your mom's arm. And I don't intend to get into an argument over your competition. . . . What I want to ask about is that Explorer you said came in yesterday morning. I talked your suggestion over with my wife, and she said if I liked it, to go for it. She's always been an SUV type of lady. The bigger the better, that's her." Rosco smiled, visualizing how much that last statement would have annoyed Belle.

Sonny produced one of his own bright and gleaming smiles. "Now you're talkin', Rick. Stu's working on it in the paint shop. Just needed a couple of dings buffed out, remember? Come on, let's go take a peek at it." But as they began to walk through the mechanic's area Sonny stopped and placed his hand on Rosco's forearm. "You know," he said, "I was just thinking. Remember I told you I was asking nineteen five for the vehicle?"

"Yes?"

"Well, see, I haven't even had a chance to flip the papers on this baby. I mean, it just came in yesterday morning, right? So, what I'm sayin' is this: If you want it, we can make like you just bought it directly from the babe who owned it. Get it?"

"Not really."

"I like to call it a *quick-flip*. I mean, it's technically illegal, but it goes down all the time in this business. We're just cutting *me* out of the picture, as far as the state of Massachusetts is concerned, that is. You know, it's half the paperwork, taxes, and registration fees. . . . And I can knock a grand off the price for you." He snapped his fingers. "Just like that; let you have it for eighteen five . . . if you're paying cash. And ready to roll on it today."

"Sure," Rosco said with feigned enthusiasm for this possible bargain. "Can I take it for a test drive?"

"As long as Stu's done with it, you bet."

They continued through the shop, past the autobody crew,

and stopped on the other side of one of the paint bays where Stu was on his knees working with an electric buffing tool on the Explorer's passenger-side door panel. He straightened when he saw Sonny approaching.

Sonny said, "This is Rick Richards, Stu. He's from ABC-TV up in Boston. He's in the market for an Explorer just like this. How's the work coming?"

"I've got everything cleaned up, Sonny. Just need to give it a couple shots of lacquer, bake her up, and she's as good as new."

Sonny leaned through the driver's-side window. "Less than six thousand miles. You're getting a real deal here, Rick."

Rosco kicked the front tire for no reason other than he assumed that was what one was supposed to do when examining a car. But when he glanced down at the tire he saw a few tiny flecks of red paint. He looked at Stu and said, "You haven't done your touch-up, right? Does that mean I can't take it for a test drive?"

Stu removed his work gloves. He wore surgical-type latex gloves beneath them. "No, I haven't done my paint work yet, so I'd rather it didn't go out right now and pick up a bunch of road grime. Anything she picks up is bound to show in the new paint job. It'll only take me twenty minutes to spray her up, and an hour to bake. It'd be better if you could swing back here this afternoon or tomorrow."

Rosco pointed to the paint on the front tire. "If you haven't done any touch-up yet, how come there's red flecks on this tire?"

The two men walked around the front of the car and crouched by the tire.

"Huh," Sonny frowned, although the expression failed to convey a sense of surprise and confusion. "Beats me. No tellin' where that came from. Any ideas, Stu?"

Stu remained silent, so Rosco opted to cut to the chase and voice his suspicion. "The Explorer hasn't been totally *repainted* has it? I mean, the entire car? Could it have been another color at one time?"

Sonny laughed, although the sound was not a relaxed one. "Hey, Rick, it's only got six thousand miles on it. Why would someone repaint it? Where's the sense in that? I mean, red's red. It's not like the babe wanted some custom color to match a new outfit or anything . . ."

"I don't know. That's why I'm asking."

Sonny took Rosco by the arm and led him away from the Explorer. "Let's go back to the office. We can work out a deal on this baby. You come back this afternoon with your cash, take your test drive, kick some more tires if you like, and you've got yourself a brand new car."

"I don't know . . ."

"Rick, Rick, I'm ready to talk turkey. I'll tell you what I'm gonna do; I'm gonna let you have this car for seven hundred dollars more than I paid for it. That's the best I can do. I've put some money into it. I've cleaned it up, but I'm not gonna rake you over the coals. How's that?"

Rosco laughed. "How do I know what you paid for it?"

Sonny draped his arm over Rosco's shoulder. "Let's step into the office, Rick. These fumes and all . . . I prefer talking where the air is clean."

The office was broken into two rooms. The first had a large steel desk on one side, and facing it were two blue metal chairs with matching vinyl cushions. The opposite wall held a couch appointed in genuine leather. The walls were decorated with prints of European sports cars. A wood-veneered door and plate-glass window opened into the second office. On the far side of the glass, Rosco spotted another desk behind which sat a woman who appeared to be in her late sixties. Like Sonny, she was immaculately attired; and her chocolate-brown helmet of hair seemed to have come directly from the hair salon. She looked up from her paperwork when they entered and never took her eyes off Rosco the entire time he was there.

"I guess that must be your mother."

"Yeah. Don't let her bother you. She's a worrier. . . . Probably thinks I'm gonna let you persuade me to let you use our shop for your shoot—or I'll run off and become a full-time actor."

Rosco nodded. His own mother could have also been deemed a "worrier"—to say nothing of his two elder sisters.

"But shouldn't I say hello? That's how things work in my family. My mom would consider it rude of visitors not to speak to her."

"Nah, she doesn't like to be bothered." Sonny sat behind the metal desk and pulled a file from a side drawer. "Have a seat, Rick."

Rosco sat, angling the chair so that his back faced the window and the scrutiny he could still feel being leveled at his shoulder blades. He had a strong sense that the brains behind the operation didn't want her son revealing certain information. But Sonny seemed unaware of his mother's watchful presence. He removed a stamped envelope from the file folder, opened it with a brass letter opener, then withdrew a check and placed it on the desk in front of Rosco.

"Ya see, Rick . . . I'm bein' one hundred percent aboveboard with you on this thing. Let's just say I'm tryin' to make up for not letting your people use the shop for their location." He tapped the check with his index finger. "This is the check I was going to mail to the woman who owns that Explorer. Pick it up. Go ahead, I want you to look at it."

Rosco picked up the check. It was for fifteen thousand dollars and made out to a Karen Johnson.

"Fifteen grand," Sonny said as he retrieved the check from Rosco. He then ripped the check up into several small pieces and tossed them into the plastic trash basket by his desk. "So that's what I was going to pay her. Now, I'm going to let you have the car for fifteen seven, just like I said would. You come back this afternoon with the cash, take your test drive, and we're all set."

"Then you pay this Karen Johnson her fifteen thousand in cash, keep seven hundred, and we have no record that the car was ever in your shop. Is that it?"

"Hey, Rick, you make it sound like *The Great Train Robbery.*

We save ourselves twelve hundred in sales tax. The car flips once instead of twice."

Rosco appeared to think for a moment then said, "Mind if I take a look at that envelope?"

"What for?"

"I just want to see if the stamp's canceled. I figure if it's a new stamp, then you really intended to mail it, and you're not giving me the runaround on the price."

Sonny laughed, and pushed the envelope across the desk toward Rosco. "I like that, Rick. That's a cool move. I'll have to remember it. I guess that's the kind of clever stuff you use on *Back Bay D.A.,* isn't it?"

Rosco also laughed, but his eyes were focused on the envelope's address. He recognized it immediately. It was the Tacete home. Rosco returned the envelope to the desktop and said, "Yeah, I see your point. Why give Massachusetts any more than we have to?" He glanced at his watch, thinking it would probably take Al Lever an hour or so to get a judge to sign an impound order on the Explorer.

"I think we've got ourselves a deal, Sonny."

The two men stood and walked back outside to Rosco's rental car.

"How about I come back just before noon for my test drive? The Explorer should be ready by then, right?"

Sonny smiled. "You got it. . . . And, Rick?"

"Yes?"

"Don't forget the fifteen seven."

CHAPTER
25

The only person more anxious than Rosco to locate Dan Tacete's missing Ford Explorer was Al Lever. Rosco had called him from his cell phone less than twenty seconds after leaving Sonny's lot. Al, in turn, had scrambled up an impound order, enabling the two of them to return to Sonny's Autobody slightly before noon. They were in Al's NPD sedan, which was the first vehicle to drive through the gate in Sonny's high chain-link fence. Immediately behind Lever's brown sedan was a blue and white police cruiser; on its tail was a flatbed traffic enforcement tow truck. The moment he saw the three vehicles grind to a halt and the officers—and Rosco—emerge, Sonny ran out of the shop like a New England Patriots' linebacker on an all-out blitz.

"What the hell is this, Rick? I thought I could trust you. You go to the cops? You turn me in for trying to skim a lousy twelve hundred bucks off the state?"

Rosco said nothing as Al removed his gold shield from his belt and held it up for Sonny to see. "My name is Lieutenant Lever, Newcastle Police Department. I'm impounding the red Explorer in your shop as criminal evidence. I'd like to ask a few questions while my boys load it up."

Sonny continued to bluster and roar. "Like I didn't know you were a cop? Like that 'unmarked' heap of yours doesn't scream law enforcement all over the place? You can't do this to me. You can't come barging in here. I'm calling my lawyer. This is a legitimate business I run here." He looked back toward the shop entrance. His mother was now standing in the doorway with her hands resting belligerently on her hips. Her hairspray glinted in the sun and made her brown coiffure seem even more rigid and fierce. "You gotta read me my rights," Sonny argued as he returned his attention to Al and pointed at Rosco. "You're not getting away with this, Rick."

"Relax, nobody's under arrest," Al said. "Not yet, anyway. . . . I just want to ask some questions and take the car in for examination."

"Sonny! Get over here," his mother demanded from the doorway. "Now!"

Al held up his hand. "I need to talk to you alone, Sonny. I don't want to have to go in there with a warrant, but I will if necessary. I'll impound your books if need be."

"Let me go settle her down a bit first, okay? My mom gets a little tense sometimes."

Without waiting for an answer, Sonny trotted back to his mother. They spoke for three minutes in harsh and angry whispers, but what they said was impossible for Al or Rosco to make out. Eventually Sonny returned to Lever, but his mother maintained her ferocious stance by the shop door.

"Okay, what do you want to know, Lieutenant?" Gone entirely was the adamant tone Sonny had used before.

Al waved to the police mechanic driving the tow truck, who then began backing the flatbed into the autobody shop. The beep-beep-beep of the truck's reverse warning system droned in the background as Lever spoke. "Are you the one who repainted the Explorer?"

"No. No way, Lieutenant. It was like that when it came in here yesterday."

"But you knew it had been repainted?"

"This is a quality shop. Any professional can tell you in a second if a car's been retouched."

"That's not what I'm asking. My question is whether *you* knew the vehicle had been repainted when you took possession of it."

Sonny's gaze shifted from Al to Rosco while his shoulders twisted in an effort not to look in his mother's direction. "Yeah . . ." he muttered.

"I didn't hear you."

"Yes. Yes, I did."

"What color was it originally?"

This time Sonny turned toward his mother; he looked as though he were hoping she could supply the answer. "White," he finally admitted. His voice was hushed and hesitant.

"And you didn't paint it red?"

"No. I told you that. I swear I didn't paint it. I only got it yesterday; and it was red. Just like it is now."

Opting not to blow Rosco's cover, Al said, "But you weren't going to tell *Rick* here, were you? That you knew it had been repainted?"

Sonny didn't reply, but his head seemed to sink into his neck.

"Are you aware that lying about a vehicle's paint job carries the same hefty fines as turning back an odometer? And that you could do some jail time if I pushed it?"

"No . . . No, I didn't know that."

Rosco thought, *Neither did I, but it sure sounds good.* He suspected that the statement might have lacked a certain amount of veracity.

Al continued to push Sonny. "I want to hear how the vehicle happened to end up in your shop."

"Let's go into the office, okay, Lieutenant?"

"No. I want to talk about this right here. I want to hear it from you, and only you."

Sonny sighed and fidgeted with his belt buckle. He glanced at the ground and once more at his mother. Then he straightened his shoulders as if preparing for the worst. "Look, a guy brought the car in yesterday morning and said he wanted to get some nicks and dings buffed out of it so he could sell it. Basically, what he needed was a top-notch detailing. It was minor stuff, really. . . ." Sonny swallowed hard and paused for the briefest moment. "So, I asked him how much he was looking to get for payment, and he said sixteen grand. I told him if he'd agree to fifteen, I'd take the Explorer off his hands. I knew I could get nineteen, maybe twenty easy. And that's it. That's all there is to know."

"But the car was registered to a woman," Rosco tossed in. "Karen something. You showed me the check. Now you're saying a man brought it in?"

"Yeah. It was registered to a Karen Johnson, but this guy said that was his wife's name."

"So the man was Mr. Johnson?" Al asked as he noted the name on a piece of paper.

"No. He said it was registered in her *maiden* name. That's why I wouldn't give him the money up front; because he didn't have the same last name. I mean, I didn't know this guy from a hole in the wall. He could have stolen the vehicle for all I knew. He looked like a bum, like he'd just come off a week-long bender; he hadn't shaved for a while and his clothes were a total mess. I told him I wouldn't pay the fifteen grand to nobody but the person whose name was on the registration. He said he'd come back later with his wife, but if I had a chance to sell it first to go ahead with the deal, to hold the cash for him and his wife. Then he left the Explorer and walked out on foot. Said he was going to catch a cab on the corner. When he didn't show, I decided to mail a check to this Karen babe at the address on the registration. I was being real straight up about all this, Lieutenant."

Al only stared at Sonny, who, in turn, tried but failed to gaze calmly back. Rosco noted that the man's right eyelid was now twitching and that sweat was beginning to streak his perfect green polo shirt.

"What?" Sonny demanded with what was clearly intended

to be a nonchalant shrug. He nodded toward Rosco, but the gesture was jerky and anxious. "Just ask Rick there. He saw the envelope. He saw the check. I was playing this completely aboveboard."

"Not if you were knowingly accepting a stolen vehicle, you weren't."

"Look, I told you I was gonna pay the babe. It's a fair price—"

"And 'aboveboard' doesn't really apply to the twelve hundred you were going to withhold from the state of Massachusetts, either." No response came from Sonny, so Al added a facetious "You wouldn't happen to have the name of Ms. Johnson's husband, would you?"

"Yeah . . . yeah, I do." Sonny suddenly appeared as eager to please as a kid in a toy store.

"Feel like sharing it with us?"

"Frank. His name was Frank. Frank O'Connell."

Rosco and Al exchanged a private look as the flatbed truck emerged from the garage. The Explorer was secured onto the load area by a series of chains.

"Fat? Skinny? Twenty? Sixty? How would you describe this Frank O'Connell, other than a guy who'd been on a week-long bender?"

"He was thinnish, as tall as me. I don't know about age. Late twenties or thirties, maybe. Red ponytail; Sox cap. He looked older, though . . . beat up, like I said. One of those guys you guess is middle-aged till they open their mouths."

"And you never asked yourself how this 'bum' might have had a 'wife' with such a swanky address and pricey car?"

Again, Sonny didn't respond. Al glowered at him, then exhaled an angry breath. "We'll be lifting fingerprints from the vehicle," he continued as the tow truck exited the lot. "I want a list of all employees who handled it. They may be asked to come to the station later to submit their prints for comparison."

Sonny shook his head. "Nobody's touched it, Lieutenant; or at least nobody left fingerprints on it. Everyone in this shop wears latex gloves and custom-fitted work gloves over them. That's our policy."

"Why is that?" Rosco asked.

"Ninety percent of the cars we get have leather interiors. My mom insists on cleanliness. She goes through the roof if one of our guys leaves a grease smudge on someone's Beamer—inside or out."

Al handed Sonny one of his card. "If you think of anything else you'd like to share with me about that Explorer, give me a call."

"So . . . so, it was a hot car, huh?"

"In more ways than you know."

"Well, as long as I didn't lose my fifteen grand, I'm a happy camper." Sonny made an effort at a collegial smile, but the attempt failed.

"Right. But better not try any camping soon. In fact, don't leave town without notifying my office. You've just made yourself a material witness."

Al and Rosco returned to the NPD sedan and pulled out behind the tow truck. The police cruiser followed them.

"I'm gathering that Frank O'Connell is Bonnie's brother," Rosco said after they'd made a left off of Clawson Street.

"Brother, uncle, cousin; gotta be one of them."

"And Karen Johnson is Karen Tacete's maiden name?"

"I'd put money on that." Lever lit a cigarette using the dashboard lighter and glanced sideways at Rosco. "Sorry, Poly—crates; my car, my rules."

Rosco ignored the smoke. "So the receptionist's brother kidnaps the good doctor. . . . Is the receptionist in on it?"

"More importantly, is the wife in on it?"

CHAPTER

26

"Okay, Karen," Rosco said, "let me get this straight. You were aware that Dan's receptionist had a brother named Frank . . . but you never actually met him?"

Her eyes raw and puffy from weeping, her blonde hair disheveled, her pale complexion drained of all color, Karen simply nodded her assent.

"Although you'd heard rumors that he had 'problems'?" Belle prompted.

Again, Karen nodded. She bowed her head in a gesture that was a study in defeat. "I'm having a really hard time talking about all of this," she finally murmured in a tone that was nearly inaudible. "It was only yesterday that they found Dan . . ." The words trailed off, unfinished.

"I know this is difficult, Karen," Rosco replied, "But time is of the essence."

Belle, who was seated beside Karen on the living room couch—a leather affair that was obviously new and expensive—resisted the temptation to put her arms around the distraught woman. For one thing, Karen's huddled form seemed to have withdrawn into itself. The other deterrent was Belle's growing confusion. With each question, Karen

Tacete seemed more unknowable; it was almost, Belle thought, as if she were deliberately keeping secrets from the very people who were trying to help her.

"Dan likes to keep his work separate from his family life," Karen now stated in a subdued monotone. "Liked, I mean. He *liked* to separate work from family." Her head sank lower; her shoulders slumped.

"But you met Bonnie?"

"Of course. At the office."

"And how did she strike you?" Belle asked.

"Strike me?" Karen finally looked up, her face a blank.

"Did she seem like an honest person when you first saw her?" Rosco tossed in.

"I guess. . . . Dan didn't hire her. Jack did. Before Dan became a partner of Smile! She's cheerful. And young. That's all I know about her."

"And that she's got a brother named Frank who may or may not have difficulties with the law," Rosco continued.

Karen shrugged. "I don't know. . . . I suspected that it might have been a drug problem . . . but I'm not sure."

"Do you have any idea how Frank O'Connell could have come into possession of your Explorer, Karen?" Rosco asked after another quiet moment.

"Dan was driving it when he . . . when he . . . No, I don't know."

"That's my point; Dan disappears in the Explorer, then Franks tries to sell it. . . . Did Dan ever help Frank out in any way?" was Rosco's next question. "Money-wise? I know he liked to aid folks who were down and out."

"He could have, I guess."

"But he didn't tell you, specifically?"

"I was just his wife. He didn't tell me everything he did, no."

Ensconced in the butter-soft and pillowy leather, Belle felt her spine straighten in protest. It took a degree of self-control not to immediately challenge Karen's remark about being "just" a wife. "But you and Dan must have had a wonderful and loving relationship . . . with Lily at the center of your life," Belle said instead, but Karen greeted this statement with another uncomprehending stare.

"So, all the cars are in your name?" Rosco asked after an additional and uncomfortable silence.

"My maiden name, yes. . . . Well, not the Corvette, but Dan said that registering them to me was like insurance, in case anything ever happened to—" Karen's mouth shut tight, curtailing the remainder of her speech. "I don't want to talk anymore," she added suddenly. "There's nothing else I can tell you. I never met this Frank O'Connell. I couldn't even tell you what he looks like—unless he resembles his sister. And I don't have a clue as to why he had our Explorer . . . or why it was red . . . or anything. . . . But it seems pretty dumb to try to sell a car that was being driven by a man whose wife reported him missing—and who then wound up being kidnapped and murdered."

Belle's ears pricked up at the word "murdered," but she decided to say nothing. Al had classified Dan Tacete's death as a homicide, but only because of the circumstances surrounding the kidnapping. She looked at Rosco, who had obviously heard and concluded the same thing.

"It seems more than dumb, Karen," he now stated. "It's criminal."

"Well, I guess you better find this Frank O'Connell."

"You're right, there," Rosco agreed with a certain amount of resignation in his voice.

Karen sat a little taller and pushed the tousled hair from her eyes. She appeared visibly relieved that the interview was drawing to a close. Then all at once, Lily thundered in; on her heels was Bear, who leapt, with his diminutive compatriot, onto the leather couch. "Hi Rock! Hi Cookie!" Lily all but shouted in her enthusiasm. Her energy and joy were so infectious Belle couldn't help but smile; but Karen's response was exactly the opposite.

She began to sob, hugging Lily close while between her tears she gasped out a spasmodic "My baby . . . I don't want to lose you. . . . Mommy doesn't ever want to lose you. . . ."

Her mother's anguish produced the same reaction in the little girl, who also began to wail out her own fear and sorrow while Bear slunk away, leaving Belle and Rosco uncomfortable witnesses to this intense family drama.

"Karen?" Belle asked after several minutes had elapsed. "Is there anyone we can call . . . perhaps, a relative you'd like to have visit for a while—?"

"No!" Karen burst out. "I don't want anyone here! I don't need anyone." She hugged Lily tighter. "Do we, Lily-bet?"

"But it might help to have family here." Even as she formed the words, Belle realized she didn't know if Karen had relatives she communicated with or not.

"I'm fine on my own. I don't need any of them. I never have, and I never will again." The tone was shrill.

"But maybe . . . just to help get you through this rough patch . . . ?"

"You don't know what you're talking about, Belle! And you sure as hell don't know the first thing about what it's like to live through rough patches."

Belle stiffened at the attack, then reminded herself that Karen was dealing with terrible emotional strain. "I know that you're unhappy and that you have every reason to feel that way . . . but I'm thinking about what might help Lily to best cope with all of this. For instance, if you had a sister, or even a professional—"

"No one's going to take my baby away from me!"

"I'm not suggesting that anyone would, Karen—"

"Just leave me alone! Both of you! You leave Lily and me alone! Now! I can handle all of this in my own way."

Then Lily took up the angry chant, leaving Belle and Rosco with no alternative other than to walk out of the house and climb slowly into Rosco's car.

"*Whew,*" Belle said as Rosco exited the driveway and entered the cul-de-sac.

"Karen's not in good shape," he agreed.

"Which doesn't make the world a healthy place for her

daughter. I think she should be seeing a professional; someone who can help her get through all of this."

They drove on in silence, although both husband and wife were pondering the same issues.

"Do you think she's telling the truth?" Belle asked after they'd traveled several blocks.

"About what? Frank O'Connell?"

"Frank . . . and everything else."

"I don't know," Rosco admitted after another pause. "Something doesn't feel right. . . . Clearly, Frank O'Connell has a lot of questions to answer. But it all seems so incestuous. . . . Bonnie and Jack . . . Rob Rossi being Dan's patient. . . . It makes me wonder if murder wasn't the original objective all along, and the kidnapping was simply for show. Which would mean that we're being led into the investigation from the wrong perspective . . . maybe even a perspective that's totally opposite—"

"I'm getting the same weird vibes. . . . Considering everything that Karen's been bombarded with, well, her reactions seem odd to me. For instance, no one has remotely suggested taking Lily away from her . . ."

"That bothered me, too."

"Because she was almost bordering on hysteria when it came to that topic, Rosco."

"I know."

"And her use of the word 'murder.'"

"Al *did* classify the death as a homicide, Belle. . . ."

"But there was something in the way Karen pounced on the term. . . ."

Rosco again nodded in agreement.

Belle thought for a long moment. "I hate to say this, but I'm beginning to wonder just how happy her marriage was."

Rosco didn't immediately reply, although he took his eyes off the road for a split second to look at his wife. Her face was tense with worry, an expression of both empathy and concern muddying her gray eyes. "What makes you suspect that?"

"Karen said she was 'just' a wife. . . . What does that mean? That Dan didn't value her as a life partner? Do you think of me as 'just' a wife? I hope not. . . . It's not how I view myself, obviously. And by Karen's own admission, he kept his business dealings from her—"

"I'm not sure how thrilled I'd be to hear nightly accounts of inlays and gum disease if you were a dentist." Rosco tried to jest, but Belle was in no mood for banter.

"And the word 'strike' had real resonance with her, too. I didn't like that. I think she completely misinterpreted what I was asking at first."

"You may be reading too much into that reaction, Belle. Karen's really shaken."

"Perhaps . . . but I definitely got the impression that somewhere someone had hit her. Call it intuition, but I believe she has bad associations with that word."

Rosco nodded. "Okay . . . so maybe her marriage wasn't peachy, and maybe her history with her family—whoever they are—is also problematic—"

"Or abusive," Belle interjected.

"Intuition again?" Rosco asked; his tone was pensive.

"I don't know what it is," was Belle's quiet reply. "But I can tell you that I'm certain that Karen is hiding something."

"You're not going so far as to suggest that *she* may have plotted to kill her husband, are you?" This time Rosco's voice had a quizzical rather than serious edge.

Belle considered the question, and as she did, she hunched her shoulders in concentration and scrunched down further in the seat. "What do you think, Rosco?"

"I'd say that was a pretty big leap, Belle, and that we don't have any means of connecting the dots. . . . Karen would have to have arranged Dan's kidnapping—"

"If he was kidnapped," Belle responded. "Because we only have Karen's word for it, don't we? And she conveniently 'forgot' to tape the extortion phone calls."

"Oh boy . . ." Rosco groaned.

"And she also *insisted* that the police not be included."

"But Karen *did* report him missing. Plus, she would have had to take Lily along for the ride, if she did."

Belle nodded. "I'm not insisting that she's one hundred percent guilty of killing Dan, Rosco. I'm just asking, What if? Stranger things have happened."

"I don't know, Belle. . . ."

"What if? That's all I'm saying, Rosco. What if?"

"Okay . . . but first things first. We need to find one Frank O'Connell."

Across

1. ET craft
4. Vitamin jar inits.
7. HS course
10. Woman in uniform; abbr.
13. Road hazard
14. Petroleum
15. Mr. Solo
16. Cigar tip
17. "Can we talk?"
20. Scouting grp.
21. Ski run
22. Part of TGIF
23. Connect the___
24. Olibanum
28. TV network
31. Part-time post; abbr.
32. Act of boldness
33. Gold and silver
35. Donkey
37. Hoppers
41. Hanks-DiCaprio film
45. "Bless you," preceder
46. Feather lei
47. Clinton's Attorney General
48. Serling and Steiger
51. ___MacDonald
53. Stitch
54. Karloff role
59. Mild oath
60. Bread choice
61. Fells
65. Mr. Lincoln
66. Patterson or Rankin title
69. Hoopsters' org.
70. Eden dweller
71. N.J. neighbor
72. Half CXXII
73. Flynn flick
74. Part of MPH
75. Have debt
76. Ford model

Down

1. Web addresses
2. 14-Across, e.g.
3. Mr. Preminger
4. Part of 19-Down
5. Expire
6. Mr. Landon
7. Zhivago portrayer
8. Dog
9. Sign
10. Auto choice?
11. Helpers; abbr.
12. See 54-Down
18. Sun blocking letters
19. JFK's Attorney General
23. Miss the turn
25. Eden dweller
26. Wall St. inits
27. Roman author
28. Cocaine source
29. Bric-a-___
30. Son of 25-Down & 70-Across
34. Jeers
36. Bro or sis
38. Crack pilots
39. Hamlet, e.g.
40. 21-Across need
42. Fishing prop
43. Yard part
44. Bulldogs' home
49. Deduce
50. Poet Gary___
52. "Hey___ ..."
54. With 12-Down, "The Creature Walks Among Us" actor
55. Religious leader
56. Mr. T group
57. "___how they run ..."
58. Negative answers

"FRANKLY, DEAR . . ."

62. Feeling fine
63. Kinks', "Who'll Be The___In Line?"
64. Lose control
66. With it
67. Fuss
68. Not 51-Across

CHAPTER

27

Belle and Rosco's desire to search for Frank O'Connell was placed on the back burner, however, because Belle found another crossword the moment as she stepped through their front door. Its title, "Frankly, Dear . . ." made her stop in her tracks the second she'd slit open the envelope. She stared at the return address and the name—Nicky O. Flanagan—then her eyes raced back to the puzzle and her mouth opened in a startled O.

"Lunch? What do we have?" Rosco asked as he entered the house behind her, oblivious to the paper in her hand. Bouncing around him were Kit and Gabby, who were displaying the kind of ardor normally reserved for humans returning from lengthy sojourns in wild and inaccessible places. The two canines and their human male companion were unaware that Belle was standing motionless in the center of the living room.

"Lunch?" she echoed as she scanned the puzzle clues. It was clear that she herself was clueless as to what her husband had just said.

"You know . . . the meal we're supposed to eat between breakfast and dinner?"

"Ahh . . ." Belle frowned, then drew in a quick and apprehensive breath.

"We stayed at Karen's longer than I'd anticipated," Rosco offered with an indulgent smile. "Let's see what I can rustle up."

"Rustle?"

"As in food . . . as in opening the refrigerator and checking to see what we've got on hand—"

"FRANKINCENSE," Belle muttered in reply.

"Not especially nutritional, I wouldn't think—"

"It's the solution to 24-Across. . . ." Belle looked up for a moment, but Rosco could see how distracted her gaze appeared. "*Olibanum* is the clue, which is its other name."

"Oh, *that* frankincense." Rosco chuckled, but Belle seemed not to notice his amused tone.

"It was never considered nutritional, but it *was* used as a medication in ancient times . . . especially in Greece and China. In ancient Rome, it was an antidote to hemlock poisoning."

"How do you know all these things? I'm surprised there's room for anything else in your brain." Rosco laughed again as he began moving toward the kitchen, the two dogs at his heels and wiggling in pleasure at the treats they knew were in store.

"I spend too much time reading the encyclopedia," Belle stated simply. Without waiting for a reply, she walked toward her office while Rosco shook his head in amusement, then he continued into the kitchen where he parceled out dog biscuits for the "girls" and began putting together a vegetable salad. Belle joined him less than five minutes later. The crossword was already spottily filled in with her signature red ink.

"41-Across . . . *Hanks-DiCaprio film?*"

Rosco thought for a moment as he sprinkled Greek olives and feta on the sliced carrots, red bell pepper, and celery. "CATCH ME IF YOU CAN."

"That's right . . . I forgot. . . . That's the story about a con artist who operated under different guises, isn't it? And the DiCaprio character was always one step ahead of the Feds. . . ."

"I guess it would be too much if I were to ask what this is all about, Belle?" Rosco asked with a grin, but his wife's response was a distracted: "And a *Patterson or Rankin title* that starts with an H and ends with a K?"

"You got me."

She glanced up momentarily. "That doesn't begin with an H."

Rosco raised an eyebrow, but Belle had already returned her focus to the crossword. H . . . I . . . D as in SNYDER at 50-Down . . . Oh, my gosh!" Her eyes, as she looked at her husband, were huge. "Here! Here's the boy who was killed in the hit and run!" Her red pen jabbed the paper.

Rosco glanced over her shoulder. "But the clue indicates a *Poet Gary,* Belle. . . . Besides, I'm sure there are lots of other Snyders out there—"

"Name one."

"Well . . . let's see . . . there's Snyder's Pretzels—"

Belle sighed and made a face. "Thank you, Mr. Nutrition."

"Just give me a minute, I'm sure I'll come up with a bunch of reasonable . . ."

But Belle was no longer concentrating on Rosco's halting answer. Instead, she was filling in the final letters of the solutions to 66-Across. "HIDE AND SEEK! That's the title of both a James Patterson and Ian Rankin book! And the name FRANK runs throughout the solutions . . . SNYDER is at 50- Down . . . Rosco! Frank O'Connell killed that little boy, and someone's blowing the whistle on him. That's got to be it!"

"Whoa . . . whoa . . ."Rosco held up his hands. "Let's not jump to conclusions. . . ."

But Belle was on a roll; she wasn't about to pause to listen to her husband's words of protest. "And that was what Sara suggested when we had supper at her house last night, wasn't it? Well, not that Frank O'Connell was the guilty party, I mean . . . but that the crosswords might relate to the crime. . . ." Belle fairly quivered in her excitement; in fact, except for the color of their hair and a certain style of walking, she and Gabby had a lot in common. "All this time I'd assumed the nursery rhyme puzzles were connected to Lily . . . but Lily's fine. . . . It's the Snyder child who died. Different authorship or not, I'm convinced the same person created every one of these puzzles."

"Belle, I love you a lot. You know I do. But this is a pretty extreme conclusion you're drawing. I don't see any evidence that supports—"

"This is not extreme. SNYDER is in the puzzle; you've been asked to look into the case; and the answer to 17-Across is LET'S BE FRANK. If that doesn't spell it out, I don't know what does!" Belle waved the crossword in the air.

"As it were."

"What?" Her blonde hair flew around her excited face. "What do you mean 'as it were'?"

"You said 'spell it out.' That's what word games do. . . . Never mind. It was a bit of a joke."

"Rosco! This is no time for levity!"

"Uh-huh . . ." Rosco folded his arms across his chest. "Okay, Miss Cruciverbalist, What about 41-Across . . . CATCH ME IF YOU CAN?"

"What about it?"

"Well, *if* you're correct about this crossword referring to the hit-and-run case—which, by the way, is a huge if—and *if* the numerous FRANKS in the puzzle refer to Bonnie O'Connell's feckless brother, then it seems to me that the title suggests that he's blowing the whistle on himself; daring us to catch him—"

"So you're thinking Frank may be our mysterious puzzle constructor?" Belle shook her head in disagreement. "I don't know. . . . A guy who hangs out at the Black Sheep, whose buddy, Carlos Quintero, all but confirmed he was into certain nefarious activities, doesn't create crosswords, Rosco."

Rosco tilted his head as he regarded his wife. "That's a pretty snobbish assessment. Besides, some criminals can be awfully clever. Not the ones who get caught. But there are some who literally do get away with murder. And let's not forget that you crossword folks love playing with people's heads."

"Ugh." Belle's frown of perplexity deepened. "I don't mean to sound like an intellectual elitist, but the personality of most puzzle constructors verges on the obsessive-compulsive. We're stubborn; we don't like to lose; we hammer away at lexical problems until we find the answers— even if it takes hours—and those aren't the overriding characteristics of people who loll away their afternoons in bars. And, 'playing with people's heads' isn't very flattering."

"How about 'whipping up their gray matter' or 'noodling with their noggins'?"

"Better . . . although they sound more like kitchen activities."

"And we wouldn't want an 'egghead' like you to be accused of culinary expertise."

"Ho, ho . . ." She sighed again, then shut her eyes tightly as she thought. " 'Sugar and spice,' " she murmured at length. "That was what Carlos said. . . . He meant Bonnie . . . but . . ." Belle opened her eyes and looked at Rosco. "Wait! Could Carlos be our puzzling Mr. Flanagan or Anderson or Isaacs or Everts?"

"I think we're getting too far afield, Belle. Besides, unless Carlos is a different type than the one you described when you came home yesterday, he doesn't seem any more 'obsessive-compulsive' than the other denizens of the Black Sheep."

"Darn it all!" Belle fumed in sudden frustration. "For a moment, everything looked so simple. . . . Now, it's just another jumble of loose ends."

"Well, dearly my Frank, I don't give a . . .' "

"I'm not even gracing that with a teeny, weeny laugh, Rosco."

"You're smiling, though."

"That's a grimace you see on my face."

"It's a smile, and you know it."

They'd only just set their two salad plates on the kitchen table when Al Lever knocked at the front door. Belle hurried through the living room and opened it, accompanied by a series of yip and barks, then led their visitor back into the kitchen. "Bonnie O'Connell sure is becoming one unhelpful lady," Al announced without wasting time on preliminaries. "I drove over to the brother's apartment right after we left Sonny's Autobody. No one home. Landlord hasn't seen the tenant in days. Or *claims* not to have seen him. He's a weird duck, though, so I'm not sure I'm buying his line. . . . Then I returned to Smile!; Bonnie also insists she doesn't know where dear, old Frankie is." At this point, Al spotted the food on the table, the two places nicely set, and Rosco, who was now obviously waiting before reseating himself. "Oh hey, sorry to interrupt you two." Lever peered down at the plates. "What is this stuff?"

"Salad." Rosco's reply sounded more like a question than a statement.

"Salad?"

Rosco chortled. "Is there a echo in this house? I went through the same routine with Belle about half an hour ago. Belle wasn't listening, but in your case, I gather you don't know what salad is."

"*Harumph.*" Lever looked at Rosco in disgust. "You can't expect to pack on extra pounds if you eat rabbit food, Poly—crates."

"Did I say I wanted to gain weight, Al?"

"No, you didn't. But you should. A married man like yourself . . . you don't want to look like a buff, young bachelor. How do you explain something like that to your wife?"

Rosco's response was another easy laugh. "Sit, Al. There's enough for three."

Belle walked to the cabinet and retrieved another plate, while Lever sat and gazed searchingly at the meal Rosco had prepared.

"Now, the cheese part I can appreciate . . . and olives . . . but the rest of it? It's so . . . so . . . so green. If you think about it, green is a very weird color for food—"

"So, what did Bonnie tell you?" Belle interrupted as she began divvying up the salad.

"What she *didn't* tell me is more to the point," was Lever's grumbling response. "First off, she pretended she was too busy to talk to me. Kept answering the phone while I was trying to question her, then made me repeat myself. Not once, but with nearly every query. Meaning that I did a lot more yakking than she did—which is not the optimal mode for interview procedure. Long story short: Ms. O'Connell insists that she and her brother aren't close. She hasn't seen him in a long time—but couldn't confirm how long—and she has no clue as to where he is. He's a sometime drummer, bounces from band to band, and she has no interest in his career or his whereabouts."

"Which is the complete opposite of the impression I got when she was talking to Carlos," Belle said. "She was genuinely distraught that she couldn't find her brother. In fact, she told Quintero she 'needed Frank now,' and she stressed the last word—just before she barreled out of the place in tears." Belle's forehead creased in thought. "Frank's disappearance and Rob Rossi's and Dan Tacete's seemed to be vitally connected—at least in Bonnie's mind."

"Where does Jack Wagner fit into all of this?" Al asked.

"You mean other than being Bonnie's clandestine lover?" was Belle's breezy reply.

"We don't know that for a *fact*," Rosco tossed in.

Belle looked at him. She looked at Lever. She shook her head. "Come on. It was Al who first made the suggestion. Don't tell me you guys are now insisting on physical evidence. Maybe this is why no one ever coined the term 'male intuition.'" She arched an eyebrow. "Maybe it's even an oxymoron."

"I've been called a 'moron,'" Al stated. "But no one's ever said I was an 'ox.'"

Belle chortled. "More salad, Al?"

"Not if it's the kind of fodder oxen munch on."

Belle laughed again while her husband turned to her. His expression had turned serious.

"Okay, Belle, let's say accept that Wagner and Bonnie are romantically involved. Where does that leave our vanished Rob Rossi? Or Frank O'Connell? Or Dan Tacete? And what bearing does any of this have on the Snyder case?"

"I'm just a crossword editor—or a 'noggin noodler'—in case you'd forgotten." She dangled the latest puzzle under their noses. "But the answer lies within this puzzle. Whoever created it holds all the solutions."

CHAPTER

28

After leaving Belle and Rosco's home on Captain's Walk, Al Lever returned to the Newcastle Police headquarters while Rosco drove to a previously scheduled meeting with Elaine Vogel, the attorney working on the Snyder case. Given everything that he and Belle and Al had discussed over their late and impromptu lunch, the timing seemed particularly apt, although Rosco needed to keep reminding himself that he had nothing of substance to share with Elaine. Not yet, anyway. Although he had a sneaking suspicion that he might in the not-too-distant future.

As Rosco parked his car and sat for a moment staring up at the tall and somber facade of the downtown office building that housed Elaine's firm, Al, simultaneously pushed open the smeary glass doors of the NPD station house. It was six minutes past three. By chance, Abe Jones had preceded Lever by less than a minute, and the two men walked in almost perfect unison toward the duty desk. The uniformed sergeant stationed there cocked his head toward Lever's office and uttered a laconic and disinterested, "You've got visitors, Lieutenant."

Lever gazed past the sergeant's shoulder. The office door with its frosted glass panel was ajar, and he could see a woman who appeared to be in her mid thirties seated opposite his desk; with her was a boy who looked about ten or eleven—twelve tops. The expressions on both their faces were tight and worried. "What's up?" Al asked the sergeant after a silent moment.

"I think you'd better hear it from the horse's mouth, Lieutenant."

Al turned to Abe. "We'll talk later."

"I'll be in the back lot," was Jones's even response. "There's a few more things I'd like to go over on Tacete's Corvette."

"Check," Al said. It was his sole reply. Then he turned away, walked past the duty desk, crossed to his office, and stepped in. "I'm Lieutenant Lever. Is there something I can help you with, ma'am?"

The woman stood. She was thin, almost gaunt, and Al could see that she was nervous. She made no attempt to smile or extend her hand or smooth the wrinkles from her navy blue suit, which appeared to be the type of businesslike outfit reserved for occasions when the wearer deemed it necessary to "dress properly." The jacket and skirt were too big by a couple of sizes, giving Al the impression that visiting homicide detectives was one of those rare occurrences.

"Lieutenant, my name is Carol Moody, and this is my son, Leo." She looked down at the boy, who had remained hunched and uncommunicative in his seat. "Stand up, Leo." The boy did as he was told, but then immediately hung his head and stared fixedly at the floor.

Al moved to his desk and said, "Please sit." The mother settled rigidly into her chair, her son plopped sullenly into his, and Lever reclaimed his own space and thoughtfully regarded them. "What can I do for you, Mrs. Moody?" Al reached for a cigarette, but halted when his eyes finally met Leo's.

"I understand from the officer at the duty desk that you're the detective looking into the death of that poor Doctor Tacete?"

"Yes, ma'am."

Carol Moody lifted a black purse from the floor and opened it. Then she retrieved a brushed-aluminum object and set it on Al's desk. The metal was in the shape of a squat T; across the top were embossed black letters that read "HURST."

"I found it in Leo's room," she stated.

Al recognized the object immediately, but his response was a noncommittal "Do you know what this is, Mrs. Moody?"

"Yes," she answered uneasily, "it's a shift knob from a car. My husband, Leo Senior, has one just like it in his Chevy."

"And . . . where did this one come from?"

"We live near—" Carol Moody stopped herself and turned to her son, who was now slumping deeper in his chair. "Leo, I want you to tell the detective where you got this."

Leo shifted sideways in his seat, but said nothing.

"Leo . . ." she repeated in a sterner tone, but the boy remained silent. "I don't need to remind you how your father's going to feel about what you did." She returned her focus to Al. "My husband is a long-distance trucker; he's been gone for over a week. He's going to be furious when he hears what Leo's done." Mrs. Moody then gave her son another chance. "Leo, I want you to speak up this minute or you'll have your father to answer to."

"I think I know where this came from, Leo," Al interjected. His tone was coaxing and kind. "I'd just like to know how you ended up with it. I don't believe you're in any kind of trouble, son; in fact, you should be commended for coming forward with this. The police department counts on citizens like yourself to help them out when it comes to crime solving."

The boy gave his mother an "I told you so" look, then said, "I found it."

"And it came from Doctor Tacete's Corvette, didn't it?"

"I guess . . . yeah . . ." He slouched back into his chair.

"Leo," his mother snapped, "you tell the lieutenant exactly how you got that shift knob this minute—from beginning to end, the whole story. I've had just about enough of this attitude from you, young man."

Al said, "Just give it to me straight, Leo. You're not in any trouble," all the while thinking, *Man, this Mrs. Moody can play good-cop-bad-cop with the best of them.*

"I . . . I . . . found it," Leo stuttered.

"Where?" Al asked.

"He didn't find it, Lieutenant; he stole it," Carol Moody interrupted with a goodly degree of irritation. "Leo, you tell Lieutenant Lever the truth."

"I wasn't talking about the shifter, Mom," Leo all but spat back at his mother. "I meant, I found the *Corvette.*"

"In the Gilbert's Groceries parking lot, right?" Al prodded. "That's where you . . . you . . . *borrowed* the shift knob, right?"

"No. No," Leo answered as tears began to form in his eyes. "I found the Corvette at the bottom of that hill near our house."

"We live out on East Farm Lane," Carol Moody explained. "About a mile from the site where you found the doctor."

"But I was there on Monday night," was Al's perplexed reply. "I didn't see you, Leo. And if you were there before me, how could you have taken the shifter from a burning car?" Lever glanced at the metal object, then looked back at Leo's mother. "There are no signs that this thing was anywhere near a fire."

"He took the shift knob on Sunday afternoon," she stated; her mouth was set and hard.

Al sat in silence as he tried to process the information. Finally he said, "Here's the problem I'm having with Leo's story, Mrs. Moody. I'm not saying he's lying, but on Monday morning Doctor Tacete's wife drove the Corvette to the parking lot of Gilbert's Groceries. I have reliable witnesses who have confirmed that fact. So how is it possible that your son removed the Hurst shifter one day earlier at the bottom of the ravine?"

"But I did," Leo shouted. "I found the car there on Sunday. I swear I did. It was covered with one of those army camouflage tarps. You know, the ones with green and brown cloth hanging on it? Like in war movies? Like someone was trying to hide—?" He looked at his mother. "Okay, I stole the shifter. I did. I did that. I'm sorry. But there," he pointed at it, "you can have it back."

"You know a man died in that car, don't you, son?" Al asked. "If you're making this up, you're going to be in an awful lot of trouble. And I won't be able to do anything to help you. You do know that, don't you? You could be prosecuted and placed in a detention center. And I'm very serious about that."

"I'm not lying. I'm not!"

"And the man's body wasn't in the car when you took the shifter?"

"No. The car was just sitting there. It was empty."

"Did you see anyone else in the area?"

"No."

"Did you look all around the area?"

"A little bit . . . kind of . . . Yeah, I did."

"Did you take anything else?"

"No. I swear, I didn't."

"How about a blue gym bag? Did you see that anywhere?"

"No."

"You're sure, Leo? Because someone had put money in it. A lot of money in it."

"No! I didn't see any bag. I promise!"

Carol Moody's eyes widened in shock and dismay, and she drew in a sharp breath while Lever leaned back in his chair, folded his arms across his chest, and sighed. "Did you tell your mother you found the car, Leo?"

"No, he did not," was her immediate reply. She directed her considerable anger to both Al and Leo. "He told no one."

"And why was that, son?" Al asked.

The boy didn't reply, so his mother answered for him. "I don't know, Lieutenant. He won't tell me anything. He won't even tell me why he failed to be the least bit honest about this. I just can't—"

Al held up his hand and gave Leo an impatient look. "A man was murdered. Do you understand that, son?"

The boy mumbled something inaudible that Lever took to be an affirmative response.

"Okay. I want some answers. I don't want to have to bring criminal charges here, Leo, but I need to know why you didn't report the Corvette the moment you found it."

"Because!" The boy's face was full of defiance, but it was clear from the way his mouth was twisting up and down that he was holding back tears.

Lever glanced at the mother, then back to the son. " 'Because'? You're going to have to do better than that."

"It was cool," Leo blurted out as he began to cry in earnest. "I mean, it was mine. Nobody else knew about the Corvette. I was going to keep it hidden, and go back whenever I wanted. . . . Then, when I was sixteen, I could fix it up and I'd have my own car, and I'd be able to do whatever I wanted to. Nobody could tell me when to go to bed or anything. Not Mom or Pop. They couldn't tell me anything ever again. If I took the knob, I figured no one could sneak the car away from me. Plus, I could practice shifting."

The two adults sat in silence for several moments while Leo sniffled and swiped surreptitiously at his cheeks. Eventually, his mother reached into her purse for a tissue, but Leo merely balled it up without using it. Then Al pulled a pad of paper and pen from a drawer and slid them across the desktop. "I think that's all for now, Mrs. Moody. If you could just write down your phone number and address for me? In case there's something I've forgotten to ask."

"Certainly."

Lever stood and walked around the desk, then he sat on the corner nearest Leo as his mother jotted down the information. "I want to thank you for having the courage to bring this shifter to me, son. You should be proud of yourself. This helps our investigation a great deal." He extended his hand to Leo's mother and said, "Thank you, Mrs. Moody. If we need to, we'll be in touch."

The moment they departed his office, Al lit a cigarette and inhaled deeply. He then crossed back behind his desk and dropped heavily into his chair. Ten seconds later his phone rang. "Yeah," he said as he brought the receiver to his ear.

"Jones, here."

"Yes, Abe, what is it?"

"Are you sitting down?"

"Just give it to me, Abe."

"The Corvette we've got back here? The one Tacete died in? It's not the same one his wife drove to Gilbert's Groceries on Monday morning."

Lever let out a small chuckle. "Great. . . . Tell me something I don't know."

CHAPTER

29

W hen Lever emerged from the rear door of the police station and passed into the evidence lot, he immediately spotted Abe Jones, who was in a crouched position on the passenger's side of the burned-out Corvette. The vehicle rested under a clear plastic tent whose support structure had been fashioned from white PVC piping. At the moment, all four sides of this temporary shelter were open, and the clean white tubing and shiny plastic flaps combined with the cerulean blue of the afternoon sky to give the wreckage a bizarre air of festivity.

Jones, however, seemed unaware of the incongruous appearance of the ruined car; instead, he was intently studying an area behind the passenger's seat. In his right hand was a plastic-framed enlarging lens. Lever approached him from behind and said, "You're looking more like Sherlock Holmes every day." The line was only partially delivered as a joke.

"Thank you, Watson." Abe stood, removed his surgical gloves, and pointed to the Corvette. "This is a new twist."

"I'll show you mine if you show me yours," was Lever's dry response.

Abe crouched back down behind the passenger seat. "I didn't get this at first because the VIN on the dash. . . ." He stopped himself and looked up at the detective. "VIN; that's the vehicle identification number—"

"Thank you sooo much, Doctor Jones," Al interrupted sarcastically.

"Hey, first time I heard VIN, I thought the car salesman was offering me a glass of French wine to seal the deal." Abe put on an over-the-top French accent. *"Un verre de vin blanc, s'il vous plaît."*

Lever raised an eyebrow but didn't otherwise reply.

"Anyway," Jones continued, "The VIN under the windshield was melted by the fire. Obviously the perp counted on this occurring, and that's why he thought he could get away with switching cars. What he *didn't* realize was that all the build codes—as well as a repeat of the VIN—are laid out on the lid of the lock box behind the passenger's seat here." He straightened. "The numbers don't match the ones on Tacete's registration card; i.e. this ain't his car. It doesn't even have the thirty-five thousand dollar LT-5 engine in it. We're running a computer check to find out the history on this junker."

"Which means that whoever killed Tacete made off with his LT-5 and left this Corvette in its place. . . . Someone definitely planned this thing well in advance. And someone wanted that LT-5 in the bargain. . . ." Lever remained silent for a long moment as he tried to assimilate the new facts; then he proceeded to describe his interview with Carol Moody and her son—at the conclusion of which he handed Leo's shifter to Jones, who dropped it into an evidence bag and sealed it.

"Forget about fingerprints. The kid's been playing with it for days," Al said. "What else have you got?"

"Well, speaking of prints, I've been able to identify three distinct sets on the car. One was much smaller than the other two, so I was thinking a child. I'm guessing they belong to your young friend, Leo. I'll double-check with whatever's on the shift knob, but I'm sure that will prove to be the case. The other set I confirmed as Tacete's—meaning we've got one set of mystery prints."

"Karen Tacete?"

"Nope. They're definitely male. Too big for Karen."

"How about Frank O'Connell's?" It was Rosco who asked the question as he sidled up alongside them.

"I won't ask how you got back here without passing the duty desk, Poly—crates," was Lever's wry reply. "I don't even want to know."

Although he'd left the police department six years before, Rosco still held most of the keys and security codes to the entrances and gates—a situation his former partner assiduously ignored when in the public eye. "I've been warning you, Al—change your locks once in a while. Change your clearance codes. Homeowners do it. Shopkeepers do it. What works for the average citizen should work for the NPD." Then Rosco pointed to the Corvette. "What's up with this baby, gents?"

After bringing Rosco up to speed on the switched cars and the discovery of the shift knob, Abe added, "We'll have to haul O'Connell in here and get his fingerprints. Although, given everything you two have told me about him, it's surprising that he's never been booked for anything. Never served in the military, either, so there's nothing on file."

"Well, it's certainly beginning to look like he's long overdue to meet our overworked justice system," Lever said. "Anything else, Abe?"

"The car was definitely torched. It didn't ignite accidentally, that's for sure. Someone doused it with gasoline and tossed a match on it, which fits nicely with what the Moody kid told you about finding it in advance of the blaze. . . . So, here's how I'm starting to put it together: The perp—or perps—plant this vehicle in the ravine . . . no telling when, but clearly before Tacete's disappearance. They pick up the LT-5 and the twenty-five grand at Gilbert's on Monday, then drive out to East Farm Lane that night with the doc. Maybe they tell him his wife paid up, and they're going to release him. Maybe they've got him so stoned he doesn't know what's happening. . . . Then our bad guys bash in Tacete's head with something—probably a baseball bat—and stick him in the 'Vette and torch it."

"So obviously Carlyle was wrong about his head hitting the windshield frame as the cause of death," Al said quietly. It was a statement, not a question.

"If Leo's story holds water, and it sounds like it does, I'd say Carlyle's theory was definitely off the mark."

Lever lit a cigarette. "Not to sound like Poly—crates here, but should we go back and review Carlyle's work? I know you said that his report looked solid, Abe, but history isn't on our M.E.'s side, and experience tells me that he could have overlooked something. What I'm getting at is this: Is it possible that Tacete might have been killed well *before* he was placed in the car? Because if he was killed back on Saturday, say, then the 'accident' was staged to cover up his death."

"Meaning that the entire deal was an elaborate and pre-meditated murder," Rosco added, "making the kidnapping nothing but smoke and mirrors. . . . That was the same con-clusion Belle and I were starting to consider after our visit with Karen."

"Well, don't forget that the perp now has a LT-5 Corvette worth over a hundred grand," Al said.

"But traceable," Rosco tossed in with a shrug.

Lever chuckled, although the sound was grim. "Right, just like the twenty-some BMWs and Benzes pinched from Porto Ristorante that you and Robbery have had so much luck in locating."

Abe smiled briefly and crossed over to a small folding table, where he flipped through a clipboard full of paper-work. "Okay . . . here." He pointed to a page of scribbled notes that only he could read. "Tacete's wife said she heard his voice on the phone on Sunday, which kind of shoots your theory that he died on Saturday." Jones looked at Lever, who replied with a pensive: "Remember that she could be lying about that call, though, Abe. Both of them, in fact. And if Poly—crates is right about smoke and mirrors . . . ?" Al didn't conclude his theory. Instead, he released a weighty breath.

"Okay. That's true. So, let's take Karen Tacete's, nee Johnson's, *alleged* phone contacts out of the equation and go back to the facts we have. At this point, there's no telling how long this 'Vette was down in the ravine. Just because Leo found it on Sunday doesn't mean it hadn't been there for weeks. But, what we do know is this: It was there *before* Tacete died. So two points hold true: Our bad guy—or gal—planned to kill the good doctor from the git-go; and the LT-5 is still out there somewhere."

Al moved away from the evidence site to crush out his cigarette. When he returned he stared at the burnt vehicle and shook his head in confusion. "Well, that LT-5 isn't an inconspicuous automobile, so I doubt if our perp will be driving it around Newcastle any time soon. And to be frank—"

Lever was interrupted by the ringing of Rosco's cell phone. "Sorry," Rosco said as he scanned the caller ID, "I should take this. It's one of the guys who had his BMW pinched at Porto Ristorante."

He walked to a far corner of the lot and tapped a button on the phone. "Yes, Mr. Gronski, what can I do for you?"

Gronski's voice crackled with the poor connection. "Yeah, listen, Polycrates, G.A.I. just paid off on my Beamer. Hundred percent. I'm a happy camper."

"That's nice, Mr. Gronski, I'm happy to hear it."

"Yeah, call me Phil."

"Sure, Phil. So, what exactly can I do for you?"

"Nothin'. I was just calling to, you know, kinda apologize. I was a little rough on ya, you know; I mean, I was sore because someone had nicked my car, that's all. I don't like to leave loose ends. You were only doin' your job."

Rosco glanced back at Al and Abe, who continued to study the Corvette. "We're still trying to solve this Porto thing, Phil. The insurers would like to recover—"

"Hey, I don't want that car back, I'm getting a new one. Next week, maybe. I got my money. I don't want no car after some joker's been driving around the world in it. Usin' the ashtray and whatnot."

"But don't you want to see these guys caught? Keep them from doing it again?"

There was a long pause as Gronski thought this over. Finally he admitted a begrudging "Yeah, I guess . . ."

Rosco glanced at his watch. "How about I buy you a cup of coffee and we talk about this in a little more detail? Can you meet me in half an hour?"

"I don't know . . ."

"Come on, be a sport about this; help out the next guy."

Gronski took a long moment, but eventually said, "Okay, where?" He sighed in resignation as he spoke.

"There's a burger joint over on Clawson Street. Actually it's not that far from Porto. I can be there in thirty minutes."

"Sure, why not?"

"You can't miss it. It's right next to that big wholesale vegetable distribution center. . . . And there's an autobody shop across the street called Sonny's."

CHAPTER

30

Having only heard Phil Gronski's deep baritone echoing from the other end of a telephone and not having met him in person, Rosco's mind had invented a brawny giant of a man: one capable of starting, and finishing, a good-sized barroom brawl all on his own. But Gronski, in the flesh, was the exact opposite. In his early forties and balding, he appeared to be five feet four inches tall at the most, and his build was slim and wiry. He looked as if he was made solely of muscle and sinew. He wore a custom-made Italian suit, a dress shirt with French cuffs and large gold and ruby cufflinks, and a matching stick pin in his glossy silk tie. Rosco wouldn't have even approached him were it not for the fact that the man looked so out of place sitting alone at the counter of Bart's Burgers on Clawson Street.

"Phil?" Rosco asked tenuously; he half expected a foreign accent instead of Gronski's blue-collar Massachusetts growl.

Gronski swiveled on the aluminum stool. His feet didn't quite reach the pockmarked and dingy fake-tile flooring. He said, "Yeah. You must be Rosco? This ain't the nicest dive in town, I gotta tell ya. Whatever you do, don't order the coffee. My wife has washed our dog in classier stuff."

"Sorry I'm late. I got hung up in that construction on Seventh Street." Rosco sat sat on the stool next to Phil. "To be honest, I've never been in here before; it just seemed like a good place to meet."

Without turning around, Gronski cocked his thumb over his shoulder and said, "So, what, you think the shop across the street pinched my Beamer?"

Rosco smiled. "In a word, yes."

"That wasn't *too* obvious," Gronski said sarcastically. He then shook his head. "Look, I've been driving BMWs for twenty years. I've never put a scratch in one, but you ask around Newcastle and everyone's gonna tell you that if you bang up your German import—your Porsche, your Benz, whatever—or you need some mechanical work and you're out of warranty, you bring your car to Sonny's. The work in that shop is top-notch. I've even met Sonny and his missus at social events on occasion. He seems like a real good guy to me. He didn't steal no cars."

"Would he recognize you?"

"Probably . . ." Gronski thought. "On the other hand, maybe not. Last time I saw him was two, three years ago at a golf club bash. I hadn't given up my toup' yet. They're dumb things, those rugs, but the wife, well, never mind. . . . Also I was sporting a VanDyke-type goatee back then, so I probably looked real different. . . . Nah, I guess Sonny wouldn't recognize me now."

The waitress stopped by, and Rosco asked for an order of fries, taking Gronski's advice and skipping the coffee. "I've been in and out of every body shop in town," he told Phil, "and Sonny's is the only one large enough to handle twenty-two vehicles in one night. I may be barking up the wrong tree, but I'd like you to just walk over there with me. There were four guys parking cars at Porto back in March, right? Would you recognize the one that drove off in your BMW?"

"Absolutely. He was about your size, six feet, maybe a little taller, with a real narrow mustache and a little scar over his left eye that cut through the brow, like so." He pointed to his own eye, then chortled in a self-deprecating manner. "Unless the bozo was wearing a toupee."

"Are you willing to go over there and see if he works for Sonny?"

Gronski thought it over for a moment, then he shrugged and said, "Sure, why not? You've got the wrong place, but why not? I'm here, right?"

Rosco went on to explain his plan of action to Phil, detailing their bogus identities, and finishing the briefing with a cautionary, "Now if you see your guy, don't do anything; and don't tell me about it until after we leave the shop. It's not up to me to arrest anyone. I don't have a gun on me, and I'm not doing any John Wayne stuff. I'll just get his name, and we'll let the cops in Robbery take it from there."

"Hey, I'm supposed to be a Hollywood producer, right? Why would I know from a robbery in a hick burg in Massachusetts?"

It was almost four thirty when the two strolled across the street; the second they stepped onto the autobody parking lot, Sonny was out of the office and trotting over to meet them.

"Jeez," Gronski muttered under his breath, "what's this guy do? Spend the day staring out the window? What do I do if he does recognize me?"

"Hey, what the hell is this, Rick?" Sonny called from twenty feet off. "You haven't caused me enough trouble for one day?" He seemed not to notice Gronski, or at least not to remember him.

"Take it easy, Sonny." Rosco held up his hands, indicating that he came in peace. He then pointed at his companion. "This is Phil Taylor. He's the producer of *Back Bay D.A.*"

Gronski grinned. "My man Rick here has told me good things about you." He extended his hand to Sonny.

The autobody shop owner declined the handshake as he studied the new visitor. "Have we met somewhere?"

Without missing a beat, Phil said, "Ya ever been to the Polo Lounge in L.A.?"

Sonny shook his head, so Gronski continued in a lofty insider's tone: "That's where I conduct my business. At the Polo. Poolside, mostly. I was the first guy in L.A. with a mobile phone. Ya ain't been there, ya don't know me. I travel with a very select crowd. I don't often—"

"Well, anyway," Rosco interrupted before Gronski could continue hamming up his performance. "We came back out here to apologize. I didn't mean to get the cops involved. . . . See, I was scouting out their station house for a possible location, and they were talking about this missing Explorer, and well, one thing led to another, and next thing you know, they're making me show them where I saw the car."

"Yeah," Phil added, "That's why I figured, since I'm the producer and all, I should be makin' with the 'I'm sorries,' myself. You know, stop by the shop, do it all personal and whatnot. Why leave it to a scrub like Ricky here?" He gave "Ricky" a small poke in the arm and then looked beyond Sonny and let out with a slow whistle. "Man, this is some operation you got." He then returned his attention to "Ricky." "I don't know, Rick-man, I think I like this place better than than the one you picked out."

"No can do, Phil," Rosco answered on cue, "Sonny says his mother put the nix on it."

"Sonny . . . Sonny . . . Sonny," Gronski said, "let me talk to your mom. I've never met the woman who could say no to me. Never. And I mean *never.* I wouldn't be a producer worth beans otherwise." He walked past Sonny toward the shop doors.

"She's not here," Sonny called after him. "She's gone for the day." He trotted up alongside Phil. "Besides, she doesn't talk to anyone. I do all the negotiating here, but she said, 'No TV shows,' so that's what it is."

Gronski looked at Rosco. "What'd you offer these people, Ricky-boy?"

"Thirty-five hundred a day."

Phil moved around Sonny once again, speaking as he walked. "I'll tell ya what I'm gonna do for ya, Sonny; I'm gonna double that. How's that? I'm the guy with the money. And I do the talkin'. How's seven grand sound to you? Huh? Let me just take a quick peek at the inner workings here to be sure I like what I see. You think it over and get back to me tomorrow morning. Your mom still says no . . . so be it. No hard feelings. We move on. I don't want to get between you and your mom. What do ya say?"

"I don't know. . . ."

"Sonny, Sonny, Sonny, what are we talkin' here? Three, four minutes? I walk to the end of your shop, turn around, and come back out again? Where's the harm?"

"Seven thousand a day?"

"Seven thousand a day. U.S. dollars; clean and crisp. Plus"—he turned and looked Sonny up and down—"you ever do any acting?" He then glanced at Rosco, nodding his head as though in thought. "Ya know Sonny here would be perfect in the part of Stryker; the guy with the three babes in the Benz convertible? What do you say, Sonny?"

Sonny considered the offer, and eventually said, "Okay. But I have to walk around the place with you."

"Sure, sure, whatever."

The three men strolled through the large entryway. Most of the workers were preparing to quit for the day. At a large utility sink just to the left of the office door, six mechanics were stripping off latex gloves and washing up using an industrial hand cleanser. They'd been telling jokes, but when they noticed Rosco their behavior turned serious and they stopped talking altogether. Rosco watched as Gronski and Sonny strolled in front of him. He became aware that "the producer," with his expensive suit and slight build, probably looked much the same as he had the night he lost his BMW. And if the man who stole the car was present, he could well recognize Gronski before Phil had time to identify him—and then quietly slip out the back door.

But Rosco needn't have worried, because the moment Gronski passed the mechanics' lifts and entered the collision repair section of the shop, he shouted an outraged, "That's the clown! That's the S.O.B who drove off in my BMW!"

A man sanding a fender on a dark green Audi straightened and stared at Gronski. He was exactly as Phil had described him: six feet tall with a pencil-thin mustache and a scar over his left eye. He recognized his accuser instantaneously, dropped his sanding equipment and began running toward the rear of the shop. Without pausing for a second, Gronski took off after him, and Rosco took off after Gronski while Sonny stood in place, dumbfounded.

Phil caught the man just as he reached the back door, slammed into him from behind, and pushed him hard into the panic-bar. Although the pursuer easily weighed half as much as the pursued, the two men tumbled through the doorway and out into the alley where they landed in a heap on the asphalt. The sprawl of bodies didn't last for long, however, as the thief immediately pushed himself clear of Phil and regained his standing position. Then Gronski also sprang to his feet and went into a low, wrestler's crouch. The position made him look as if he were only four feet tall, and his suit jacket, which was torn apart at the shoulder seams, and his trousers, which were ripped at the knees, gave him a curiously simian appearance, as if he were a trained chimp auditioning for an ad campaign or a TV spot.

The sight brought a quick chuckle from Gronski's adversary, but it lasted less than a millisecond as Phil spun on his left heel and, in a perfectly executed karate kick, brought his designer loafer straight into the man's solar plexus.

"Hey!" Rosco shouted, running over. But Gronski wasn't finished. His right fist pounded up into the man's cheek and nose, causing him to crumple unconscious onto the pavement. "I've been waiting to do that for months," Gronski growled with a satisfied smile. Then he straightened and dusted his ruined sleeves.

Rosco looked down at the comatose body shop worker and then back at Gronski. "Your suit didn't fare too well," he observed as he dialed 911 on his cell phone.

"I got a closet full of them. This was worth it."

"Do you mind if I ask you what you do for a living?"

"Franks."

"Franks?"

"Franks. Frankfurters. Hot dogs. Wieners. I manufacture Phil's Franks. You can get them at Gilbert's Groceries."

CHAPTER
31

Rosco had no sooner returned home from the melee at Sonny's Autobody than Belle greeted him with a hyper-excited, "We have to drive up to Boston! Now! We have to leave right now!"

"Well, hello to you, too." He leaned toward her. "I don't suppose you'd care to give your adoring husband a kiss . . . tell him how much you love him . . . or ask how I spent my afternoon."

"I know already. You saw Elaine Vogel."

"Wrong. She didn't show. Guess again."

Belle tapped her foot on the wooden floor. "Rosco! Come on. You can tell me all about what you did while we're driving. . . . Time's a-wasting."

"What about supper?" Rosco gave his wife a wry smile. Her enthusiasm was infectious, although it was sometimes hard to rein in.

"We'll grab something on the way. Let's go. I've been waiting for you for hours and hours and hours." The tips of Belle's shoes all but jumped up and down in impatience.

Rosco looked at his watch. It was precisely two hours and fifty-three minutes since he'd left home. "I don't know about 'hours and hours and hours.' I take it you've sleuthed out our invisible Frank O'Connell? Found all the missing pieces? Got the whole thing solved?"

But Belle's response was an unexpected, "Dan Tacete went to Boston last Thursday afternoon—instead of heading home as promised. And he was back here, in Newcastle, late Thursday night. So the kidnappers must have grabbed him after that."

Rosco's eyes grew serious. "And how might you have discovered these pieces of information?"

Belle looked at her husband as if he'd just asked one of the dumbest questions known to humankind. "His credit card, of course."

"Wait, wait, wait. We checked those cards on Friday. Nothing showed up."

"Right, Rosco, but both gas charges were made at the full-service island. The attendant apparently uses one of those old-style imprint machines, and the charges aren't generally posted to the credit card account for forty-eight hours."

"Ahhh . . . So much for the consumer's right to privacy and confidentiality."

"Rosco! I didn't do anything illegal. After all, Karen originally supplied the necessary background information. I simply pretended to be her, that's all. Besides, it's exactly what you would have done if you'd thought of it, so don't give me a hard time. . . . Come on, let's go!"

Rosco shrugged and turned back toward the door through which he'd just entered. Belle grabbed the sleeve of his shirt and said, "Wait! So, where have you been if you weren't talking to Elaine Vogel all this time?"

"Hah. Wouldn't you like to know?!"

"You're kidding!" Belle said after Rosco had finished describing the scene at Sonny's Autobody, as well as Al and Abe's discovery of the exchanged Corvettes. "Wow!

That's a lot of suspicious vehicles turning up in a single day. . . ." She bounced up and down in the passenger seat of his leased car; although it was excessive energy that made her body jounce around rather than an uneven stretch of Route 24. "So Sonny's a big-time crook. . . ."

"It would appear so."

"Wow," Belle repeated in an awed voice. "I wonder if his mom had any clue."

"Aren't mothers supposed to be the last to know?" Rosco asked with a small smile. "Although, in this case I have a feeling she's up to her ears in it, too. 'Like mother, like son?' Doesn't have the same ring, does it?"

But Belle didn't share his amused approach. Instead, she shook her head gravely. "What if Sonny's involved in this Corvette situation, too? I mean, Frank had to get the replacement model somewhere, right? *And,* someone has to fence the high-end job."

"We'll work out that connection later. Right now, Sonny's got a lot to answer for in the Porto case. Although I've got to say that it would be pretty darn weird if he'd gotten his mitts on both Corvettes *as well* as the Explorer."

"But he was trying to sell *you* the Explorer, Rosco—"

"That he was."

"And not the Corvette."

"No . . . I would have bought that one . . . and kept my mouth shut," he added facetiously.

"And where would Kit and Gabby ride, I might ask?"

Rosco reached across and placed a loving hand on Belle's thigh. "You have a lap, don't you?"

"Wow . . ." Belle echoed for a third time, bringing her mind back to the case. "So Sonny's just a latter-day Jeremy Diddler."

"Who?"

"It's a character from an early nineteenth-century farce. The name's come to be synonymous with a bamboozler or doubledealer."

"Not to me, it hasn't."

"Well, now you know, Rosco. A diddler is a flimflammer, a cozener, a chiseler—"

"How about a plain old felon?"

Belle laughed. "Have it your own way, Mr. Private Eye." Then she settled in to tell her own story; as she did so, her body shifted in the seat until she was turned toward Rosco, making her appear to have forgotten she was riding in a car rather than sitting in a comfortably upholstered chair. "Remember Karen telling us that Dan was supposed to get home early last Thursday? That he'd promised to join her on their afternoon trip to the dog park? She was going to make him a special lunch and then they'd have the rest of the day together."

Rosco nodded, but didn't otherwise respond.

"And then Karen and Lily waited and waited for him to return, and Lily went missing—?"

Again, Rosco nodded but didn't speak.

"Well, what I want to know is, what was he doing purchasing gas in the Boston area"—Belle glanced at a notebook she had open on her lap—"at two twenty-seven in the afternoon, according to the credit card company, when he was *supposed* to be with his wife and little girl? And how come he put another six dollars in the tank at eleven seventeen the same night back in Newcastle—*after* his wife had already reported him missing? And six measly dollars of gas? That's nothing for an SUV. It barely gets you down to the corner."

Rosco shook his head. "I don't know." Then he added a thoughtful, "Could it be that Dan was nabbed at noon or a little earlier as he was preparing to drive home from Smile!, and that it was the *kidnapper* who was using his credit card? And also driving by Explorer at that point?"

"But why would this person—or persons—go all the way up to Boston, and then come back again?"

"Maybe they needed to meet someone up north," Rosco offered. "Maybe they stashed Dan in a safe house up there and came back to Newcastle without him."

"I don't know, Rosco. It seems like a really sloppy way to handle things. Wouldn't this person be aware that there might well be two photos on two different security cameras? Plus there's the attendant, right?"

"Do you happen to know the location of the security camera that covers the ATM across the street from Lawson's?"

"Ahh . . . no."

"See? People don't pay attention to that kind of thing anymore. We've become inured to it. It's *1984,* and Big Brother's just part of our lives."

Belle frowned and tilted her head. "You're right. . . . Maybe . . . although I still think something weird's going on."

"Homicide and switched luxury sport cars aren't enough to worry about?"

Belle looked through the windshield and distractedly touched the dashboard. "Cars . . ." she murmured, "we keep coming back to them, don't we? Karen's insurance . . . Frank peddling a vehicle registered in her maiden name . . ." Belle sighed and turned back to face her husband. "So, is Al leaning toward Karen as a suspect?"

"All I know is that he's as disturbed about those unrecorded phone calls as we are. 'Alleged contacts' is how Abe put it. And you know Al; he doesn't count anyone out until he has a confession."

Belle didn't speak for another moment. "She'd have to have a partner to pull off something like this, wouldn't she?"

"I assume so."

"Then who is it?"

"That the sixty-four-thousand-dollar question."

They drove on in silence for several more minutes. "Are you hungry?" Rosco asked as a highway signboard came into view. It advertised dining and lodging—discreetly, of course. This was coastal Massachusetts, after all. Giant billboards in neon colors were relegated to less tradition-bound regions of the country.

"Rosco . . . jeez . . . How could I be hungry?" Belle cocked her head to one side, her expression perplexed.

"Because it's getting dark? Because it's close to eight o'clock? Because generally people have an evening meal before Letterman comes on TV."

"Not when they're on the trail of a cold-blooded killer!"

"Mmmm . . . You've got a point—which explains why most homicide detectives I've encountered are so scrawny and undernourished," he said sarcastically. "Oh, wait! There's Big Al, who's probably tucking into a nice juicy steak right about now. Or maybe he's already polishing off his meal with a caramel-fudge sundae. . . . Anyway, I thought you suggested 'grabbing a bite on the way.'"

"We can do it on the way *back*. After we have a chance to talk to the attendant or at least scrutinize the first security camera video."

"We should have just gone to the gas station in Newcastle first. We could have zipped down there in ten minutes, max, had supper at home, and then driven to Beantown in the morning. If you didn't drive me to distraction so easily, I would have thought this out better."

"We need to view the videos in order, Rosco. You know that. If your stomach weren't growling at you, you'd have made the same assessment. In fact, you would have been the one to inform *me* of the routine."

"Well, ignore me if I starve to death first. Grab the wheel if I look as if I'm about to black out."

"You can't," was Belle's breezy reply. "I forgot my driver's license, and you have to get us both home."

"Don't ever say compassion isn't your strong suit."

"Anyway, it's good to be hungry once in a while. It gives us an edge and makes our thought processes fire faster."

"I believe that applies to four-footed predators rather than humans, Belle."

"Well, everyone knows we can learn a great deal from animals."

"And if you think about it, the only reason their thought processes are firing faster is because they're looking for something to eat."

* * *

The Petro-land gas station attendant who had filled up the Explorer the previous Thursday had left for the day, and the video taken from the security camera was grainy, but the figure leaning against the car's front fender was easy to distinguish: a tall man in what appeared to be grubby jeans and a stained T-shirt. He wore a baseball cap. Through the snap-back protruded a greasy-looking ponytail, and although his face was somewhat blurred and shadowed, it was obvious he sported a mustache that looked as unkempt as he.

"I'd say we've got ourselves a photo of Frank O'Connell," Rosco said.

"I'd say you were right on target, my love."

"Does that mean I get my supper now?"

Belle beamed. "When have I ever denied you sustenance?"

With the videotaped image of Frank O'Connell watching the attendant pump gas into Dan Tacete's Explorer seared into their brains, Belle and Rosco left Petro-land and went in search of food. The area immediately surrounding the service station boasted a truck-leasing business, a muffler shop, an autobody shop, a tire warehouse, and a specialist in auto glass replacement—none of which were open at nine twenty at night. Nowhere in the space of two blocks was there any indication of a place that offered meals.

"This is bleak," Belle said.

"Not if you're a car," Rosco answered.

They drove back toward the interstate and finally found a fast-food restaurant where they wolfed down two burgers each and fries, every particle of which tasted like salt-covered cardboard. "I gather this food's supposed to be in the nutritional family," Belle said, although her tone was hesitant.

"It's a family of something," Rosco remarked. "But I think it might be more closely related to cellulose, or possibly birch bark."

Then they returned to Newcastle, where it took some wrangling for Rosco to convince the security guard of the local Petro-land to play back the video detailing a six-dollar purchase by a man driving a Ford Explorer the previous Thursday at eleven seventeen P.M.

Again, it appeared to be an image of Frank O'Connell. And again he leaned against the front fender, watching as less than three gallons of gas were pumped into the car by the attendant. But the difference between the two video representations of man and machine was striking, because by the time the white Ford Explorer had reached Newcastle it was no longer white; it was red.

"So that's why Frank went to Boston," Belle said in a stunned whisper. "He was getting the car painted—out of town. It must have been at that body shop across from the first gas station. Maybe he's not so dumb after all."

CHAPTER

32

B y the time Rosco arrived at the apartment building at nine thirty the next morning, yellow crime scene tape had been stretched from the railing of the wooden porch down to the sidewalk and across the property's narrow front yard. A uniformed police officer stood before the ribbon barrier; he was smoking a cigarette and bending slightly to listen to a stooped and elderly woman who, despite her fragile appearance, seemed determinedly inquisitive. Even at a distance, it was clear to Rosco that she was in a talkative vein—permitting the officer only a few brief nods of response to her running commentary.

The remainder of the block was dotted with the usual curiosity seekers who had gathered in groups of three or four around the medical examiner's van and the various marked and unmarked police cars that lined both sides of the street. It was an unusually large crowd for a weekday, and the message etched on every face, and marked by every tenuous stance, was clear: Something horrible had happened. Something horrible right here in the neighborhood.

As Rosco threaded his way through the onlookers, he overheard the elderly woman repeat a plaintive, "But he seemed like such a nice young man, officer. . . . I simply can't believe he'd do something awful like killing himself. Of course, you detectives and so forth know far more about such things than old-timers like me. Still, it doesn't seem right, does it? Not someone *his* age. If he'd been infirm like me with my chronic back and bowel problems, well, I could understand. You have to be tough to endure the health issues I've been facing all these years. Why, just last week, my rheumatologist, my new one, told me it was a miracle I—"

The officer caught sight of Rosco and began to loosen a knot in the crime tape. He seemed immensely relieved to have someone other than his current companion to talk to. "How ya been, Rosco? Long time, no see. Lever's inside. . . . Said you'd be stopping by."

Rosco slid through the space in the tape as the woman turned to gawk at him. She seemed about to speak; instead, she scowled, knitting her brows together in a dark and unforgiving line. "Thanks, Will. . . . How's Will Junior these days?" Rosco said.

"Pitched a two-hitter at the Little League opener last weekend."

"Must have the old man's arm."

Will grinned. "No doubt about it." He would have continued the conversation—as would the old lady at his side—but Rosco cut them both short with an affable "You tell him hi from me and to keep up the good work. Who knows? Maybe a scout from the Sox will be knocking on your door one day."

"I'll tell him. It'll make his day." Will's erstwhile companion said nothing, but Rosco nodded to her pleasantly anyway.

After that, he proceeded up the concrete walkway, where he passed two more officers and stepped inside the house. There, he climbed the stairway and walked to the rear of the building.

When Rosco entered Frank O'Connell's apartment he was glad to see that the body was no longer in the position Al had described over the phone: hanging from the overhead light fixture of the dingy one-room studio. Carlyle had taken down the corpse, but had yet to cover it with the sheet that was folded beside his medical bag. The skin on Frank's face and hands was a waxy gray color, and his eyes were open. His lips were a mottled blue. His red hair was now cut short; there was no sign of the ponytail or mustache that Rosco and Belle had seen in the service station videos, but his clothes appeared just as unkempt. In fact, the only thing that looked tidy was the mark above his upper lip where the mustache had been shaved off. Judging by the variance in skin tones, it was clear that the dead man had rid himself of his facial hair shortly before he died.

Rosco moved his gaze from the corpse and looked toward Abe Jones and Al Lever, who stood in the center of the room beside a convertible couch that was open into its bed position. From the amount of trash that had collected around the bed's base and on its surface, Rosco guessed that the convertible had been in the same position for some time. As with the sofa-bed, all other surfaces of the apartment—two folding chairs, a green resin table near the cramped galley kitchen, two window sills, a TV stand, and a battered bureau—were covered with trash. There were stained takeout food containers, beer cans that had been either crumpled or not, a couple of empty bottles of Jack Daniel's, a stack of free weekly newspapers, yogurt containers, opened potato chip bags, red pistachio shells scattered over the floor, soda cans, a paper plate of half-eaten Oreos, balled-up wrappers from prepackaged sandwiches, and several orange-yellow plastic prescription drug vials. One of Abe Jones's assistants was dusting a soiled drinking glass for fingerprints while another was shooting flash photographs with a motor-drive Nikon camera.

"So Frank hung himself?" Rosco said as he approached Al and Abe. "That's not going to make his connection to the Tacete situation any easier to prove."

The men exchanged handshakes and Abe said, "Not definitively, maybe."

"Who called it in?"

"The landlord," Al answered. "He said he'd been poking his head in twice a day, knowing that we were looking for his tenant. He's kind of a kook. In fact, I think he was hoping for a little gore, but at least he informed us in a timely fashion."

"Did our boy leave a note?"

Lever pointed to the table near the galley kitchen. Sitting atop a discarded Hawaiian-print shirt was an old manual typewriter. In its roller was a letter.

Rosco walked to the table and began to read in a subdued and level voice: *"What's the point? What's the point of going on? Okay, so I did it. I killed him. You'll have no trouble piecing things together, but if you think you're going to get a blow by blow confession, you're crazy. Because the real deal is; I'm bored. I don't see anything left for me here so I'm moving on. Just moving on. I'm going to a better place, and I won't miss a one of you in the slightest, so please don't waste your energy crying into your beers. Except you, Bonnie. You're the only one I really loved. You I will miss, but I couldn't stand it here anymore. So, adios, amigos. Hasta la vista, sayonara, and all that stuff."*

Rosco's gaze returned to Abe and Al. "Does his sister know?"

"No," Lever replied. "Carlyle will move the body to the morgue in a bit, and she can come in and identify it before he does his autopsy. I don't need an hysterical relative in here until Abe's done with the place."

"Find anything interesting?" Rosco asked Abe.

Abe nodded. "I thought you'd never ask. Here's where my 'not definitively' gets a little help. . . . We've got an army tarp that's fits the description of the one Leo Moody saw covering the Corvette in the ravine; we've got Tacete's

Rolex watch; we've got a few of his credit cards; we've got about six thousand dollars in fifties, which is the denomination Karen was instructed to leave in the gym bag; and we've got this . . ."

Abe's gloved hands reached down toward the tangled bedding, produced a legal-sized manila envelope, opened it, and proceeded to show and describe to Rosco what it contained. "We'll want Belle to examine this, of course, to see if she can discover any hidden clues; but for starters, we have five sheets of graph paper with crossword grids penciled in. They're in varying degrees of completion—lots of erasures and restarts. . . . I'm guessing they're probably prototypes for ones O'Connell later completed. There are also two blank sheets containing lists of words, quotations, and what I gather must be possible puzzle titles. . . . The "Frankly, Dear" crossword has a solution that runs the width of the grid: CATCH ME IF YOU CAN. The words are written in red, as you can see."

Rosco nodded; his expression had turned very grave. "I've got to admit that this doesn't make me feel any too comfortable. It looks like our dead man spent a lot of time emulating Belle—down to the red pen and the same gauge of graph paper. And we know he was targeting her. . . . She received four of these puzzles under different authorships."

"Well, Poly—crates," Lever tossed in. "The guy's a goner. He can't bother your wife now."

Rosco turned back to Abe. "So, Frank went missing in order to take care of the Tacete business, left the place a junk heap, and then sneaked back in and hanged himself? What's his motive? And don't tell me it was remorse."

"I'm not sure there's a motive, per se." Abe indicated the vials of medications. "My guess is that he wasn't lucid when he decided to take his own life."

"The letter looks clear enough."

"There's no telling when he wrote it," Lever responded. "He could have been clean and sober when he was pounding away on the keys, and then needed a little help to get on with the job."

Rosco returned to the typewriter, studied the letter again, and frowned in thought. "Doesn't this confession seem a tad too easy to you both?"

Al shrugged. "The guy was about to take his own life. My guess is that he wanted to keep it sweet and simple. There's no hedging your bets when you've decided to check out."

Rosco's frown of concentration deepened.

"Okay, Poly—crates," Lever said, "what's eating you?"

"I don't know, Al. . . . Something seems wrong. The guy was a total slobola—"

"And slobs don't get depressed?"

"That's not the problem," Rosco answered, shaking his head.

"C'mon, Poly—crates, give. Whatever it is, I'm sure it'll be good for a few laughs."

"I keep coming back to the fact that the Tacete deal was carefully orchestrated. To be honest, I don't think Frank was capable of pulling off such a sophisticated plan alone."

"You knew him?"

"No, but . . ."

"Okay, then who? Bonnie?"

"Or Karen . . . Remember, we've got a whole slew of possible suspects. . . . We could even be looking at a group effort."

"And one of those sweethearts was about to rat, and Frankie couldn't take the pressure," was Al's acerbic response.

"That's possible," Rosco said, but his tone wasn't enthusiastic.

"Come on, Poly—crates. What's O'Connell's M.O.? A guy who was into a lot of iffy stuff, who believed he had more on the ball than anyone had ever given him credit for, who'd spent his life dreaming up small-time cons—and whose substance abuse issues could easily have been escalating. Which means he was probably strapped for cash. Look at the letter he wrote. Maybe being 'caught' by those security cameras wasn't an accident, and the same thing goes for his attempt to sell Tacete's Explorer. Maybe our boy knew exactly what he was doing. Maybe he wanted us to nab him. It wouldn't be the first time."

"Or else someone was setting him up, and he was either too vain or too dumb to realize it," was Rosco's quiet answer.

"And you think it was a woman?"

"Wouldn't be the first time."

Across

1. Pea coat?
4. See 53-Down
7. Plead
10. Goose___
13. "The Greatest"
14. Edge
15. Altar words
16. 34-Down inspiration
17. ___Pan Alley
18. Stubborn
20. Put-down
21. Quote; part 1
24. Philly Pops leader, Peter___
25. Rug
26. Helpers; abbr.
28. Collection
30. Quote; part 2
32. Mr. Yale
34. In debt
35. Fishing pole
36. Quote; part 3
41. Mr. Franklin
42. Poetic contraction
43. Word to 22-Down
44. Quote; part 4
47. Colorful fish
51. "After you," in Italy
52. Heating no.
55. Groan
56. Quote; part 5
60. The limit
61. Refine
62. Spanish uncle
63. Do away with
64. Fib
65. Revolver
66. Mr. Cheney
67. Wallet item
68. 007
69. Tie breakers; abbr.
70. Ship's heading

Down

1. ___leather
2. Stanley's partner
3. Scratch
4. Waiter's prop
5. Black___
6. Muscat native
7. Prejudice
8. Ms. Ferber
9. Exploded
10. E. U. moneyman's concern?
11. 5 miles No. of Kenton, OH
12. USA output
19. Ms. Ryan
22. Many a dog
23. Kyrgyzstan City
27. Forlorn
29. Wapiti
30. Overwhelm
31. "___at 11"
33. "Got it"
34. See 16-Across
36. Hide of 29-Down
37. Wife of James VII
38. Imperfect; abbr.
39. Smack
40. 2nd on the agenda
41. Power rating; abbr.
45. It may be huge
46. A & E
48. Stroll
49. RCA output
50. Whosoever
52. Lei
53. "It takes 4-Across to___"
54. Raw, film-wise
57. Cut
58. "___Died with Their Boots On"
59. Urges
60. Hit sign

"AND THE COW JUMPED OVER THE . . ."

1	2	3		4	5	6		7	8	9		10	11	12
13				14				15				16		
17				18		19						20		
21			22								23			
24					25					26				27
28				29				30	31					
			32		33		34					35		
	36	37				38				39	40			
41				42				43						
44			45	46						47		48	49	50
51						52	53	54		55				
	56				57	58				59				
60				61								62		
63				64			65					66		
67				68			69					70		

CHAPTER

33

" Oh, this is so sad. . . ." Belle murmured over and over again while Rosco perched in the canvas deck chair near her desk and watched her fill in a Xerox copy of Frank O'Connell's final crossword. The afternoon sunlight made the bearded irises outside the window glow like the flowers in van Gogh's famous painting, but neither husband or wife seemed aware of the lovely sight. "Because, from the evidence of this, as well as of his previous puzzles, Frank was obviously brighter than anyone believed. He was certainly better read."

"He's also the prime suspect in a homicide, my dear."

She sighed. "I know . . . I know that, Rosco. . . . And I realize that we were hot on Frank's trail last night, ready to accuse him of everything and anything, and full of righteous indignation—at least, I was."

"I expect we both were. But that's what happens when the bad guys ride into town. They get folks angry and upset."

Belle released another pensive breath, but didn't immediately reply. " 'And the Cow Jumped over the . . . ,' by Frank T. O'Connell," she read aloud, then paused again in thought. Beside her lay a duplicate of the entire file Al Lever and Abe

Jones had found in the dead man's apartment; its contents were spread across her desktop. "It's interesting that he used his middle initial, and also added them to each phony name on the other puzzles; and then built *this* crossword around a lesser-known step-quote from Mark Twain; a man who was famous for poking fun at personal pretensions."

"Whoa, hold on." Rosco craned his neck toward Belle's desk. "I didn't see any mention of Mark Twain when Abe showed me the file."

Belle tilted her head and looked at her husband in innocent surprise. "That's because the quotation wasn't attributed in the puzzle."

"Don't tell me you have this Twain thing memorized, along with everything else in the world?"

"All right, I won't." Belle gave a brief smile.

"Very funny. . . ." Rosco also smiled lightly. "No wonder you have such a hard time recalling the really important things, like recipes for meatloaf. Your brain is already stuffed with aphorisms and poems and derivations—"

" 'Man is the only animal that blushes. Or needs to,' " she interrupted.

"That's what Frank wrote? He sure wasn't blushing when I saw him. He was as blue as Paul Bunyon's ox."

"Thank you, Mr. Sensitive. . . . No. It's a quote from *Pudd'nhead Wilson's New Calendar,* which is the book Frank referenced. 'When in doubt, tell the truth,' is from the same work."

"So what did O'Connell use?" Rosco asked.

Belle's face returned to its thoughtful expression. She pointed to the crossword in her hand. "Start here at 21-Across, continue with 30, 36 and 44-Across, and conclude with 56-Across."

" 'EVERYONE'S A MOON AND HAS A DARK SIDE WHICH HE NEVER SHOWS TO ANYBODY,' " Rosco read aloud.

"I guess that theory must have summed up Frank T. O'Connell's life," was Belle quiet comment. "All this time,

I assumed those child-themed crosswords were intended as a threat, or else a reference to the Snyder case . . . when they may simply have been the product of a lonely soul wanting to connect with something he'd never had: a carefree youth." She lined up the five puzzles. " 'Baby Steps,' Frank's first attempt at contacting me . . . Even its nursery rhyme stepquote has a sinister tone. A MAN OF WORDS AND NOT OF DEEDS IS LIKE A GARDEN FULL OF WEEDS . . . then 'Sugar and Spice,' which was probably inspired by Bonnie. . . . 'As Time Goes By'; 'Frankly, Dear.' . . . I feel as though we're witnessing an entire life unraveling within these crosswords." She grew silent once again; at length she sighed and returned her gaze to her husband. "So, we're supposed to meet Al at Bonnie's apartment? I don't know if I'm up to it, Rosco."

He nodded and glanced at his watch. "Al said he'd give us a shout when he was on his way over there, which should be soon. He wanted to allow Bonnie time to process the information after she identified Frank's body at the morgue."

"Which was only a couple of hours ago. . . . Not much chance to 'process'—"

"This is a criminal investigation, Belle. Al doesn't let grass grow under his feet; he never has. Besides, Bonnie could well be as involved in this situation as her brother."

Belle wrapped her arms around herself. "I wish I didn't have to go with you two. . . ."

"I know. I'd tell you to skip it, but Al needs you to question her about the crossword puzzles; act as a foil, if nothing else."

"I realize that, but it's not bringing a smile to my lips." Belle winced as the word "smile" escaped her lips and her mouth turned downward in dismay. "Maybe the dental practice should have been named Grimace! instead of Smile!" she complained. "Or perhaps Bite the Dust is closer to the truth."

"Not too customer-friendly," was Rosco's gentle response before his cell phone rang. He answered with a hurried, "Yes,

Al," then finished with an equally businesslike, "We're on our way. See you in fifteen."

"To the *toothsome* Bonnie's?" Belle asked with a marked lack of enthusiasm.

"You got it."

" 'That one may smile, and smile, and be a villain,' " she recited in a flat, dejected tone.

"*Pudd'nhead Wilson* again?" Rosco queried.

"You're off by about fifty-five hundred miles. It's Hamlet. And humor wasn't his strong point."

"Good with a sword, but no rapier wit, huh?"

"Stop, Rosco!"

He stood and looked down at the two dozing pooches. 'Let sleeping dogs lie.' . . . Charles Dickens."

"Very good."

"Well, I knew it wasn't the . . . Great . . . Dane."

"I never saw any of those puzzles before!" Bonnie insisted for the fourth time. "You people need to start listening better. Besides, they all have different names on them; what makes you think Frankie made them up?" Her red, swollen eyes moved from Al, who'd posed the question, to Rosco and finally to Belle before letting her glance slide to her carpeted floor.

In the several minutes the threesome had been questioning Bonnie O'Connell, Belle had come to realize that the young woman was more comfortable in the company of men than with her own sex. In fact, Belle had begun to identify Bonnie's attitude toward her as one of wholehearted mistrust. "I mean, yeah, Frankie liked to play around with word games and stuff in the newspapers, and the ones in the magazines, too, but so what? The last I heard, that wasn't a crime."

"So you have no idea why he constructed these particular crosswords and sent them to me?" Belle asked as she indicated the puzzles she'd spread across Bonnie's glass-topped coffee table.

"Maybe he wanted to be famous?" was the offhand reply. "You know, see his name printed in the paper? Frankie was always hoping for a big break."

"But, as you said, they weren't sent to me under his own name. Your brother used four different pseudonyms, as well as a fake post office box. Do you know where he got the names, Bonnie? Are you acquainted with this Everts person, or Randy Isaacs, or Sal Anderson, or Nicky Flanagan? Because none of them are in the Newcastle phone book, and the post office box belongs to a woman who died six months ago."

Bonnie only shook her head slowly.

"And there's nothing in the clues or quotations or titles that rings a bell, either? Or that might prove useful in Lieutenant Lever's investigation?" Belle continued to probe. "Because if it's there, I sure can't see it."

Bonnie tossed her head and shrugged in a show of disinterest. "Nope. I already told you people. I never saw those crosswords before. Maybe you shouldn't be wasting your time with me. Maybe you should be looking for the person who really killed Dan Tacete. Cuz it sure as hell wasn't my Frankie."

Belle glanced at Rosco and then at Al, who was the next to speak. "I know you're upset, Miss O'Connell, but I don't need any flippant remarks. You realize that it's a crime to withhold evidence, don't you?"

"I'm not withholding anything!" Bonnie spluttered. "I told you Frank was into a lot of things he didn't feel like sharing. I mean, how does that saying go? About not being your brother's keeper or something? Well, that's me and Frankie in a nutshell! And he's giving you this 'dark side of the moon' business? That about says it all, if you ask me. . . . I mean, c'mon, look at the letter he wrote . . . the one you found . . ." Then her shoulders suddenly sagged, and her defiant chin dropped toward her chest. Reflexively, she patted the leather couch on which she sat, rubbing her fingers against the smooth grain as if the expensive expanse could bring her relief. Instead, it produced the opposite effect. "Oh, Frankie . . . how am I going to afford this place now? Where's the money going to come from?" she muttered under her breath.

Belle and Rosco and Al shared a look. "What do you mean 'now'?" Al asked. "Has the picture changed financially in some way? Isn't Doctor Wagner keeping you on——?"

"Jack?" Bonnie's head jerked up, her expression now full of fury. "Jack's a louse! A complete and utter louse. Frank told me not to trust him, but I didn't listen. Boy, didn't I listen!" But this confession only served to increase Bonnie's pain, and she again resorted to stony silence.

"So it's all over between you and Doctor Wagner? Is he . . . is he firing you?" Belle asked.

Bonnie stared at Belle in confusion. "Why would he do that?"

"Well, I just thought . . . when you said he was a——"

Rosco interrupted. "Then your brother was helping support you because your salary at Smile! wasn't enough to cover this"—he waved his hand to indicate the room—"this lifestyle? Is that what you're saying?"

"Oh, honey, are you ever out to lunch! Frank give *me* a nickel? Frank? Mr. Mooch himself! I was the one carrying him along." Then Bonnie's face crumpled again. "Why did he have to kill himself!? Why did he have to do a dumb thing like that? I could have kept giving him dough. I could have! I could . . . we could have figured things out . . . gotten him back on track and everything . . . He could have stopped using all that junk. . . . He . . ." She began to weep, wrapping her arms around herself and giving in to her enormous grief while Belle, Rosco, and Al looked at each other in growing perplexity.

"Your brother was dealing drugs as well as using them, wasn't he?" Al asked after a brief pause.

Bonnie nodded and sniffled. "I guess . . . maybe . . . yeah, probably . . . Look, Frankie did what he did. And he didn't like me asking a bunch of questions. So I didn't. End of story. . . . Anyway, he told me he was into something big. It was gonna turn his life around." Her chest heaved convulsively, and she started to cry afresh.

"I assume he meant the kidnapping." Al's voice was level and professional.

"Look, mister, everything you've got on him is circumstantial—"

"Did you help him set up the Tacete situation?" Al continued in the same measured tone.

"No!" Bonnie exploded.

"But you knew he was involved?"

"No! I already told you! Frank didn't like me knowing what he was up to. Besides, you don't know for certain he was part of that deal."

"Yes we do, Bonnie. When we found him, his apartment was full of incriminating evidence," Lever told her.

"Evidence can be planted. I know how these drug cops operate. You're all the same," was Bonnie's ferocious reply.

"I hope you're not suggesting items were planted by the Newcastle police?" Al responded. His lips were now tight. "That's not going to get you very far with me."

"I'm just saying it happens, is all," Bonnie grumbled, but her voice had grown muffled and cowed.

"But you *did* connect your brother to the crime as soon as you learned that Doctor Tacete had died." It was Belle who made this next statement. "You went looking for Frank back on Tuesday after you left work early, didn't you? And you were concerned about Rob Rossi's whereabouts, too."

Bonnie's unhappy eyes had turned into bitter slits. "What is it with you, sister? You think you can read my brain or something? Well, you can't. I don't give a fig about what Rob does or where he goes or anything!"

"That's not what you told Carlos Quintero."

Confusion swept across Bonnie's face. She studied Belle for a moment, then said, "Ah, right . . . you're the one who was looking for the waitress job at the Black Sheep. I thought I'd seen you somewhere before. . . ."

"So where is Rob Rossi?"

"I don't know!" Bonnie all but shouted.

"So, if your brother *didn't* nab Doctor Tacete," Rosco interrupted in a surprisingly harsh voice. "How did Frank get possession of his Ford Explorer?"

Again, Bonnie's body appeared to collapse into itself. "I don't know," she whispered.

"And who was supposed to pose as Karen Tacete when he went to sell it, if it wasn't you? The police will be checking that car for fingerprints, Bonnie. You're not going to be able to lie about this forever. Or is Karen in on this, too? Were you all working together? Are your fingerprints on the Explorer?"

She covered her ears with her hands in an effort to block out Rosco's words. "Stop. Stop! Look, Frankie would never have hurt Dan. I know he wouldn't!"

"Well, surprise, surprise," was Al's pointed reply. "He did a hell of a lot more than hurt him."

"He wouldn't!" Bonnie snapped back at him. "Okay, so my brother was no saint. And maybe he did a bunch of bad things . . . and was high a lot of the time, and couldn't keep a job . . . and maybe he liked playing around with these dumb paper puzzles. . . . But he's dead now, okay? And that's all I'm saying. I need to talk to a lawyer. There's nothing you can pin on him. Or me."

"Well, that's where you're wrong, Bonnie," Al told her. "Because from where I'm sitting, you look like an accessory to murder. And I've got a strong hunch that you and Frank and possibly Karen—"

"But I loved Dan!" Bonnie blurted out. "Why would I want to kill him?"

Neither Al nor Rosco nor Belle made a move. They didn't even exchange a glance; instead, they kept their astonished eyes glued to Bonnie's face.

"So there!" she fumed with another mutinous toss of her head. "And I don't care who you tell. I loved Dan. I loved everything about him. He found me this apartment and gave me money to get all this nice stuff . . ."

"Wait a minute," Lever finally muttered. "You mean you and Tacete were . . . and not Jack Wagner . . . ?"

"What's that creep Jack got to do with the price of eggs?" Bonnie spat out.

Rosco sat back on the couch. When he spoke, his words were slow and thoughtful. "Was your brother aware of your relationship with Dan?"

"So what if he was?" was Bonnie's belligerent retort.

"Was Frank putting the squeeze on Tacete?" Al asked her after another silent moment. "Dan was a married man, after all."

"They had their own deal going," Bonnie shot back. "I don't know what it was. And I don't care." Then her chest started to heave with sobs again. "Look, maybe Frankie was involved in something shady; maybe he was squeezing Dan; maybe he even found out who nabbed him. Or . . . or Frankie knew all along. But he didn't kill Dan. He wouldn't have done that to me. Not ever."

CHAPTER

34

The top floor of the Newcastle police station consisted of a long, dreary hallway that culminated in two large, facing rooms. The space to the east was the evidence room and was kept locked at all times. The space to the west was an employees' lounge. There was a television that seemed incapable of receiving anything but sporting events, a pool table, three couches in various states of decay, a collection of folding chairs, and an assortment of vending machines. It was not a place for quiet or confidential discussion. That type of activity was reserved for the eight smaller rooms that lined the sides of the corridor: four of which were connected by two-way mirrors and used for questioning detainees, and four of which were utilized as meeting areas. Each of these spaces was soundproof, and it was in one of them that Al Lever decided to have his tête-à-tête with Abe Jones and Herb Carlyle. Needless to say, he wasn't looking forward to it. If Carlyle and Rosco were water and oil, Carlyle and Jones were potentially a more combustible mix; and the present situation wasn't improved by the fact that Al had requested that Abe sit in on the O'Connell autopsy.

"So what have we got?" Lever asked as the two men joined him at the utilitarian, formica-topped table. The room had witnessed countless such interviews, and the table's surface bore the marks of every discussion: the nicks, the gouges, the charred marks of cigarettes left in overfull ashtrays. As if adhering to an unspoken tradition, Al lit up his own cigarette while simultaneously grabbing the empty but dirty glass ashtray from the table's center.

"Why don't you have *Doctor* Jones fill you in on the situation," was Carlyle's acid response. "That's why he's here, right? To weigh in with his *expert* opinion? That's why you had him peering over my shoulder all the time I was examining O'Connell."

Lever took a long, slow drag and leaned back in his chair. "You know what, Herb? This whole case has got me going in circles. And I'm not happy about it. So, I intend to use every thing, and every individual, at my disposal to get to the bottom of it. And to be honest with you, I don't care who likes it and who doesn't—from the mayor on down. Do we understand one another?"

Carlyle didn't reply. Instead, he removed a manila folder from his briefcase, plopped it showily on the table, then opened it, bringing his reading glasses up to the bridge of his nose. He glanced down briefly at the paperwork, then all but glared at Al. "Frank O'Connell didn't kill himself. He was murdered."

Al sat up straight and looked at Abe, who nodded in silent agreement with the assessment. "Okay, Herb . . ." Lever said after a moment. "Let me have it."

"First off, O'Connell was loaded up with OxyContin to the point of an overdose. That isn't what killed him, though. . . . Of course, being stoned or drunk isn't necessarily inconsistent with a suicide; a lot of people have to get high as a kite in order to get up the guts to take their own life."

Lever didn't respond, and Carlyle interpreted the lack of interruption as tacit approval. He continued to catalog his findings. "Cause of death: asphyxiation. But our killer was slick; he knew what he was up to. The angle of the bruises around O'Connell's neck are almost exactly what a suicide by hanging would have produced." One of Carlyle's ghoulish smiles spread across his face. "But *almost* ain't good enough. . . . My theory is that our boy was strangled with the same piece of rope he was then left hanging from."

Lever opened his mouth to ask a question, but Carlyle raised a hand to silence him.

"I know what you're going to say, Al; ropes can slip; angles can shift. But in this case, the garrote was almost too precise—like someone with military training did the job. . . . However, the real kicker is this: As you can see in the photo I've marked number four, there are faint bruises on O'Connell's arms, just up from the elbows. They were covered by his shirt when we found his body. My belief is that the parallel positioning of the discoloration indicates that he'd been tied, arms behind his back, right up until the time he expired. I also have reason to think he'd been gagged. White cotton samples were detected within his mouth, perhaps from an athletic sock. It was most likely held in place with a ski mask to avoid leaving marks on his face. There's no indication that duct tape, or the like, was used."

"Our murderer knew what he was up to by faking a suicide," Lever echoed Carlyle's statement. There was a good deal of resignation in the tone.

"No doubt about it. . . . Now, although O'Connell's arms were bound, his wrists were not. Obviously, our perp was hoping no bruises would surface on the upper arms after the victim stopped breathing. Also, his hair and mustache were cut *after* death, which is consistent with Jones's findings."

Al glanced at Abe, who then continued. "We found a number of hair samples in the carpet at Frank's apartment."

"Any thoughts as to why?" Lever asked Carlyle.

"Why the murder was set up to look like a suicide or why the guy's hair was cut?"

"Either one."

"Not a clue, Lieutenant. That's your business not mine." There was a discernible level of glee in Carlyle's voice.

"Boy, oh boy . . ." Al stubbed out his cigarette and immediately lit another. "You know the longer we walk in these woods, the more lost we're getting, and I have a really bad feeling we may end up with more than *two* cases of homicide before we find the right path out of here."

Abe nodded. "It's a curve ball, all right."

"I guess there's a possibility that O'Connell's murder has *nothing* to do with Tacete's death. . . ." Lever pondered aloud. "It could have been a drug deal gone south, maybe even a mob hit . . ."

"It's a possibility, Al," Abe agreed, although his tone indicated he didn't believe those two scenarios applied. "But let's be realistic; O'Connell was driving the doctor's car around. That only points to one conclusion."

Lever returned his focus to Carlyle. "Time of death?"

"I'm placing it between two and four A.M."

"And did he die there? Or was the body brought in?"

It was Jones who answered. "I'm guessing he was killed in the apartment. There's no way someone carries a body up those narrow stairs without leaving marks on the corpse or the hallway. Plus, there are neighbors. Bringing a buddy home late at night, drunk or doped up is one thing. Carrying a dead man is another story altogether. My hunch is that Frank was so wigged out on the Oxy that he didn't know where the heck he was. . . . And he was in no condition to fight back once he felt the noose go around his neck."

Lever pulled a pen from his breast pocket and made a note in his own file. "Have you been able to match O'Connell's fingerprints with the odd set on the Corvette?"

Abe shook his head. "We're working on that right now. But I'm certain—" He was interrupted by a loud cough from Carlyle.

"Yes, Herb, what is it?" Lever said.

Carlyle tapped his wristwatch. "It's five o'clock. If you're

done with me, I'd like to leave here at a decent hour today."
Without waiting for a reply, the medical examiner stood and
pushed his report closer to Lever. "It's all in there, Lieutenant.
If you have any questions, I'll be back at nine tomorrow
morning." Carlyle then turned and walked out the door.

After he left Jones said, "No one would ever accuse Herb
of being a workaholic, would they?"

Lever chuckled and stubbed out his cigarette. "Yep, he's
a happy camper when people have the good sense to get murdered nine-to-five." Then he leaned back in his chair once
more, raised his arms, and placed his beefy hands behind the
back of his head. "I got an interesting little tidbit back from
Craigor Autobody about an hour ago. That's the body shop
in the Boston area that's across the street from the gas station where Frank fueled up the Explorer. The guy at Craigor
said O'Connell brought the vehicle in for a paint job immediately after he'd left the filling station. He paid in cash.
The car went in white, came out red. A real quickie. Frank
had it back in four hours."

"So that confirms Rosco and Belle's theory."

"Yeah, but there's more. Craigor is known for quick turnaround time, but it's an appointment-only shop. Frank scheduled the paint job almost three weeks prior to bringing it in
on Thursday."

"Which supports the notion that this was a well-
orchestrated crime."

Al chortled. "It gets better, my friend. Apparently, the
same vehicle was brought in nine months ago for body work
on the right front fender. The owner said she hit a deer."

"She?"

"She. The Explorer's registered to Karen Johnson Tacete,
remember?"

"And nine months ago?"

"What the man said, Abe."

"You're not going to tell me he was still able to describe
the woman after all that time, are you, Al?"

" 'A babe. Blonde. A gorgeous blonde.' Exact words."

Silence hung in the room. Neither Lever or Jones looked at each other; instead, they stared into the middle distance, but it was clear from the intense concentration apparent on both faces that they were pondering the same thing.

"A deer, huh?" Abe finally muttered. "And she didn't go to a local shop?"

"It kinda makes you wonder, doesn't it?"

"Nine months ago was when the Snyder kid was killed. . . ."

"That's what I was thinking, too."

Jones fell silent again as he drummed his fingers on the table. "I know it's a real longshot . . ."

"Since when did that stop you, Abe?"

"Let me see if I can lift any DNA from the vehicle. *If* the tires are still the same, and *if* it's the crime vehicle . . ." Jones let his words trail off while Lever brought his hands back down to his lap, another thoughtful expression crossing his face.

"Which brings us back to, Who killed Cock-Robin?" he said. "What do you make of all this, Abe? Any theories?"

"Are you talking about Tacete, O'Connell, or the Snyder boy?"

"Take your pick."

Jones reached for Carlyle's folder, opened it, and began leafing through the photos and papers. "Leaving the Synder situation alone for the moment . . . let's go back to Frank, and let's assume he was involved in Tacete's death. . . . I realize Frank's sister claims he wouldn't have hurt Dan, but, from my point of view, the evidence refutes that statement. I would also guess there were at least two people involved in the doctor's kidnapping and death and that O'Connell either had an accomplice—or that someone else masterminded the scheme and solicited his help. And that *other* person then killed Frank. Maybe it was a matter of a deal gone sour . . . or maybe someone was trying to cover their tracks."

"But why was so much of the cash left in O'Connell's apartment?"

"To make us believe that Frank was a lone ranger; i.e., the perp hangs himself because of his terrible remorse. Case solved; the party's over." Jones brushed the palms of hands together two or three times to emphasize the point. "No more police investigation. Whoever killed O'Connell must have been banking on the NPD dismissing the death as what it originally appeared: a drugged-up murderer checking out."

"Which means that whoever was working with Frank didn't need the money that desperately. So what did they want?"

"A dead Dan Tacete seems the logical answer; Frank's *supposed* suicide may have been part of the plan from the git-go."

Lever reached for another cigarette, but Abe held up his hands. "This room's awfully small, Al. Could you hold off on that one? For me?"

Lever grumbled and returned the pack to his shirt pocket. "If your theory's true, Abe, and I'm inclined to agree with you, then we have a wealthy killer on our hands—which *could* lead to the partner, Jack Wagner."

Jones only shrugged.

"What?" Al asked incredulously. "It goes like this—" Lever began ticking off his reasons on his fingers. "Wagner's sick and tired of working with Tacete. We know that for a fact. But if he breaks up the business, he loses half his customers—who follow Dan to a new location. . . . Then Jack happens to meet his receptionist's lowlife brother and decides to set him up—while supplying Frankie as much OxyContin as he wants. Wagner also has enough cash to buy the second Corvette without breaking stride—"

"You don't know how much I'd love to take that bet," Abe interrupted with a laugh. "But I'm too fond of you. . . . I've already gone there, Al. Wagner's still in the Army Reserves.

His fingerprints are on file. He's one of the first people I checked out. The prints on the 'Vette aren't his."

"Okay, so they belong to Frank; that doesn't change my theory. I still say Jack Wagner's our boy. Who else would leave that much cash in O'Connell's apartment? And the garrote? Carlyle described it as 'military'; and you just said Wagner's in the Reserves."

"As a *dentist*, Al." Jones smiled and shook his head. "Not Special Forces. And dentists aren't supposed to strangle people—no matter how much they squawk about root canals. . . . But here's my theory. I'm a passionate guy, re-member, and murder's very often a crime of passion. I say go back and question Karen Tacete. You might want to ask her why she went up to Beantown nine months ago while you're at it."

"What about this missing Rob Rossi?"

"Ever hear of a love triangle?"

CHAPTER

35

Belle and Rosco turned into Karen Tacete's driveway shortly after six P.M. Al Lever's brown sedan had preceded them by half a minute, and Al was in the midst of exiting his unmarked NPD vehicle as Rosco pulled to a stop and set the emergency brake. "I hate doing this good cop/bad cop routine," Belle grumbled aloud as she watched Al shove the driver's door closed and begin ambling toward them.

"Better than doing an all bad-cop act," was Rosco's wisecracking retort.

"Har, har. Very funny . . ." Belle produced a resigned sigh. "First Bonnie, now Karen. . . . Why can't I just be a crossword editor, without having crime investigation added to my job description?"

"You're the one who refers to herself as 'an operative with the Polycrates Agency'; or was it sub-contractor?"

"Twice, Rosco! I've only used that term two times! . . . Okay, maybe a little more . . . but the last I heard cruciverbalists weren't moonlighting as criminologists."

"Well, cheer up, then. You've discovered an important

niche market—Belle Graham, the Celebrated Cruci-crimi-verbologist."

"Cruci-crimi-verbologist isn't a word."

"Maybe it should become one. Why don't you submit it to the O.E.D?" Rosco chuckled while Belle suppressed a second lengthy sigh, his lighthearted tone failing to win her over.

"Okay," she muttered after another quiet moment, "no point in postponing the inevitable."

By this time Al Lever had reached their car. Rosco and Belle climbed out of their seats; the two men shook hands, and Al turned to Belle. "I can't tell you how much I appreciate your help in all this. . . . I know it's not easy, Karen being your buddy and everything. . . . So, all I can say is thanks. Really. From the bottom of my heart."

Belle smiled at him, her grousing all at once a thing of the past. She kissed him on the cheek. "What a secret softie you are, Al."

"That's not the scuttlebutt at the NPD."

"I'll keep the good news to myself, then," was Belle's teasing reply. "There's no point in polishing up a reputation that's been so carefully scoured into a dull and rusty finish."

The three walked toward Karen's house. "She knows we're coming, right?" Rosco asked Al.

"Correct. But she's not happy about it. In fact, the only reason she agreed to meet this evening was because Belle would be joining us."

"So much for *my* popularity," Rosco jested, although his tone had taken on a serious edge. "And she was offered an opportunity to have a lawyer present? I'm more than a little surprised she opted to pass. It doesn't sound like the wife of a professional, if you ask me."

"Her position appears to be 'bereaved and innocent widow done wrong by the slackers in the police force.' Why would she need a lawyer?"

"Maybe because that's the truth," Belle added in an undertone, but Al made no reply.

* * *

Lily was nowhere in evidence as Karen led the trio through the house and into the kitchen, where she pointed to the breakfast nook, indicating that she preferred the conversation take place there and not in the larger space of the living room. Her body language was hostile and wary, but the rigidity of her spine and the tightness of her jaw couldn't conceal an overall effect of great weariness. She looked like a person who'd taken one too many punches.

"Lily's out. A neighbor's daughter is babysitting for me," Karen explained in an exhausted voice that also contained a goodly share of anger and hurt. "The kid needed some money, and I, well, I just don't want my baby involved in this mess. She doesn't need to overhear things she isn't meant to hear." Karen's face had flushed an aggressive hot pink. Still standing, although her visitors had already seated themselves, she crossed her arms over her chest and glared down at Al. "What is it you want from me this time, Lieutenant?"

"Let's understand something, Mrs. Tacete: All I'm trying to do is find the person who killed your husband. I assume it's a question we'd both like to see answered."

Karen remained stony, so Al pushed on. "What can you tell me about Rob Rossi?" was his even response, and Karen's face grew redder.

"He's a patient of Dan's—*was* a patient of Dan's."

"You've met him?"

"Yes."

Al waited; when Karen didn't continue, he added a probing, "But you hadn't met all of Dan's patients, so why do you know Rossi?"

"*Former* patients," was the icy answer. "Dan's dead, remember?"

This time it was Al who bristled. "If you'd come to us when the kidnappers first contacted you, Mrs. Tacete, there's

264 ■ NERO BLANC

a chance your husband would still be alive. If, indeed, there *were* kidnappers."

"What's that supposed to mean?" Karen demanded.

"What it sounds like: that we have cause to believe the entire ransom situation could have been one big hoax."

Karen stared at Al. "A hoax? But—"

"Someone wanted your husband out of the way, Mrs. Tacete. His death was a carefully orchestrated event."

Karen's mouth fell open; she didn't speak, but her fingers began to loosen their steely grip, leaving white impressions on her bare arms. "What do you mean by 'orchestrated'?"

It was Belle who answered. "Karen, I realize this is a hard concept to accept—"

But Dan Tacete's wife was having none this placating attitude. "You're telling me someone murdered Dan and just *faked* the kidnapping situation?"

"That's right," Al said, his eyes never leaving Karen's face. "The kidnapping angle was only a ruse to throw us off the track."

"But what about the money . . . and the instructions I was given?"

"You tell me, Mrs. Tacete; by your own admission, you're the only one who heard this alleged kidnapper's voice—as well as your husband's."

"You're not suggesting I'm mixed up in this, are you?"

"I'm not 'suggesting' anything, Mrs. Tacete," Al replied in an even tone. "I'm merely asking questions. . . . Now what can you tell us about Rob Rossi?"

"He's a bartender," she replied after a long moment of silence. "Dan said he worked at a local joint. A kind of grungy place. Dan was interested in the place from an 'anthropological' viewpoint. I'm not sure what he meant by that, but it was his term. . . ."

"The bar is called the Black Sheep," Al interjected. "So you went there with your husband?"

Karen shook her head. "No. I met Rob Rossi, but not there. In fact, I don't recall the circumstances."

"But you *do* know Rossi?" Al continued to push.

"Yes, I do," Karen pushed back. "And I know Belle. And your good pal, Rosco, too. So what? Are you putting all my friendships under scrutiny now?"

"So Rob's a friend?"

"Look, Lieutenant, I don't know what you're getting at here. . . ."

"I'm just trying to clear up some loose ends, Mrs. Tacete. And one of them involves Rossi."

"Well, I can't tell you any more about him than I already have."

Lever sat back and regarded Karen. He seemed to be making some private assessment of the situation. "It may interest you to know that the Black Sheep was also a favorite hangout of Frank O'Connell."

But the information seemed to have no effect. "The same O' Connell who tried to sell the Explorer?" Karen asked. "The brother of the receptionist at Smile!?"

"That's right," Al said.

Karen's glance swept across the threesome seated at the table. "Are you telling me that he and Rob Rossi are involved in Dan's death?"

Belle sidestepped the questions with one her own. "Karen, let me ask you something. . . . Did you ever suspect Dan of being unfaithful to you?"

Karen's face flushed a brighter pink. She opened her mouth to speak, but immediately closed it.

"Did you?" Belle pressed.

Karen turned away. "Yes . . . well, not at first . . . but recently . . . yes, I did. . . . I don't want to talk about this. I really don't."

"Did you know the woman's identity?" It was Rosco who posed this question.

Karen shook her head in denial, then added a sarcastic, "I don't suppose this hot little number is on your and your crony's list of possible suspects, is she?"

"As a matter of fact, she is," Lever answered, "And she's

confirmed that she had a relationship with your husband. It was his receptionist."

"Bonnie O'Connell?" Disbelief rang through Karen's voice. She stared at Al and then at Rosco. "*Bonnie?*"

Rosco nodded.

"Dan couldn't do better than her?" Karen sat down abruptly, her jaw clenching and unclenching in wrath, although it was clear her rage was no longer directed at her visitors but at her husband. "He was cheating on me with an idiot like *her?*" Karen looked at Belle. "How did you find out?"

"As Al said, it came directly from her."

"She told *you* people. She admitted it to *you?*"

Belle nodded while Karen released a spiteful groan. "Well, that situation certainly must have thrilled her brother. . . . I'll bet he was Johnny-on-the-spot to take advantage of that situation. Ready money . . . I can just picture it. So Dan was being blackmailed over his little honeybun, was he?"

"We don't yet have evidence to substantiate that claim, Mrs. Tacete, but it may very well be the case."

Karen shook her head. "Well, my bet says he was." Then her open hand slammed the table. "That creep," she swore, "giving away what belonged to Lily and me. . . . Giving it to some tramp and her druggie brother!"

"You already know that Frank O'Connell attempted to sell the Explorer, Mrs. Tacete," Al stated. "What you possibly don't know is that he drove it up to the Boston area the day your husband disappeared"—Karen hunched forward as if to interrupt, but instead remained silent—"where he had the car painted," Al continued, "at Craigor Autobody." Lever paused as if expecting a reaction to the name, but Karen made no move. "Craigor is an appointment-only operation. The paint job had been scheduled three weeks before."

Karen shrugged; a bitter smile twisted across her face. "I guess the O'Connell duo has more smarts than I gave them credit for."

"I was also told that Craigor had worked on the same vehicle prior to that time. Nine months ago, in fact. The person who brought it in was identified as Karen Johnson."

"What?" Karen said as a bewildered look covered her face. "I . . . How? I don't . . . know anything about—!" she insisted, but Lever overrode her.

"Who claimed she'd hit a deer . . . The owner of Craigor was told that she'd hit the deer up in New Hampshire, but on the drive back the steering seemed to be acting up, and she was afraid to continue on to Newcastle—which is why she'd stopped at the out-of-town shop. When O'Connell showed up with the same vehicle for repainting, the owner was then told that he'd returned because Craigor had done such good work earlier. Clearly you have more than a passing relationship with Frank O'Connell."

"I know nothing about this!" Karen repeated.

"The Explorer's registered to you, isn't it, Mrs. Tacete?"

"You already know that, Lieutenant. All Dan's cars are registered in my name. It was because he wanted me and Lily to have financial security, in case . . . in case . . . because the mortgage on this place and the lack of savings . . ." Then Karen's head suddenly dropped into her hands. When she next spoke, her voice was a strangled moan. "They're going to take my little girl away from me again, aren't they . . . ?"

Belle looked at Rosco who returned her perplexed gaze.

"That's what you're trying to tell me, isn't it?" Karen looked up; her face had gone dangerously white. "That's why you're here. This has nothing to do with Dan."

"Who is 'they,' Karen?" Rosco asked.

"The Feds . . . D.H.S. . . . the creeps who put her in foster care in the first place. . . ." Karen batted tears out of her eyes, squinting hard, as if will-power alone could keep her from crying.

"Lily was in foster care?" Belle couldn't disguise the shocked surprise in her tone. "Where was Dan?"

But Karen seemed not to hear the question. "She was only three months old, and those hags snatched her away. . . . three months old. I didn't get to see my baby again until she'd already passed her first birthday."

"But what about Dan?" Belle repeated.

Karen stared at her, her expression blank and confused. "Dan?"

"Yes. Where was he in all of this?"

Karen glared at an empty space above Belle's head; then her focus dropped back to the table's surface as though she were studying something written there. "It's what the social workers wanted. . . . I promised them I was clean and sober, that I was going to stay that way, too, but it wasn't good enough. They insisted I get a permanent job, but it was hard, you know, because my record wasn't so hot. I'd done some things . . . well, not the kind of stuff you put in a resume . . . And then I met Dan, and we fell in love, and he wanted to marry me. . . ."

"So . . . Lily isn't Dan's child? Is that it?" Rosco asked.

"No," was Karen's leaden response. "No, she's not. . . . I used to think he'd saved my life, you know? I used to think we could still make it work. That *I* could make it work. What a laugh." She tightened her lips in a silent grimace while Rosco, Al, and Belle sat straighter in their chairs and shared a long and troubled look.

"What about family?" Belle asked at length, and Karen's head jolted upward as though she'd been slapped.

"Family? Me? Don't make me laugh. If I never see one of those cretins again, it'll be too soon. Lily's my family, and that's it." But no sooner had these fierce words been spoken than Karen's shoulders again sagged in defeat. "We were all set, Lily and me. It was clear sailing, until all this happened. But now we've been left with nothing. Nothing except those damn toys of his."

"Which are worth a fair amount," Rosco offered in a quiet tone.

"What a prince he was! A house mortgaged to the hilt. No savings; nothing!" Karen burst out. "You know something? That brother of his that I was never introduced to?

The one I kept trying to call when my dear husband went missing? Dan told me the guy refused to see me because of my past. Because his saintly little brother had married beneath himself! Why would Dan have told him all that junk in the first place? Why would he have done a crummy thing like that?"

It was with heavy steps that Belle and Rosco and Al returned to their cars. "Do you think she's telling the truth?" Lever asked when they were out of earshot of the house. "Something seemed very off there."

"You mean about Lily's background?" Belle asked.

"No, that part struck me as true. It's the rest of it that bothers me: her denial of the first Craigor job, her dancing around her relationship with Rossi and O'Connell, even her *seeming* surprise at learning that Bonnie was the other woman in Tacete's life. . . . How about you, Poly—crates? What's your read on the situation?"

"If she's lying, she's a real pro, Al. But we know that whoever pulled this stunt off was very slick, and experience tells me that—"

Belle spun on the two men. "If you two aren't the most cynical—"

"It's happened before, Belle," Lever said, holding up his hands in a gesture of truce. "Karen's got one heck of a motive. She knew her husband was being unfaithful—"

"Well, *I* believed her," Belle insisted, although even as she made the statement, her forehead clouded in perplexity. "We didn't ask if Dan had a life insurance policy. . . ."

"Now who sounds cynical?" Al asked. But no sooner had he spoken than his cell phone rang. He grabbed it from his belt and said, "Yes, Abe, what's up?"

Al nodded several times as he listened to the voice on the other end. "Well, I'll be damned," he finally admitted as he released a long, unhappy breath. "Okay, Abe . . . Yup . . . Which means we're back to square one on that third set of fingerprints on the 'Vette . . . ? Yeah, I'm on my way in. . . . See you in a half hour." Lever clicked off and turned to Rosco and Belle. "I've got bad news, and I've got bad news. Which do you two lovebirds want to hear first?"

"Doesn't sound like much of a choice you're offering, Al," was Rosco's caustic reply.

"Smart boy." Lever cocked his head to one side. "You remember that big robbery that occurred the same night Tacete's car was torched? Abe was at that site while I was enjoying my fun-filled chitchat with Carlyle?"

"You mean when Papyrus was hit?" Rosco said.

"Correct-o, Poly—crates. It turns out our Frankie was involved. He left his fingerprints all over the store's safe; which just happens to be twenty miles away from where the Corvette was torched—at basically the exact same time."

"Which means that Frank couldn't have killed Dan."

"Not unless O'Connell was capable of being in two places at once. Our dead puzzle-man just got himself an alibi."

CHAPTER

36

The sun had almost set, and Munnatawket Beach was in the process of turning a gentle coralline hue that simultaneously reflected and softened the more vivid colors of the sky. The ocean's expanse had become a pale crimson, the foam on the breaking waves was strawberry-pink, and the light beaming into Belle and Rosco's faces was so rosy and healthful that it made them appear rejuvenated and carefree rather than anxious and careworn.

"So now the Feds and Abe have confirmed that the fingerprints on the Corvette belong to none other than Rob Rossi—which, in turn, is currently inspiring a major manhunt for a guy whose previous notoriety was how fast he could open beers. . . ." Belle was thinking aloud as she walked, head down and heedless of the beauty of the evening.

Rosco didn't bother to respond. They'd been analyzing Abe's newest discovery for the past twenty minutes, which was why they'd driven to the beach. As similar seaside trips had done many times in the past, this evening's ocean air and sand-between-the-toes stroll was intended to clear their brains and give them a much-needed time out, as well as providing Kit and Gabby with ample opportunity for stick and ball chasing.

"So Frank *wasn't* involved in Dan's death, but Rob *was*. . . ." Belle continued to mutter while Rosco picked up an ancient and now salt-soaked tennis ball and heaved it back down the beach from whence it just had been retrieved. Both dogs tore after it, sending up small clouds of russet sand in their wake.

"I guess you wouldn't want to fetch a stick if I threw it, would you?" Rosco said to his wife. He raised a piece of driftwood in the air. "On your mark—"

She looked at him in bewilderment. "What?"

"I said, I guess you wouldn't like chasing after this."

"Chasing after . . . ?"

"Never mind. It was a joke."

"A joke?"

Rosco shook his head. "As in, what I said was supposed to be *amusing.*"

Belle frowned in thought. "You're not comparing me to one of our four-legged friends, are you?"

Rosco chuckled. "To both of them, actually. When have you known either of those two to relinquish something they're wrestling with?"

"Is this a hint to get me to stop talking about murder accomplices?"

"Boy, is your brain clicking tonight."

"Very funny." But instead of following Rosco's suggestion, Belle returned to her examination of the Tacete case. "If Rob killed Dan, and Frank had a legitimate—or *not* so legitimate alibi—then was Rob setting Frank up to take the fall? Look like the guilty party? Ergo: Did Rossi strangle Frank?"

"Belle, this is supposed to be a relaxing walk."

"It is, isn't it? I know I'm relaxed."

"Liar, liar. You are not. Your shoulders are tensed; your forehead is in knots."

"Well, this is a *knotty* problem," was her swift reply, "*not* the least of which is how all these suspicious characters are *tied* together."

"Well, let's see, there's the Karen connection," Rosco offered.

"You mean as the mastermind behind her husband's murder?"

"It's happened before. And by her own admission a little over an hour ago, we know that Karen comes from a less than savory background. . . ."

Belle deliberated quietly as Rosco continued his thought. "I realize Karen told us otherwise, but what if she knew all along that Dan was sleeping with Bonnie? What better way to hurt Bonnie than to pin Dan's death on her brother—and then have the brother killed?"

"By Rob?" Belle asked.

"Sure, why not? Al and Abe have connected him to the Corvette. . . . And you just mentioned him as Frank's potential murderer."

Belle released a slow and pensive breath. "That's an awfully evil scenario, Rosco."

"Homicide isn't generally applauded for its niceties."

Belle cocked her head to one side. "Thank you for reminding me."

"Don't mention it."

She sighed again while her brain went back into high gear. "Why stop there, Rosco? Why not toss Jack Wagner into the witches' brew, too? He could have been lusting after Karen . . . and then connived to get Dan out of the way for good. Jack must have realized Bonnie and Dan were an item; maybe Wagner even knew the sordid truth about his partner's less-than-peachy marriage. Perhaps he convinced himself he was rescuing the lovely Mrs. Tacete."

"*If* Wagner killed Dan. Which, I admit, is still not out of the realm of possibility."

"Or he found someone to do his dirty work for him.

Namely, Rob Rossi. We know Rob spent some time at the Smile! office. Wagner certainly had the opportunity to approach him." Belle picked up a stick and began doodling in the damp sand while Rosco accepted the tennis ball from the triumphant Kit and threw it again. As before, both dogs took off like a shot.

Belle wrote FRANK, then drew a line joining it to BONNIE, and another connecting them both to ROB. She squinted at her work. "Wait, I'm forgetting CARLOS and ED. . . . So much for my tidy triangle. . . ." She added those names, rubbing out lines and creating new ones, and in the center of the circle drew a poor facsimile of a sheep.

"I take it that refers to the notorious tavern," Rosco observed.

Belle studied the picture. "I guess the beast looks more like Gabby than a member of the *ovis* family," she admitted. "I must be better at depicting dogs than ruminants."

"Well, you're good at *ruminating,*" Rosco said before adding, "Is this supposed to be leading us somewhere, Belle?"

"I don't know. . . . I just like writing things out."

"Maybe you should put all these folks in a crossword."

"That's right! I forgot Frank's crosswords . . . and the money found in his apartment." She scratched dollar symbols into the sand and beside them wrote X-WORDS.

Rosco chortled, and pointed at Belle's scribbles in the sand. "X marks the spot."

"If you're not going to help, I'd appreciate your keeping your comments to yourself." But her heart wasn't in her gibe, because she'd already refocused on her expanding diagram. Belle added KAREN to the list, then drew an arrow from her name to the dollar marks.

"What's that for?" Rosco asked.

"She needs money, doesn't she? If what she told us is true, that Dan left her high and dry."

"Which your outline definitely isn't. There's an ocean about six feet behind your back."

"Rosco! Stop!"

"No humor. I forgot. We're deadly serious tonight." He took up his own stick and began making additional arrows connecting everyone at the Black Sheep to the money symbols. "Looks like cash is everyone's motive," he muttered aloud. "However, don't forget that it was Karen who gave up the ransom money in the first place."

"Maybe she expected a bigger payoff down the road, and we're not seeing it," was Belle's deliberate response. Then she added JACK to her suspects, and began rattling off a number of words. "Jack . . . dough, beans, cabbage, lettuce, mint leaves—"

"Mint leaves?" Rosco asked her.

"It's slang for paper money."

"Ahhh . . ." Any potential retort was interrupted as Gabby returned with the ball clutched in her mouth. Her curly topknot and little beard appeared the essence of smug pride. "You finally beat your big sister to the prize, did you, Gabsters?" Rosco chortled. "Good for you." He threw the ball for the two dogs again, then turned back to Belle. "Maybe we need some *tea* leaves to help us solve the puzzle."

But Belle wasn't listening because she was too busy writing DAN TACETE in the sand. "It's weird how names sometimes mirror people's professions, isn't it?"

"You mean like Doctor Brayne for a brain surgeon or Fischer for an oceanographer?"

Belle nodded. "The first time I met Karen Tacete and learned what her husband did for a living, I thought, wow, that's sure an odd coincidence." Belle paused to look into her husband's face. It was obvious he didn't have a clue what she was referring to. "Didn't I tell you about this already?"

"Not that I recall, but that doesn't mean—"

Belle interrupted. "The name's an Italian slang term taken from the verb *tacére,* which means to be silent. *Tacete* translates to 'Hold your tongue!' or 'Hold your jaw!' "

"That's quite a moniker for someone whose profession is dentistry. . . . More subtle than Doctor Paine, though."

"Mm hm . . ." Belle agreed as she returned to her diagram and began making additional lines. "Okay . . . here's DAN . . . and he's having an affair with BONNIE who's brother's a felon. . . . KAREN'S the wronged wife, JACK's the partner who may or may not be involved in shady business practices . . . ROB and CARLOS and ED are some of the patients DAN has been treating at a reduced rate, and JACK doesn't like those scroungy types hanging around his swanky office." Belle's words suddenly ceased. She looked at her husband.

"Maybe we've been looking at this situation from the wrong perspective, Rosco!" she said in a quick, excited gush. She jabbed at the names in the sand. "All these folks are connected to DAN, which is true, but look, here he is, at the center of everything: FRANK, ROB, KAREN, everyone . . . ! What if none of them were conspiring against Dan . . . ? What if *he's* the one who's been plotting against *them,* all along . . . ? Including you and me by getting us tangled up in this mess by staging a phony kidnapping. Dan knew we were friends of Karen's and that she'd turn to us right away. Maybe he's been one step ahead of us at every turn."

"Whoa . . . whoa . . . whoa . . . Hold on. . . . You're saying Tacete staged his own death?"

Belle scarcely heard her husband's question. "Rob's prints are on the burned Corvette. He vanished at the same time Dan went missing. . . . The body Carlyle examined was so badly damaged it could only be identified by dental records. What if it *wasn't* Dan who died in the Corvette? What if it was Rob?" Belle gazed at her husband, her expression triumphant. "Which would make it a perfect crime, Rosco! Dan kills Rob, but makes it looks as though Rob killed *him!*"

This time Rosco frowned. "Let me get this straight. Doctor Dan Tacete, an otherwise respected member of the community, arranges to murder a fairly marginal guy who holds down a job in a local dive and in the process fakes his own death . . . I'm afraid I just don't see the motive, Belle."

"That's because we haven't gotten to that part."

"I see . . . but you're about to explain it. Is that it?"

"Well, no . . . I don't have a handle on that quite yet."

"At the risk of being critical, I think I should point out that homicide usually involves a motive. It's a cause and effect kind of thing."

"Hear me out, Rosco!"

"I'm all ears."

"Okay . . . whatever Dan's motive was—and I agree he had to have a compelling reason for his actions—he arranged the scenario months ago. Maybe he even solicited Rob to become a patient. They were more or less the same physical type . . . all Dan had to do was exchange Rob Rossi's dental records for his own."

"Uh-huh . . . and he keeps Rob happy as a patient while luring the guy to his death. . . ."

"You're not taking me seriously, Rosco!"

"I'm trying to, Belle, but logic keeps getting in my way. And how does Frank play into this . . . uh . . . *inventive* scenario?"

"Dan killed him, too, of course—after setting him up to look like a kidnapper. He needed a clean ending to it all, so that the police would think the entire matter is wrapped up."

"Ohhhh, Belle, I don't know . . ."

"Sure . . . Dan must have known all about Frank's nefarious dealings because of Bonnie, so he was able to coerce him into going up to Boston the night of the supposed kidnapping . . . and putting in an appearance at Sonny's Autobody—" Belle gasped again. "Unless . . . No, wait . . . Why not . . . ? This works. This really works. It wasn't Frank in those gas station surveillance videos, after all; it was Dan wearing a wig and baseball cap. And the mustache! The one Dan recently grew that Karen thought was sexy, but that Lily didn't like . . . ? Frank and Rob both had mustaches, so Rob's body—!"

"Belle, stop. This theory of yours is getting a little crazy. Besides, I keep coming back to motive. Dan's a successful guy, has a nice home, a good practice. Okay, maybe he shouldn't have been fooling around on the side, and maybe O'Connell was threatening to expose his affair with Bonnie. But all Dan had to do was 'fess up to his wife. It wouldn't have been the end of the world. Besides, she'd already guessed he was cheating on her. . . . Arranging two murders to cover up his tracks seems overkill to me."

"As it were," Belle said, then frowned.

"Right. And what about the crossword puzzles? Did Tacete construct those, too? And then leave them in the apartment as some sort of proof that Frank was, in reality, a brainy and misunderstood guy?"

"That's a clever touch, besides fitting perfectly into my supposition that Dan was using us from the very beginning. He was convinced that we'd get involved, and he was right."

Rosco shook his head and stared down at the diagram.

"You don't like my theory because you didn't dream it up," Belle groused.

He laughed and then said, "No, I'm not buying it because I don't see a *reason* behind the crimes."

As the couple stood there talking, a larger wave than the others crashed behind them and sent a pool of water speeding up the beach. In a moment, their bare feet felt the shock of cold, May water; a second later, Belle's picture was wiped away.

"A clean slate," Rosco observed with a half-smile. "So . . . do we start all over from the beginning?"

Belle gazed at her husband. "A clean slate. Maybe, that's exactly what Dan wanted—a perfectly clean slate."

CHAPTER

37

"I gotta tell you, Poly—crates, this is not the kind of thing that will improve your endearment-rating with our buddy, Herb Caryle. . . ." Al Lever's voice rumbled out of the speaker-phone in Belle's home office. Despite the hardboiled-detective act, it was abundantly clear he was relishing the fact that the mayor's brother had dropped the ball yet another time. In proof of which, Al permitted himself a self-satisfied chuckle while Belle and Rosco exchanged a knowing glance. Perched atop the desk, she leaned closer to Al's disembodied voice while Rosco hunched forward in his chair to better hear the words. "Coward that I am, Poly—crates, I sent Jones down to check up on Carlyle's Tacete file. I was in no mood to confront Mr. Personality first thing in the morning. . . . Anyway, it seems your lovely lady just might be on to something."

"Meaning?" Husband and wife demanded in unison. After explaining Belle's theory to Lever the previous evening, the couple had spent a restless night awaiting Jones return to the NPD and his positive confirmation—or lack thereof—of Carlyle's autopsy report on Dan Tacete. It was now ten A.M., and sleep deprivation, coffee, and only a cursory nod at

nourishment had made the pair jittery and apprehensive—
Belle, especially. "Meaning what, Al?" she repeated.

"Arrgh . . ." Lever replied with another chortle, "You
have me on the speaker phone? I can't believe it. This completely shatters the image I've always had of you two; cozy-
ing up the telephone receiver, ear-to-ear, listening to your
incoming calls as though you had Krazy Glue stuck to the
sides of your heads."

"Get to the point, Al. Please." Belle released a sigh that
indicated eagerness rather than indignation.

"The *point,* Miss Impatient," Lever continued, "is that
your supposedly harebrained notion may very well be correct. Ostensibly, the quickest method of corpse identification
is through dental records, especially when the remains are
charred beyond recognition. So when Carlyle made the match,
he never looked further. And in Herb's defense, there's no
listing of blood type on many dental records, so he assumed
Tacete was type A—same as the corpse. If our favorite dentist
hadn't had an emergency appendectomy a year and a half ago,
no one would've been the wiser."

Belle and Rosco could hear Al strike a match and inhale
on his cigarette. Belle half expected smoke to begin drifting
through the phone. "So the blood types don't match?" she
asked. Her voice quivered.

"Nope. They sure don't. Tacete's a type O. The body in
the Corvette was type A."

"And Rob Rossi?" Rosco said. "Do we know his blood
type is yet?"

"Oh, yeah, that was all with his military records. He's A,
as well."

"I was right," Belle murmured, and then her spine un-
expectedly bent as though a heavy weight had been thrust
upon her shoulders. She'd expected that confirmation of her
hunch would please her, but it only produced a wave of
sadness.

"I'd say the chances are ninety-nine percent that you're
on the money," was Al's response. And considering the fact

that we have Rossi's fingerprints all over the 'Vette, and that
no one has seen him since well before the accident . . . Who
else's body could be sitting in the morgue? I'm having Abe
run the DNA tests now for a positive confirmation, but that
almost seems a moot point."

"I take it you've already notified the federal agencies?"
Rosco asked, although he knew exactly what his ex-partner's
response would be.

"Absolutely. I'm not waiting around for any DNA tests,
that's for sure. One thing is certain: If Tacete's alive, and it
sure looks like he is, then he's gonna do his best to get the
heck out of the country. The Feds have transmitted his
photo to every airport and Canadian border crossing in New
England. If he's still in America, he's staying in America."

"Belle and I also discussed the fact that it may have been
Tacete who took the Explorer to Sonny's Autobody, as well
as tanking up at those two gas stations and getting the vehicle repainted in Boston—which means he was successfully
impersonating O'Connell by wearing a wig and coloring his
mustache."

"I imagine he's already tossed that disguise Poly—crates,
but you're right, he may be sporting another. I'll pass the info
along."

They said their goodbyes, and Belle tapped the button to
disconnect the call. Then she looked at her husband. "This
all seemed so . . . I don't know . . . otherworldly and unreal
as a theory. . . . But here it is, and instead of feeling vindi-
cated and proud, I simply feel sick."

Rosco stood and walked behind his wife, placing his
hands on her shoulders and rubbing them. "I know what
you mean. . . . The idea that Dan was so premeditated . . .
finding someone his own weight and build—Rob Rossi;
luring him into his office, growing a mustache, switching
the dental records, all the while knowing full well that he
was going to murder the poor schlub. . . . And then setting
O'Connell up as the ineffectual kidnapper; and again,
knowing Frank was going to die. . . . It takes a special kind

of brain to maintain that level of emotional disconnect."

"Not to mention the effects on his wife and step-daughter. At best, he realized he'd leave them with the memory of a kidnapping and fiery death; at the worst . . ." Belle's words trailed off; her head bent in empathy.

Rosco had no answer; instead, he massaged his wife's weary muscles.

"Do you think Dan had help?" Belle asked at last. "I mean, did he do this by himself, or could Bonnie have acted as an accomplice?"

"I can't believe she'd set up her own brother to be murdered."

Belle thought for a long moment. "I'd like to agree with you, but the fact is that some siblings loathe one another. Fratricide is a word of Latin origin. And let's not forget Cain and Abel." Belle grew silent again, then, at length, added a resigned "I'm guessing—just *guessing,* mind you—that Bonnie may be in on the crime, and that she's planning to hang around Newcastle for another few months and then hook up with Dan somewhere out of the country."

"If that's the case . . . she gave us one heck of a performance yesterday."

Belle's head jerked up. She stared hard at her husband. "Yesterday, we were accusing Frank of killing *Dan* . . . which Bonnie was denying up and down. She didn't have to pretend because Frank *didn't* kill Dan."

"I don't know, Belle. . . . That's an awfully messy picture you're painting; and Dan planned this thing too carefully to leave behind a flake like Bonnie—and then trust to heaven that she was going to keep her mouth shut about the entire thing. That's a dangerous loose end to leave dangling."

"*Tacete* . . ." Belle murmured, giving the word a proper Italian accent, and then offering up its translation, "Shut your mouth. . . ." She closed her eyes briefly, then opened them. When she did, their gray color had darkened with resolve. "He's killed two people, already. Why not a third?"

Rosco folded his arms across his chest. "Bonnie?"

"If she helped him carry off this scheme, he doesn't really have a choice, does he?"

Rosco and Belle drove directly to Smile!, where they learned that Bonnie had called in sick first thing that morning. It was now ten to eleven; time seemed to be conspiring against them. "Maybe she's already flown the coop," Belle said after the couple had returned to their car and begun driving toward Bonnie's apartment complex. "Maybe our interrogation yesterday sent her running to Dan; maybe he's—" Belle bit off her words, reflexively gripping the door handle.

"Don't do this to yourself," was Rosco's quiet reply. "You're not responsible for Bonnie's actions—or for Dan's. Besides, if the theory you've been spinning out is correct, then Bonnie's an accessory to murder. Two murders, in fact."

"Nobody deserves to be killed in cold blood," Belle observed in a hollow tone.

"I take it you're not referring to Rob and Frank?"

She sighed but made no further answer, and they continued on in silence until they pulled up in front of Bonnie's home. As luck would have it, Bonnie was just emerging from her front door with Carlos Quintero. "Well, at least we're not too late," Belle said as she threw open the car door.

"Assuming we're looking at the real Carlos and not Dan in disguise," Rosco tossed in, but there was nothing amused in the sound of his words.

As Belle and Rosco approached the pair, Carlos stepped in front of Bonnie. He'd assumed full bodyguard pose: arms straight, palms out as if preparing for a shoving match, knees bent, feet firmly planted.

"Bonnie told me all about you, doll. You weren't looking for any waitress job, and your hubby here is a PI. Bonnie, ain't answering any more of your questions, so you'd better just clear out. Go back where you came from. Both of you."

It was Rosco who responded. "There have been two homicides in Newcastle county during the past week, Quintero.

Either one carries with it a life sentence. If you're involved, then your behavior here is probably justified. However, if you're not involved, and you choose to interfere with any conversation with Ms. O'Connell, then you're in danger of becoming accessory to the fact and being charged with obstruction of justice."

Before Carlos could answer, Bonnie pushed her way forward. "What do you mean, *two* murders?" Her voice was raspy and frightened.

"Your brother didn't commit suicide, Bonnie," Belle said in a level tone, "he was murdered and—"

But before the sentence could be completed, Bonnie had fainted. Carlos caught her upper body in his arms, and then he lowered her slowly onto the concrete sidewalk, where he began fanning her face. Her skin was bluish-white and covered with a sheen of perspiration. There was no faking her physical distress.

"What do you mean Frank was murdered?" Carlos asked in utter confusion, "Bonnie said he hung himself."

Rosco handed Carlos his jacket. "Here. Put that under her head, and get her legs in the air. Sit down by her feet, and put them in your lap." Rosco dropped down onto one knee and checked Bonnie's pulse. Belle moved to the other side of the prone woman so that she would cast a shadow over her face. Rosco added a businesslike, "The autopsy concluded that Frank was first strangled and then hung in his apartment. The killer's intention was to make the death look like a suicide."

Bonnie's eyes flickered as she slowly regained consciousness. She gazed up at Rosco, Belle, and Carlos, and then closed her eyes again as if hoping the bad dream would disappear.

"Did you hear me telling you what happened to Frank?" Belle asked her.

Bonnie nodded, but instead of responding with speech, she began to cry. Abundant tears flowed from her cheeks into the red hair spread upon the pavement.

"You know who killed your brother, don't you?" Belle continued.

Bonnie opened her eyes and stared straight up into the sky. She made no other movement.

"And you know about Rob, too?" Belle prodded.

"Rob?" Bonnie echoed. She stared at Belle.

"That it was *his* body found in the Corvette."

"No . . . it was . . . Dan . . ." Bonnie began struggling into a sitting position. "It was my Dan. . . ."

Above Bonnie's head, Belle and Rosco looked at each other.

"You're certain of that?" Rosco asked.

"That's what the police told me." Bonnie's eyes searched first Belle's face and then Rosco's. "And that lieutenant friend of yours—"

"Bon, you know you shouldn't be talking to these people here without a lawyer present," Carlos interrupted, but she was having none of his advice.

"Shut up, Carlos! I haven't done anything wrong!" She turned back to Belle. "You said someone killed my brother."

"And we think you know who it was," Rosco replied.

Bonnie looked at Carlos. "How could I . . . ? I don't know all the lowlifes Frankie used to hang out with. . . . He was into a lot of dumb things. I already told you people that. . . ." Again her words faltered. Then she gasped.

"It . . . was . . . Dan, wasn't it?" she mumbled at length. "He's not dead. . . . He . . . he . . . he set all this up, didn't he?" Her eyes jumped toward Belle, then as rapidly fell away. "That note . . ." she whispered, "I knew that note couldn't be Frankie's. It wasn't his language . . . it was Dan's. It was *Dan* saying goodbye to *me*. . . . He knew the letter would end up in my hands. He knew I'd be the one reading it over and over. And he must have done those puzzles, too, because Frankie—" Bonnie's words halted abruptly; she sat fully erect, hugging her knees to her chest and lowering her head until her face was nearly hidden. Her shoulders shook with grief.

"The police believe you helped plan this," Rosco lied as he rose to his feet. "That you and Tacete—and your brother—arranged to drug and murder Rossi—"

"Hey . . . hey!" Carlos piped in. "You gotta read the lady her rights. She's allowed to have a lawyer present if—"

But Bonnie overrode him. "What you're saying would mean that I let Dan kill my brother! Why would I do that? Why would I do anything as horrible as that?"

"That's right," Carlos insisted. "Bonnie wouldn't ever have—"

Rosco wasn't finished, however. "And you and Tacete then placed Rossi's body in the driver's seat and set the car ablaze. . . ."

"No!" Bonnie yelled, and Carlos immediately came to her aid.

"Back off, buddy, why don'tcha? Can't you see the lady's upset? Look, if you're saying Tacete's still alive and that he killed Frankie, then that's that. But I know Bonnie; she wouldn't do nothin' to hurt her brother. Never in a million years."

"Why would Tacete have wanted to kill Frank O'Connell?" Rosco demanded of Carlos.

Carlos shrugged; his gaze left Bonnie and began instead to wander across the grass. "Frankie was into this . . . blackmail stuff. . . . Sorry, kiddo, but your bro told me all about it. . . . I mean, like, he was kinda proud, like he'd invented the greatest scam of all time."

Rosco studied Carlos. "What did Frank have on Dan?"

"He knew about Bonnie and the doc. I guess he was threatening to tell the wifey."

"So, Frank was demanding money . . . ?"

"Nah, man, OxyContin. See, Tacete wrote prescriptions, and then Frankie sold the Oxy to other dudes at way-out prices. . . . Well, yeah, sometimes there was cash, too."

"Just can it, Carlos," Bonnie snapped. "Nobody needs to know that stuff!"

"Sure they do, Bon. Because if these people are right about

the doc, then he's gettin' off scot-free. Don't you want to see Tacete do time for killin' your brother, even?"

"Shut up, Carlos," Bonnie snarled again. "Don't say anything else, okay?"

"What else is there?" Carlos asked; his face was clouded in confusion.

"Just don't say any more. That's all."

"How long had you and Doctor Tacete been having an affair?" Belle's query was gentle. She sensed that Bonnie was still concealing something, and she hoped that a nonconfrontational manner would keep the words flowing.

"I don't know," was the nervous reply, "three or four months maybe."

Carlos shook his head. "Come on, Bon, that's such a crock. You've been foolin' around with Tacete for at least a year now. 'Cause last summer, Frankie told me you—"

"Butt out, Carlos. You don't know what you're talking about."

Again, Rosco and Belle shared a look, and an almost imperceptible nod of agreement passed between them. "Frank knew you took Dan's Explorer to Boston to be repaired, didn't he?" Rosco said.

Bonnie didn't reply, although she gripped her knees tighter.

Rosco leaned down. "You put on a blonde wig and you told the mechanic you'd hit a deer while driving through New Hampshire. But it wasn't a deer, was it? It was the Snyder boy, and it happened right around the corner—"

"No!" Bonnie cried out.

"DNA samples lifted from the Explorer's tires match perfectly with the Snyder case," Rosco once again lied. "We know it was the same vehicle."

"I didn't do it. I swear I didn't!"

"Then why did you take the car to Boston be repaired?"

Bonnie hunched her shoulders and lowered her chin, but she refused to answer.

"Come on, Bonnie," Rosco growled. "You never went to

New Hampshire, but you were using Dan's car. . . . Or you and Frank had borrowed the Explorer, and Frank killed that boy, and you knew the cops would throw the book at him—"

Bonnie began to sob. "No! That's not how it went. . . . Okay . . . okay, yes, I was there when the boy died . . . but Frankie wasn't. He wasn't anywhere near the place. . . . Dan was driving, not me. . . . I know Dan should have stopped. I begged him to stop and go back. It wasn't right to just leave that poor kid lying in the street like that . . . but Dan said the boy was dead, and there was nothing we could do. He told me if we got involved and called the cops that Karen would find out about us."

"But your brother learned the truth."

Bonnie nodded. "I should never have told him . . . but I was so shook up. And then Dan made me pretend to be Karen when I took the car to be fixed. He said it had to be a woman because of the registration. He got me the wig and everything—even some of Karen's clothes. . . . But I was just so scared." Bonnie's tears increased. "That's why Dan kept paying Frankie. Money, real money, not just the Oxycontin like Carlos says. . . . I begged Frankie to leave it alone, but he just wouldn't. He said he wanted to be on easy street for once in his life. And Dan, well, I mean, he didn't seem to mind that much. He kept telling me he was helping my brother through a rough patch. . . . And now Frankie's dead—" By this time Bonnie was sobbing heavily. "I should have told the police about the Snyder boy. I know that. But Dan said I'd be blamed, too. He told me we'd both go to jail . . . and . . . and what I'd done when I took the car to Craigor was illegal, too. Like you said, an 'accessory,' or something . . ."

"So Tacete arranged it so that you'd be forced to take the fall for the Snyder death." It was Carlos who made this gloomy observation. "Man, Bonnie . . . I always said that guy was a snake. I knew he was no good for you from the git-go. A married guy with a kid. A person like that shouldn't have no chick on the side. . . ."

Carlos didn't continue, and Bonnie made no effort to challenge or correct him.

"And you truly believed that Dan had been kidnapped and then killed?" Belle asked.

"Yes," was the muffled reply. "Yes, that's what I thought. That's what everyone said. Why wouldn't I think it was true?"

"You should have come forward after the Snyder accident," Belle said, as sympathetically as she could. "It was an awful situation, but it *was* an accident."

"I couldn't. Don't you see? I mean, a thing like that . . . and me in the car. What would it have done to Karen and that cute little girl of theirs? I loved Dan. I didn't want to ruin his good name."

Belle looked down at Bonnie. "Maybe you should have been worrying about your own good name."

CHAPTER

38

"Let me get this straight; see if I'm putting two and two together and coming up with four . . . ," Martha said as she doled out a second cup of coffee to Abe Jones; at the exact same moment, her other hand passed a stainless steel pitcher containing heavy cream toward Belle. Lawson's and its loyal patrons didn't believe in heat-sealed, personalized creamers—either for the genuine cow-produced variety or for artificial "whitening agents." Cream was cream, just as maple syrup was maple syrup; they were thick and comforting liquids that needed proper pouring spouts and handles that were easy to grasp. "So, Bella-Bella, you and your hubby, and Big Al here, just learned that Tacete had pulled this same weird stunt before?"

"Well not precisely the same, Martha," Belle answered. "But we did find out he'd successfully accomplished two previous vanishing acts—"

"That you know of," Sara interrupted.

"Correct," Belle said. "That we know of."

"And did the others also involve murder?" Martha demanded.

"No one's certain yet," Al said in response, "but the prognosis sure points in that direction. One of the cases involved what was originally termed a 'suspicious death.' That was in Indiana where his *then* wife accidentally died of carbon monoxide poisoning. At the time, the police in South Bend didn't like the looks of the situation, so they listed her husband as a 'person of interest.' But they weren't able to pin anything on the apparently grief-stricken widower—who then just up and disappeared. Of course, his name wasn't Tacete back then."

"But they're reopening the investigation?" Martha prompted.

"Oh, you betcha," Al replied evenly. "Both cases. The one in Indiana *and* the one in Florida. Our boy was a real rolling stone before the Feds nabbed him for 'allegedly' killing Frank O'Connell and Rob Rossi."

"Allegedly, shmedgedly," Martha barked out. "Rob Rossi *accidentally* put himself in a car and dropped into a fiery ball at the bottom of ravine? And O'Connell strangled himself by *mistake?* Tell me another one, Al!"

"Oh, they'll pin those deaths on our tooth doc, all right," Lever answered in a grimmer tone, "with a little help from yours truly and Doctor Jones, here." Al took a sip of his coffee. He didn't seem to notice that it was no longer piping hot, or even lukewarm.

"Wow . . . Two other times . . . and maybe even more . . ." was all Martha could think to respond. Then she did the unthinkable. She plunked herself down at the table with Sara, Abe, Belle, and Al, the current stalwarts of the Breakfast Bunch. Rosco was missing from the group. He'd told Belle he had a couple of details on the Porto case to tie up before he could join the Lawson's crowd.

"Wow . . ." Martha repeated while the others regarded her with concern, wondering if she'd suddenly taken ill. "What a creep!" she muttered. "Sneaking out on his wife and step-kid . . . and trying to pin the Snyder boy's death on that poor doofus, Bonnie—"

"Not to mention what he did to his buddies O'Connell

and Rossi," Abe Jones observed in his own steely tone.

"You know something, gorgeous?" was Martha's swift retort. "In my book, killing a couple of guys is a lesser sin than *plotting* to desert a wife and little girl. Okay, so the crumb-bum sets up Rossi and O'Connell, acts all friendly and helpful—probably even tells Rob he admires his 'stache and wants to grow one just like it—all the while thinking, *You're dead meat, fellas. Adios, amigos. . . .* But at the same time, the cretin's *also* inventing the special hell he's going to inflict on his family. . . . Imagine dreaming up that kind of scheme! That's a twisted brain, that's what it is! It's downright evil. Just think how that child's going to grow up after the horrible shenanigans committed by her supposedly loving step-dad. Just think what she's been through."

"And her mother," Sara added.

"Right. And Karen," Martha said with a heavy sigh. "Boy, oh boy . . ." She slumped against the table, her usually bird-sharp eyes glazed over and sad.

"Are you feeling okay, Martha?" Belle asked after a moment.

"Huh? Sure . . . yeah . . ." But Lawson's ruling waitress didn't look too certain.

"I could take care of your customers if you want to sit here and rest for a bit," Belle offered. "I worked as a waitress in college. I was actually pretty good."

"I can help," Sara tossed in, swinging her legs genteelly toward the side of the banquette.

"No way, Sara." Martha shook her head and smiled, albeit feebly. "The day Newcastle's reigning queen-mum starts slinging java in a Pyrex carafe instead of serving it in an antique silver coffee set is the day I resign." Then she made a sound that was half chuckle and half groan. "Look at me, sitting down on the job! I must be losing my marbles. If Mr. Lawson saw me acting like this he'd call the padded wagon."

"Well, it's a rotten situation," Belle responded in a gentle tone. "It's upset us all. The fact that Dan—or whatever his real name is—was so knowingly cruel can't help but give us the willies. . . . And then there's the whole bizarre situation with the crosswords he kept sending me under various aliases. I don't know why I never thought to line up the initials in the names instead of merely studying solutions and clues—W.H. Everts, the supposed creator of 'Baby Steps'; Randy E. Isaacs who allegedly submitted 'Sugar and Spice'; Sal D. Anderson, fictional author of 'As Time Goes By'; Nicky O. Flanagan, the bogus constructor of 'Frankly, Dear'; and a phony Frank T. O'Connell—all of which spell out WHERE IS DAN OFF TO? Talk about playing nasty mind games!"

"No one could have imagined Dan Tacete would put his own name in the crosswords, Belle, dear," Sara said. "I would employ the word hubris to describe his action, but there was something far more vicious at work."

"Which fit the perp's M.O. to a T, Mrs. B," Al interjected.

"Sounds like you're aiming to start writing song lyrics, Big Al. Though you don't particularly fit the natty Cole Porter or Noel Coward image." Martha made this lackluster attempt at a wisecrack, then she stood and distractedly smoothed the wrinkles from her rustling pink skirt. "What on earth is keeping that hubby of yours?" The question verged on the petulant. Her ordinarily breezy manner had definitely not returned.

It was Al who answered. He forced a companionable chortle as he spoke. "Poly—crates sure opened a big can of worms with that Porto scam. Now Sonny's lawyer's screaming at Sonny's *mother's* lawyer, accusing her of being the mastermind of the entire heist while Sonny was just a stooge with a big smile and engaging manner. . . . Seems he really didn't know anything about the Porto thefts—if you can believe his attorney. His loving mom was running the entire operation, both the legit business and the chop-shop sideline and keeping her baby boy in the dark. I gather she believed 'ignorance is bliss' is the only way to raise a child."

"Another happy family," Martha threw in darkly. "Well, all I can say is, you're a fortunate gal, Belle. Rosco's true blue—besides being a handsome son of a gun."

"I know, Martha," was Belle's thoughtful reply. "And I thank my lucky stars every day."

"How come you're not passing out compliments in my direction, Miss M?" Abe jibed.

"You may be gorgeous, Doctor Jones, but you're not married like my man Rosco. And married men who are good and kind don't grow on trees. Look at Dan Tacete or whatever his name is. . . . And look at those poor women who trusted him . . . Karen, Bonnie . . . the dames in Florida and Indiana . . . What's wrong with us gals, anyway? Why do so many of us need to be victims?"

The question silenced them all again, and Martha continued to stand beside the table, the now cold carafe forgotten in her hand while the restaurant's other patrons tried without success to catch her eye. "At least the doc's locked up for good," she insisted loudly and angrily, "and I hope they throw away the key. In fact, I hope they forget he's in a jail cell and don't bother to give him any chow."

"Well, we're all going to need to rally around Karen and Lily," Sara said after another somber pause. "They'll need our help and support."

"*If* Karen decides to stay in Newcastle," Belle replied.

"Well, I hope she does," Sara insisted. "I realize she'll have to move to a less-costly domicile, but well, I'm prepared to do my part and supply any aid she might need in future."

Belle looked at the old lady and smiled in gratitude and love. "You're a peach, Sara, do you know that?"

"When I wish to be. Only when I wish to be."

"No, all the time." Belle touched her friend's hand, and as she did she caught Martha's eye. Belle was surprised to see two tears rolling down the rouged and powdered cheeks of Lawson's famous wiseacre and skeptic.

"You know what?" she murmured. "That damn guy nearly got away with murder. And he would have, too, if it weren't for certain people sitting right here at this table."

"But what were Dan's plans for Bonnie?" Belle interrupted in a small voice, although she'd intuited the answer already.

"Another homicide, in all probability," Al said. "He couldn't have left her alone to blab to the whole world, which she would have done eventually. Especially if he had no plans to take her with him."

"Who knows," Abe added with a taut and unforgiving shrug, "maybe that's why he was heading back toward New-castle when the Feds picked him up on Friday."

"And to think that the brother Karen never met didn't even exist. . . ." Belle continued in her subdued tone. "He was just another one of Dan's manipulative fictions. Dan had to know how much that hurt her—"

"As opposed to his affair with Bonnie?" Abe interjected. "Or the circumstances surrounding his 'loving' marriage? Or the fact that he was living high off the hog all the while knowing that his wife and step-daughter would be left with nothing?"

"Except his expensive collection of automobiles," Sara said.

"Which is what ultimately did him in," Jones continued in the same embittered voice. "He just couldn't let his pre-cious LT-5 Corvette burn up in the ravine. He had to take it with him. It was a *car* thing all along. I believe I said that a month ago at this very table."

"And to think I once considered that Karen might have arranged to have her husband killed," Belle admitted with a guilty sigh.

"We all came to that conclusion," Lever told her. "Your hubby, too. Speaking of whom . . ." A genuine grin began spreading across Al's face as he looked out the window and across the street. Rosco was in the process of parking his "new" car directly in front of the fire hydrant.

Martha followed Al's gaze, she looked at Rosco's car, then she glanced down at Belle. "Oh, honey . . . ," she murmured in real sympathy, "I'm so, so sorry . . . but you should never let men go shopping by themselves. . . . You never know what they'll drag home. . . ."

Belle and Abe and Sara turned in their seats and watched as Rosco flipped down the sun visor to display a police parking permit he considered part of his NPD retirement package. Studying the scene, Abe Jones couldn't help but laugh. "I guess there's a certain amount of truth to the adage that you can't teach an old dog new tricks."

"Well, I think it's a . . . it's a . . . delightful vehicle, Belle, dear," Sara offered in a hesitant manner while Belle stood and dropped her napkin on the table. Instead of looking mournful, however, she was smiling brightly, almost seraphically.

"Where on earth did he find it!? It's an exact double for the red Jeep he was driving the day I met him." She hurried out of Lawson's, rushed across the street, and gave her husband a long and loving kiss. Through the window, their friends could see the couple in excited and animated conversation. Whatever anyone else's assessment of Rosco's surprise purchase, it was clear that both husband and wife were thrilled.

Al chuckled as he leaned back against the pink vinyl seat. "The ride's twenty years old, only has forty thousand miles on it, and no body-rot, from what I could tell."

"You knew about this scheme in advance, Albert?" Sara asked. Her chiding tone conveyed the fact that she thought he'd taken a mighty chance in not persuading his friend that a more modern and comfortable vehicle might have been a wiser choice.

Al ignored the gentle rebuke. "He bought the Jeep yesterday, Mrs. B. When he called me to describe his great 'discovery,' I knew there'd be no stopping him. He had it detailed this morning—thus his excuse for not joining us for breakfast."

When Abe Jones's laughter finally subsided, he asked the question they were all wondering. "Where in blazes did Rosco find it? It's like a clone of his old car."

Lever rolled his eyes. "Where does he find anything, Abe? Poly—crates lives a charmed life; you know that. . . . But I'm not sure the vehicle you're looking at was always red. . . ."

Across
1. Evil
4. Toss
7. Boxing org.
10. French salt
13. Operate
14. Water off Mass.
15. Mr. Rossi
16. Record label
17. Fib
18. Birth of 1817, in Concord, Mass.
20. Dr. Tacete
21. Who'll be the clerk? "I," said the___
23. ___Steven
24. Wood preserver
26. Loafed
28. Who'll make his shroud? "I," said the___
29. Play hockey
32. Mr. Silverstein
34. Quiz
35. Montana capital
37. Gnawed away
39. Who'll dig his grave? "I," said the___
40. Who killed Cock Robin? "I," said the___
42. Who saw him die? "I," said the___
45. Discourage
46. Desert sight
48. Mr. Kojak
51. Set down
53. Types
54. Mary Chase classic
56. False
58. Some poems
59. Fright, often
60. Mr. Anan
64. French one
65. Cut out
68. Place for toys
69. State & Main; abbr.
70. Put on
71. Tiger league?
72. Jor. neighbor
73. Pre DDE
74. "Rah!"
75. Born
76. "All___king's horses . . ."

Down
1. Who'll toll the bell? "I," said the___
2. Where Bombay is
3. Bambi, e.g.
4. Mr. Boone
5. Lucy's pal
6. Hand warmers
7. Who'll bear the pall? "I," said the___
8. Feather stole
9. Treat harshly
10. Drug
11. Internet missives
12. Who'll bear the torch? "I," said the___
19. "As many as___grow in the wood"
22. Who'll carry his coffin? "I," said the___
25. Head of France?
27. Thick
28. Aster or rose
29. No___
30. ___Gardens
31. "___the king's men . . ."
33. Goof
36. Appropriately
38. Paddles
41. Actors org.
42. Passing fancy
43. SM-MED___
44. Quite so
45. Who'll be chief mourner? "I," said the___

"WHO KILLED COCK ROBIN?"

47. Who'll be the parson? "I," said the___
48. Who'll sing his dirge? "I," said the___
49. Hangouts
50. Mr. Hemingway
52. Murders
55. Test part

57. Collection
59. Verdi opera
61. Last words?
62. Who caught his blood? "I," said the___
63. In the matter of
66. Alphabet run
67. "A pocket full of___"

The Answers

"BABY STEPS"

1 F	2 A	3 C	4 T	5 O	6 R	■	7 S	8 P	9 R	10 Y	■	11 A	12 B	13 C
14 E	T	H	A	N	E	■	15 H	O	E	R	■	16 G	E	O
17 A	M	A	N	O	F	18 W	O	R	D	S	■	19 R	A	P
20 T	O	R	■	■	■	21 H	O	T	■	■	22 H	E	R	E
■	■	23 A	24 N	25 D	26 N	O	T	O	27 F	28 D	E	E	D	S
29 I	30 O	D	I	D	E	■	■	■	31 T	O	M	■	■	■
32 P	R	E	T	T	Y	33 M	34 A	35 I	D	S	■	36 S	37 T	38 P
39 O	G	R	E	■	■	40 E	T	C	■	■	41 C	I	A	O
42 S	S	S	■	43 S	44 I	L	V	E	45 R	46 B	E	L	L	S
■	■	■	47 Y	U	K	■	■	■	48 R	A	R	E	L	Y
49 I	50 S	51 L	I	K	E	52 A	53 G	54 A	R	D	E	N	■	■
55 S	T	O	P	■	■	56 T	U	G	■	■	■	57 C	58 E	59 E
60 A	R	T	■	61 F	62 U	L	L	O	63 F	64 W	65 E	E	D	S
66 A	I	T	■	67 U	S	A	F	■	68 R	E	T	R	I	M
69 C	P	O	■	70 N	E	S	S	■	71 A	D	E	S	T	E

"SUGAR AND SPICE"

¹S	²O	³C	■	⁴C	⁵O	⁶T	■	⁷H	⁸A	⁹M	■	¹⁰C	¹¹A	¹²P

Crossword grid:

Row 1: 1·S 2·O 3·C ■ 4·C 5·O 6·T ■ 7·H 8·A 9·M ■ 10·C 11·A 12·P
Row 2: 13·H B O ■ 14·U S H ■ 15·E L I ■ 16·A D O
Row 3: 17·E R N ■ 18·R T E ■ 19·L O C 20·A T E R
Row 4: 21·L I 22·T T L E B 23·O P E E P ■ ■ ■
Row 5: 24·F E R R Y O U T ■ ■ ■ 25·S 26·A 27·L 28·T
Row 6: ■ 29·N A I L ■ 30·T O 31·M ■ 32·L O S E R
Row 7: ■ ■ 33·B O 34·A C ■ 35·A 36·S U ■ 37·E T A
Row 8: 38·A 39·N 40·T ■ 41·C F H ■ 42·R O C ■ 43·A S P
Row 9: 44·B O O ■ 45·K B E ■ 46·G U Y 47·S ■ ■
Row 10: 48·B O O 49·T S ■ 50·R 51·O E ■ 52·L A 53·S 54·A
Row 11: 55·A N T I ■ ■ 56·C R 57·E O S O T 58·E
Row 12: ■ ■ 59·M 60·O 61·N 62·D A Y S C H I L D
Row 13: 63·F 64·O 65·R E V E R ■ 66·D I K ■ 67·L A G
Row 14: 68·U R E ■ 69·E R A ■ 70·A R E ■ 71·E S E
Row 15: 72·N E D ■ 73·R O B ■ 74·W A T ■ 75·D T S

"AS TIME GOES BY"

1 O	2 H	3 M	4 S		5 A	6 T	7 P		8 S	9 C	10 A	11 M
12 S	P	E	A	K	13 D	I	E	14 P	E	A	C	E
15 P	E	R	R	Y	16 I	M	P	17 E	A	T	E	N
18 E	R	A		19 H	O	E		20 I	R	M	A	
21 C	A	N	22 D	23 L	E	S	24 T	I	C	K	25 N	26 N	27 W
	28 U	R	I	S	29 O	D	E	S	30 D	O	E
31 O	P	A	L		32 B	E	D		33 T	H	E
34 K	A	T	Y		35 B	R	A	36 C	H	I	P
37 I	S	H		38 C	O	E		39 C	H	E	T
40 L	I	E	41 E	L	S	A	42 G	O	O	F
43 L	S	C	44 J	A	C	K	45 B	E	Q	U	I	46 C	47 K
	48 L	49 O	E	W	50 D	O	T		51 D	L	I
52 B	53 R	O	N	C	54 W	O	N	55 S	56 I	D	E	S
57 F	A	C	E	T	58 A	W	E	59 E	R	L	E	S
60 A	S	K	S		61 R	N	S	62 W	E	E	K

"FRANKLY, DEAR . . ."

1 U	2 F	3 O		4 R	5 D	6 A		7 S	8 C	9 I		10 W	11 A	12 C
13 R	U	T		14 O	I	L		15 H	A	N		16 A	S	H
17 L	E	T	18 S	B	E	F	19 R	A	N	K		20 G	S	A
21 S	L	O	P	E			22 F	R	I		23 D	O	T	S
		24 F	R	25 A	26 N	K	I	N	C	27 E	N	S	E	
28 C	29 B	30 S		31 T	D	Y		32 F	E	A	T			
33 O	R	E	34 S		35 A	S	36 S			37 T	O	38 A	39 D	40 S
41 C	A	T	C	42 H	M	E	I	43 F	44 Y	O	U	C	A	N
45 A	C	H	O	O			46 B	O	A		47 R	E	N	O
		48 R	O	49 D	50 S		51 O	L	52 D		53 S	E	W	
54 F	55 R	56 A	N	K	E	57 N	S	T	E	58 I	N			
59 R	A	T	S		60 R	Y	E			61 D	O	62 W	63 N	64 S
65 A	B	E		66 H	I	D	E	67 A	68 N	D	S	E	E	K
69 N	B	A		70 E	V	E		71 D	E	L		72 L	X	I
73 K	I	M		74 P	E	R		75 O	W	E		76 L	T	D

"AND THE COW JUMPED OVER THE . . ."

¹P	²O	³D	■	⁴T	⁵W	⁶O	■	⁷B	⁸E	⁹G	■	¹⁰E	¹¹G	¹²G

Grid answers:

- 1 P O D — 4 T W O — 7 B E G — 10 E G G
- 13 A L I — 14 R I M — 15 I D O — 16 U R N
- 17 T I N — 18 A D A M A N T — 20 R A P
- 21 E V E R Y O N E S A M O O N
- 24 N E R O — 25 W I G — 26 A S S T S
- 28 T R O V E — 29 E — 30 A N D H A S A
- 32 E L I — 34 O W E — 35 R O D
- 36 D A R K S I D E W H I C H
- 41 B E N — 42 E R E — 43 S I T
- 44 H E N E V E R — 47 T E T R A
- 51 P R E G O — 52 B T U — 55 M O A N
- 56 S H O W S T O A N Y B O D Y
- 60 S K Y — 61 E N H A N C E — 62 T I O
- 63 R I D — 64 L I E — 65 G U N — 66 L O N
- 67 O N E — 68 S P Y — 69 O T S — 70 E S E

"WHO KILLED COCK ROBIN?"

[1]B	[2]A	[3]D	■	[4]P	[5]E	[6]G	■	[7]W	[8]B	[9]A	■	[10]S	[11]E	[12]L
[13]U	S	E	■	[14]A	T	L	■	[15]R	O	B	■	[16]E	M	I
[17]L	I	E	■	[18]T	H	[19]O	R	E	A	U	■	[20]D	A	N
[21]L	A	R	[22]K	■	[23]E	V	E	N	■	[24]S	[25]T	A	I	N
■	■	■	[26]I	[27]D	L	E	D	■	[28]B	E	E	T	L	E
[29]S	[30]K	[31]A	T	E	■	[32]S	H	[33]E	L	■	[34]T	E	S	T
[35]H	E	L	E	N	[36]A	■	[37]E	R	O	[38]S	E	■	■	■
[39]O	W	L	■	[40]S	P	[41]A	R	R	O	W	■	[42]F	[43]L	[44]Y
■	[45]D	E	T	E	R	■	■	■	[46]M	I	[47]R	A	G	E
[48]T	[49]H	[50]E	O	■	[51]L	A	[52]I	D	■	[53]M	O	D	E	S
[54]H	A	R	V	[55]E	Y	■	[56]N	O	T	[57]S	O	■	■	■
[58]R	U	N	E	S	■	[59]A	G	E	R	■	[60]K	[61]O	[62]F	[63]I
[64]U	N	E	■	[65]S	[66]C	I	S	S	O	[67]R	■	[68]B	I	N
[69]S	T	S	■	[70]A	D	D	■	[71]I	V	Y	■	[72]I	S	R
[73]H	S	T	■	[74]Y	E	A	■	[75]N	E	E	■	[76]T	H	E